A PLACE TO SHINE

A PLACE TO SHINE

Marie Arnold

VERSIFY
An Imprint of HarperCollinsPublishers

Versify® is an imprint of HarperCollins Publishers.

A Place to Shine

Copyright © 2024 by Marie Arnold

Illustrations by grondetphoto/Adobe Stock (rays)

and Oqvector/Adobe Stock (curtains)

Library of Congress Control Number: 2023943860

ISBN 978-0-06-325175-5

Typography by Jenna Stempel-Lobell

24 25 26 27 28 LBC 5 4 3 2 1

First Edition

This book is dedicated to all
the children in the foster care system.
May you find your forever home . . .

This book is also dedicated to
Ethel Greenspan.
Thank you for leading the family
with grace and fortitude.
And most of all, thank you for
the blankets that always made us feel safe.

Chapter One
A "Grave" Mistake

I WAS JUST STARTING to like being ten years old. And I heard good things about turning eleven. But I might not make it that far. In fact, I'm pretty sure this is my last day on earth. If I had known that this morning, I would have eaten a yummier breakfast. Instead of cheesy grits and eggs, I would have had chocolate chip banana pancakes with extra syrup. My name is Sundae Williams; everybody calls me Sunny. And in about five minutes, I'm a dead girl.

How do I know I only have five minutes left to live? That's how long before Tessa Graves gets out of band practice and wipes me off the face of the earth! Tessa is taller than the Statue of Liberty, her hands are wider than the Grand Canyon, and she has a glare meaner than any supervillain. I didn't plan on getting into a fight today, especially not with Tessa Graves. I mean her last name is "Graves," for crying out loud. But that's exactly what's about to happen.

It all started this morning in the schoolyard. I ran into Tessa at top speed and sent her flying to the ground. But it wasn't my fault. My little brother, Miles, brought his pet hamster to school. His name is Noodle, and he got out of his cage. I had to help catch him. I was so focused on Noodle, I didn't realize I was about to collide with Tessa. After it happened, I said, "Sorry," but she wasn't interested in my apology. She said she wanted to fight. It didn't take long before the whole school was talking about it.

So now I'm standing in front of the back entrance of the school, waiting for Tessa to come out. I bury my hands into the pockets of my fluffy pink coat to warm them up. It doesn't work. Right now, nothing in my body is working the way it's supposed to. My stomach is a pretzel, there's a desert caught in my throat, and my heart is a Ping-Pong ball, bouncing around in my chest, trying to escape.

It's the end of September and Chicago doesn't usually get that cold yet, but today even the buildings are shivering. I thought the weather would make the kids stay away but nope. The kids of Washington Carver Elementary won't let a good fight go unseen. There are about twenty of them out here, all with Christmas-morning levels of excitement.

"Are you sure about this, Sunny?" my best friend, Folake, whispers in my ear. Folake is a circle—everything about her is round; her head, her big eyes, and her rainbow-frame glasses.

One of the things that I really like about Folake is her hair. Every Monday, she comes to class with it in a different pattern. Sometimes it forms an actual maze! We started hanging out together because we have a lot in common. We're good dancers, we're left-handed, and we love to put ketchup on pizza.

The first time I went to a sleepover at Folake's house, I learned two things: One, she has a lot of siblings. She has six in all. They come in from every direction of the house, always rushing off to go somewhere. Her house is busier than Union Station. But their mom, Mrs. Musa, always makes them come home in time for dinner. That brings me to the second thing I learned: Nigerian food is suuuuuuuper spicy!

One time when I had dinner at her house, her mom made white rice over red chicken stew. The food smelled so good, it made my mouth water. I didn't know then that the food would be spicy, so I started eating as fast as I could. I exhaled and flames leaped out of my mouth and singed the curtain across the room. So now, whenever I go over there for dinner, they always have a glass of milk waiting for me, so I can smother the fire building up in my belly.

I look at Folake and see my reflection in her glasses. I've been wearing my hair in two gigantic, fluffy pigtails. I want to change it, but Nanna made my part so straight, I'm afraid if I undo it, I'll never get my part that straight again. So I comb out the ends and leave the part where it is.

"Sunny, you still have time to go and hide," she says.

"I can't. I have to face Tessa," I reply. Folake sighs. She thinks agreeing to the fight was a mistake. She might be right.

But sometimes even when you know you should not do something, you do it anyway. Like the time this kid in my class, Benny, bet me five whole dollars that I couldn't eat an entire jar of mayo. It only took three spoonfuls to know that I had made a big mistake, but I had to see it through.

A few kids walk out the front door of the school holding their clarinets. It's official—band practice is over.

"Last chance," Folake says, sounding worried.

I think about running away, but then I take another look at my hair in Folake's glasses. I remember something.

Back when I was a kid, like seven or eight, people used to tease me about my hair. They made fun of it because it wasn't smooth and silky like some of the other kids in my class. But then Nanna explained that my hair had a story. I couldn't believe it when she said that. I always thought hair was just . . . hair.

"Oh no, child! Although Black hair comes in many different textures, they all tell the same story—a story of triumph and resilience!" Nanna Jo said.

I didn't know what "resilience" meant back then. I had to look it up. It basically means that my hair won't be bossed around. So if my hair is strong, maybe I am, too.

"Nope, I'm not running. Let Tessa come," I tell Folake as I swallow hard and pray that I am right. But what if I *am* wrong? What if the only strong thing about me is my hair?

I turn away from the entrance and look around the playground. Is there anything here that can help me? I feel a chill on the back of my neck. Chicago is one of the windiest cities in the whole world. Maybe a gust of wind will come our way and blow us all to different corners of the earth?

Okay, that's probably not going to happen, but maybe a strong breeze could blow Tessa back to her house? I close my eyes and feel the wind on my face. It's blowing kind of hard but not hard enough to carry anyone away.

I saw a video once on YouTube where a kid was chewing bubble gum and blew a bubble with so much air, it grew to twice the size of his head. What if I could blow a bubble so big, it would trap Tessa and bounce her out of the school? I dig inside my pockets, but there is no gum.

Folake tugs on my coat sleeve. I look at her face; her eyes are as big as a great horned owl. I know all about owls because Miles talks about them all the time, even when I ask him not to.

"What is it?" I ask her.

"Look!" she says. I follow Folake's stare. Another student has left the building and is coming our way—Tessa.

How did she manage to grow even taller since this morning? I look her over from head to toe. I never noticed her feet—they are huge! She's going to crush me. She'll go home, and her mom will say, "Tessa, what is that stuck to the bottom of your shoe?"

Tessa will look and then turn back to her mom and say, "Oh, that's nothing. Just leftover chunks of Sunny."

Tessa will then leave her sneakers on the porch, where her dog, Bebe, will chew right through them. I know her dog's name is Bebe because she talks about her all the time. I'm about to be dog food—literally.

"I didn't think you'd be dumb enough to actually show up," Tessa says.

I shrug my shoulders and give her what I hope is a friendly smile. "I heard it's rude to cancel last minute," I joke.

She's not amused.

I swallow hard.

She comes closer.

She wears her meanness on her face; that's why her lips are so twisted and her eyes so beady. She pounds her fist into her palm. It makes a loud *thud*, causing ripples on the surface of the puddle a few feet away. Each time her hammy fist smashes into her palm, the earth shakes. I think even aliens, in galaxies far, far away, can feel it.

"Hey, you leave her alone!" someone calls out.

We follow the voice. It's coming from a swollen, blue-colored blob waddling its way toward us. It's my kid brother, Miles—or what I can make out of his face. His puffy blue coat swallows up most of his head.

Miles and I have the same big hair, big eyes, and big lips. But his skin is the color of almonds, and he has freckles on his nose. He got them from my mom. She had freckles in the same spot. My skin is the color of a plum. I don't have freckles, but I do have dimples. I got them from my dad.

"Miles, you're supposed to be in Homework Help!" I remind him as Folake and I rush over to him.

One look at Folake, and Miles turns to mush. "Hello, my queen," he says in a dreamy voice. I roll my eyes.

"Hi, Miles," Folake replies patiently. Miles is looking so hard at Folake that he forgets the rest of us are there. That happens a lot when he's around her.

"You know, won't be long until I start shaving . . ." Miles says proudly as he tilts his chin up and raises his left eyebrow. Folake has no idea what to say.

I try to snap my little brother back to earth. "Miles, you're supposed to be in Homework Help."

"Mrs. Goldsmith is out sick, so it's canceled. Good thing because you need my help," he says in his favorite "hero" voice. Miles is a pretty good little brother when he's not touching my stuff or asking a million questions. We argue sometimes, but Nanna always tells us, "It's okay to disagree with family, but when that's done, you best be closer than you were when it started."

I whisper, "Miles, I'll be fine."

"Shine, I wanna help." Shine is another nickname. But no one calls me that except my family. "You need me," he says stubbornly.

"Yes, I need you alive. If Tessa has anything to say about it, you won't be. So go!"

He looks over at Tessa and shouts, "I know kung fu! I'm not afraid!"

I groan and roll my eyes.

"Oh, you know kung fu, huh?" Tessa snickers. "I was o gonna take care of your sister, but keep it up, little man I'll take care of you, too!"

Miles quotes one of the old movies Nanna Jo has over and over again with him. "You have offended You have offended the Shaolin Temple!"

He tries to do a one-legged kung fu pose, ance, and falls over. Folake and I run over and

Once he's up, he says, "I meant to do that

"Miles, I can handle this," I promise hir

"Are you sure?" he asks.

"Yes," I reply.

Miles thinks for a moment and then agrees to go to the basement and wait for me. Just before he walks away, he leans in and whispers, "Just remember the Central American cichlid."

"What?"

He sighs loudly and puts his face in his palm. "The Central American cichlid fish plays dead to trick its predators. It's in the book I gave you!"

"You know possums do that, too. You could have said that," Folake points out.

"There are so many other animals that play dead better than *Didelphis* marsupials. When will people learn?!" He shakes his head and walks away.

"I'm done waiting!" Tessa says.

"Tess, crush her!" Tessa's best friend, Leigh, says, stand- a few feet away.

"Tess, beat her butt real good!" another girl chimes in.

"ah, let's see a fight!" someone in the crowd yells.

"t! Fight! Fight!" The crowd cheers loudly as she marc hrough them to get to me. My heart finally finds a way out of my body and takes off down the block. Shame, nna miss having a heartbeat.

"Let's Tessa says, now only a few feet away from me. From th ner of my eye, I see a dog walker going by with six dogs struggling to get one of the dogs to let her put its col. "Oh, c'mon, Lucy! It's against the law

8

for you not to have on a leash. It's not my rule—it's the city of Chicago!"

That's it!

I quickly whisper something to Folake, and she nods, although she's not really sure if what I said makes sense.

"Okay, Tessa, let's fight! But first I will need to see your battle bracelet," I inform her.

"What?" Tessa says, confused.

I extend my arm and show her the bracelet I'm wearing. It's a black plastic chain link with a pink plastic star in the middle. Folake and I made them from a kit Nanna bought us; we each have one.

"Where's your battle bracelet? You need one to fight," I tell her.

"No, I don't!" Tessa shouts back.

"Yes, you do. You are not allowed to fight without one. It's not my rule. It's the city of Chicago's rule," I reply.

She folds her arms over her chest and furrows her brows. "I have never heard of that. You're just trying to trick me. I won't fall for it."

"It's true," I reply, elbowing Folake in her side.

"Ouch," Folake mumbles under her breath.

"You can ask Folake. She has one, too. So we can fight each other if we want. But we can't fight someone who doesn't have a bracelet. It's a Chicago city rule: no bracelet, no battle."

Folake shows off her bracelet to Tessa. Tessa thinks about it for a moment and then looks to the crowd and says, "Anyone ever fight without a stupid bracelet?"

Almost everyone raises their hand. I clear my throat and ask the crowd another question. "Anyone ever mysteriously lose something? Like a sock or a favorite toy?" Almost everyone in the crowd raises their hand again.

"See, that's what happens when you fight without going through proper fight procedure—something of yours mysteriously disappears," I warn Tessa.

"I don't care if I lose a sock. Let's go!" Tessa says, about to charge ahead.

Folake steps in front of me and says, "It might not be just a sock. It could be someone much more important."

I quickly join in. "Yup! Something like . . . a pet."

Tessa's eyes go wide with panic.

"You don't have any pets do you, Tessa?" Folake asks.

"I have a German shepherd named Bebe," she says.

"If I had a dog I loved, I would *never* take the chance that she could disappear. But okay. Let's fight." I take my backpack off, put it on the ground, and face Tessa.

Tessa thinks for a second and then growls, "Next time, watch where you're going, Sunny!" She turns around and stomps away.

Chapter Two
Home

FOLAKE IS WALKING HOME with us today because my nanna said she could come over for a little while. It's cold out, so there are very few people around. In the summer, everyone on the block is outside. There's hip-hop music blaring, kids hustling in and out of the corner store, and the basketball court up the street is full. But right now, it's just too cold for all that. So the block is nearly empty.

I take a handful of Sour Skittles and give the rest to Folake and Miles. I love when Folake hangs out with us, but sometimes it's just too much excitement for Miles. He gets all giddy and can't focus on anything but her. That's why as we walk toward our apartment building, I make sure I stay in between them. I think if Miles had to walk next to her, he'd forget how to use his legs, trip, and fall.

"I can't believe you messed with Tessa and you're still alive! I thought you were gone for sure!" Folake says.

"Yeah, me too!" I confess. We both look at each other and burst out laughing. That was a close one. Phew! Now, all I have to do is make sure I never bump into Tessa again. But since we go to the same school, that might be hard.

"So, what are your thoughts on marriage?" Miles asks as we pass the laundromat we go to every Saturday. Folake and I look at each other and try not to laugh at my little brother.

"Marriage? Aren't you too young to be thinking about that stuff?" Folake asks.

"I may look seven, but inside . . . I'm a man," he assures her as he tries to make his voice sound deep. He moves his left eyebrow up and down and gives Folake a crooked smile. I roll my eyes and groan.

"Thanks for letting me know, Miles. If I ever feel like getting married, you're the first person I'll talk to," she says, politely squeezing his cheek. Miles blushes.

"Hey, how come you don't get mad at Folake for pinching your cheek, like you get mad at me?" I ask.

Miles replies in a breathless whisper, "Because there's only one Folake."

I shake my head and wonder if I can trade him in for a new brother, one who doesn't have a big crush on my best friend.

We have just turned the corner when Folake stops walking, even though we still have half a block to go.

"Why'd you stop?" I ask.

"Look!" she says. I follow her eyes; there's a cop car parked in front of the building. The two of us start running; Miles isn't far behind. We get to the front, and I take out my keys and open the lobby door. We're about to run up to Nanna's apartment, on the third floor. We start up the stairs but freeze when we hear heavy footsteps making their way toward us.

We peek through the bars on the railing and look up to see who's coming. It's two police officers. They're helping someone make their way down the steps, telling the person to be careful and to hold on to the railing.

"It's okay, ma'am, we got you. Take your time," one of the officers says.

"Well, all right, I guess. But what about my grandbabies? I got to go see about them. They need a snack. None of that sugar cereal; they need real food, you hear?!" the person says. The three of us look at each other; we all know that voice—Nanna!

Miles bolts toward the sound of Nanna's voice. I take off after him. I grab on to his coat and pull him back. He looks at me, upset and puzzled. I put my finger to my lips, telling him to be quiet. The footsteps are getting closer. The three of us silently walk back down to the landing. I signal for them to follow me to the small nook under the staircase.

We can't see them from where we are, but we hear them, coming closer. The officers speak in calm, friendly voices.

"It's okay, no rush. Take your time, ma'am," one of them says. The three of them get to the landing. I take a chance and quickly peek out. Nanna is with two Black police officers. She looks calm as they gently guide her to the exit. I have to put my hand over my mouth so I don't shout Nanna's name and run to her, just like Miles tried to.

Before the three of them can walk out, our neighbor Mr. Wynn opens his door. His apartment is right next to the exit, so he's always keeping a lookout on who is coming and going. Mr. Wynn has light skin, hazel eyes, and always looks like he's about to yell at someone. But he just looks grumpy; he's actually pretty nice.

"What's going on here? Where you all taking Ms. Williams?" he asks the officers. They look at each other, not sure they want to answer him.

"Please, Officer, we look out for each other around here. Is she okay?"

"We received a call from one of your neighbors," the shorter of the two officers replies. "They wanted us to do a wellness check on Ms. Williams. She had been seen earlier walking the street, disoriented."

"Where are you taking her?"

"We're going to take her to meet some nice folks at the Shady Glen Nursing Center. She needs a social worker who can get her the help she needs."

My heart sinks. I have thought about this day for a long time, but I didn't think that day would be today.

Nanna hasn't been well for a while now. It first started when she let us leave home with ashy elbows. A few weeks later, she oversalted the hot water corn bread. And then the unthinkable: she was doing my hair on washday, and she forgot to comb out my kitchen! I knew then something was very wrong. Things just kept getting worse; sometimes Nanna would forget where she lived.

I saw on TV that when older people start forgetting things, they are taken to a home to live with other old people. But that can't happen. We need our nanna here with us. I know every kid thinks that their grandma is the best, but mine is *actually* the best. When Miles was sick and didn't want to take his medicine, she convinced him to drink it by promising that they would go dinosaur hunting at Lincoln Park once he was better.

Sometimes grown-ups say they'll do things but then they forget. But not Nanna—she kept her promise. A few days later, she burst into our room wearing a large tan hat with netting and hiking boots.

She said, "Let's go, baby, dinosaurs wait for no one!"

That's not all—Nanna knows how much Miles loves insects and bugs, so she lets him bring them into the apartment. It doesn't matter if the bugs are slimy, wiggly, or stuff oozes out of them. So long as Miles doesn't let them loose, the bugs can stay.

Last year, I wanted to go to Taste of Chicago. It's the biggest food festival in the world, and it's right here in our city! I had a plan; I would go to the festival wearing my favorite blue dress, with my high-top kicks and strawberry-kiwi lip gloss. I'd get to act fancy like one of those famous judges on the cooking shows Nanna and I watch.

The two of us would enter the festival, and everyone would stop and look. We'd get all the attention because we're famous master chefs. I'd walk up to the table, sample a small bite, and smack my lips as I judge the food. I even worked on my dramatic pause before giving my opinion, just like the judges on TV do.

But the tickets were too expensive, especially for all three of us to go. Miles offered to stay home with a sitter. Nanna offered to buy me a single ticket to go with a friend of hers, but I said no because it wouldn't be the same.

On the last day of the festival, Nanna said, "Sunny, if you want to try new foods, that's just what we will do." She made me get dressed in my blue outfit, and we headed out the door. A few minutes later, we were standing in front of our destination.

"We got all pretty to go to the corner store?" I asked, confused.

"Just because we don't have money doesn't mean we can't have a good time! Now, let's go in and show out!" she said gleefully as she made her grand entrance.

I followed right behind her, also making a head-turning entrance.

We paraded around the store as if we were superstars on the red carpet. We studied different items on the shelf; Nanna held up a snack and asked the clerk questions.

"Excuse me, young man, what is the name of these orange sticks with the red powder featured on the front of this bag?" she asked.

He looked at her oddly and then slowly replied, "Um . . . that's Flamin' Hot Cheetos with Límón."

"Well, that sounds very exotic! I will try one," Nanna said as she opened the bag. She put a Cheeto in her mouth, and I put one in mine. Together we smacked our lips, looked up at the ceiling like we were really thinking hard, and then we both took a big, long pause.

Then she suddenly clapped. "Bravo! This 'Cheetos' thing will be a hit at corner stores all over Chicago!"

"It's simply divine!" I added.

The clerk looked at us like we were from another world. Nanna and I laughed. We tried out all sorts of chip flavors and snacks. And we washed them down with fancy Lipton Iced Tea. (It was on sale, two for the price of one.) I don't mean to brag, but that day, we were the best-dressed shoppers at Tom's Mini Mart.

Nanna Jo loves adventure, and she told us there was no better place to find it than in books, especially fantasy books. We loved reading stories that featured extraordinary creatures, wondrous worlds, and of course magical mayhem. Our favorite tale is *The Girl of Fire and Light*. We read that one a lot. We read other stories, but we always go back to that one. Nope, they can't take her away.

"Ms. Williams, you all right?" Mr. Wynn asks.

"Oh, yes! I'm going to see some very nice people. Isn't that right?" Nanna asks the officers.

"Hold on, let me write down where you're taking her. Half the building will come and visit. We all love us some Williams," Mr. Wynn says. He disappears behind the door and comes back quickly with a pen and notepad. The officers tell him the address.

"Now what about her grandchildren, Sunny and Miles?" Mr. Wynn asks.

"Social services came by earlier and picked them up."

"And took them where?" Mr. Wynn asks. My tummy flips. My heart beats out of control. I know the answer even before the officer replies.

"Emergency foster care."

We wait until Nanna and the officers are gone and Mr. Wynn goes back inside his apartment. I signal for Miles and Folake to follow me up to Nanna's apartment. And as soon as I enter, I can tell something has changed.

"There must have been some kind of mix-up! They think someone already came to pick you two up!" Folake says.

"Yes, but soon they'll see they made a mistake and come back to get us," I reply sadly as I look around our home. Whenever I enter this apartment, I always feel warm, like I'm being hugged. But right now it feels cold and empty. I think the apartment is sad. I think it knows that she's gone.

"Sunny, don't cry," Folake says.

"I'm not crying," I lie, turning my face away from her. It's useless. The harder I try to stop, the more tears overflow. Miles starts to cry, too. Soon, Folake's eyes are wet!

I see my reflection in the mirror on the wall. I see my hair; Nanna made the straightest part and put my hair up in two puffy pigtails. That was just a few days ago. I remember asking her, the same thing I always ask when she does my hair, "Nanna, why can't my hair go *whoosh* and swing around, like some of the kids I see on TV?" And I hear her voice, like she was standing right next to me. "Baby, you got the same hair I got. Same hair your mama had. It won't bend and sway in the wind like other folks'. Your hair will stand its ground. It's strong. You're strong."

I'm strong like my mom. I'm strong like Nanna . . .

I wipe my face with the back of my hand and tell myself to stop crying. This is no time for tears. We have to find a way to get Nanna back.

"Okay, no more crying. Miles, stop it!" I demand. He's sniffling, but he's stopped sobbing.

"We have to get our nanna back!" I announce.

Miles looks over at me, wipes his eyes, and nods. "Yeah! She's ours!"

"What do we do? How do we help your nanna?" Folake asks.

"Before we figure that out, we have to find a place to hide so they don't make us go to foster care. I saw videos online of kids who had been in foster care and everyone looked like they would rather be somewhere else. They didn't get to stay in a real home and be a real family. There were a lot of kids, too many kids. I don't think any of them were tucked in or read to. And I'm pretty sure they wouldn't allow Miles to have pets."

"I don't want to go!" Miles says, clinging to me. I hold him close and vow that no matter what, we are not going to foster care.

"So, where do we hide you two?" Folake asks.

I look at Folake and smile. "We know a secret hideout."

She doesn't get it at first, but soon her face lights up. "The kitty door!"

A few weeks ago, Folake and I were at recess and found a

cat in the schoolyard. She had bright white fur and patches of black fur around her eyes. She got in through an opening in the fence. We followed her to the back of the dumpster, where she slid inside a small ground-level window. We squeezed inside and ended up in a small room in the basement. The cat strolled by our feet and took a nap on an old, dusty, empty bookshelf. She would come take a nap the same time every day. We never told anyone; it was our "best friend secret." And besides, the cat looked really tired. It deserved to nap in peace.

"Okay, we're gonna hide out in the school basement. Miles, shove some clothes in your backpack, hurry! They'll be coming for us once they realize no one picked us up. And no animals!" I warn him.

"Awww, c'mon!" he begs.

"We're on the run! You can't just take pets on the run!" I point out.

"But Noodle is already in my backpack. Can I at least keep him?"

I want to say no, but then Folake whispers to me, "Maybe he'll be so busy looking after Noodle, he won't have time to be sad about Nanna."

"Okay, but only Noodle. Your other pets will have to stay here," I reply. Miles looks like I just told him I didn't love him.

Folake saves me. "Tell you what, Miles. I'll take them to my house so they are safe. All your bugs are sealed in a cage, right?"

"It's called a terrarium," he informs her.

"Okay, great. As long as they can't get out," she says, swallowing hard.

"Thanks," I tell her.

She smiles and goes with Miles to help him get his bugs. In the meantime, I throw a few clothes into my backpack and grab our favorite storybook, toothbrushes, and a picture of Nanna. And then I pack for Miles. When we're all ready to go, I run into the kitchen and climb the stepladder. I reach for the metal coffee can that Nanna keeps on top of the fridge. It has twenty bucks! I grab it and we run out of the apartment. Folake goes home with all of Miles's pet bugs. We agree to meet up in the back of the school.

Miles and I know better than to wait for Folake out in the open. We've watched enough spy movies to know we have to stay hidden, just in case they come by the school. We go to the corner store and head to the back. We pretend to look over the chips like we don't know which ones we want. Thankfully Folake soon appears with a bag in her hand.

"I told my mom I was keeping the bugs for Miles because your landlord was coming to spray the apartment. They did that for us a few days ago. She bought it! I also told her that I left a book at your place and had to come get it. So I can't stay long," she says.

"Thank you!" I reply, embarrassing her. She hands me a bag with sandwiches, snacks, and water.

"Okay, so you have everything you need?" Folake asks with sad eyes.

"Yup! I'm great!" I reply with a grin. It's important I show

Folake that I am happy, even though I'm really not. I don't want her to worry. But even though I flash the biggest smile I can, it never fools her. I guess that's what makes her my best friend and not just a friend.

"Nanna Jo was reading us a story once and it was late, and she said we could not finish the story because it was way past our bedtime. But the people in the story were in really deep trouble, so I begged her to finish it. She told me when things get really bad in a story, it means the story is not over. We just have to have faith and hold on. It's not easy. But if we have faith and hold on, we'll get to the end of the story."

"How do you know when it's the end?" she asks.

I smile back at her. "When you're happy."

She hugs me really, really tight. I blink back tears because, again, they don't help. "Thank you for the food," I say as she pulls away.

"So, you know how much I love combining foods to make it something new and awesome?"

Oh no . . .

I recall all the times Folake surprised me with her food "creations." There was the pickle and peanut butter sandwich, the tuna and banana taco, and the grape jelly and mayo dip. (My stomach still hasn't forgiven me for that one.)

"What did you combine?" I ask, bracing myself.

"I won't spoil the surprise. But I'll tell you what it's called." She inhales proudly and announces, "Tonight you and Miles will be dining on my latest invention: Cauliflower Courage."

"Is there any way that could mean ham and cheese?"

She laughs. "You're so funny! Like I would ever feed my best friend something so common! Next thing you know you'll want a grilled cheese!"

I am about to protest, but she just looks so pleased with herself, I don't want to make her sad. Also she's doing me a favor by coming here with supplies, so I guess I shouldn't complain. We send Folake out first, and she tells us that the coast is clear. We quickly go to the schoolyard and enter through the hole in the fence. The two of us cram ourselves behind the dumpster and wiggle inside the window. We wave goodbye to Folake. We take a look at the room; it's full of dusty shelves, broken chairs, and gym mats.

Well, I guess we're home . . .

Chapter Three
Ruined!

I CAN TELL BY the look on Miles's face he's not too happy about our new home. I try to cheer him up by telling him we're on an adventure. But that doesn't work. So I try a different way.

"Oh, man, I hope there aren't any bugs around here. There can't be bugs in a basement, right?" I ask.

His face lights up. "Bugs! There might be!"

"Okay, why don't you look around the room and see if you find any. I have to go upstairs to the bathroom. When I come back, we can have dinner," I reply, trying to make it sound like it's a normal day.

"Folake's sandwich?" he says, sounding a little grossed out.

"Well, let's at least try it and see. If not, maybe we can sneak over to the corner store and get something. Deal?" I reply.

"Deal!" he says, turning his focus to bug hunting.

The basement smells like moldy socks and tuna. There's

dust everywhere. I make my way down the hall and up the stairs. I keep seeing Nanna being taken away. The flashback makes my chest hurt and my stomach queasy. I hated watching her go, but if I had come out, they would have taken us away, too.

I miss her so much, I start to cry again. Suddenly questions pop into my head that won't go away. Was it the right thing to do? Will Nanna be mad at us? Is Nanna okay? Will anything ever be okay again?

Stop that, Sunny! You got this! You're strong, remember? You can save your family. You must!

I get upstairs, and even though I know the school is closed, I still peek around the corner to make sure no one is out in the hallway. When I am sure it's all clear, I go down the hallway. The squares on the floor are painted blue and gray, the school colors. They are shiny and reflect the lights overhead. The school feels creepy when no one else is here. I use the girls' bathroom, then take a deep breath and wipe my eyes. I don't want Miles to see me like this. I wash my face and make sure there's no sign that I have been crying. I head back to the basement and enter our little room.

"Miles, I'm back!"

Silence.

"Hey, Noodle. Have you seen Miles?" I ask the hamster eating inside his little bubble cage. Noodle is no help.

Something outside the window above Noodle's cage catches my eye. I look closer, and across the street, I see a man in a suit lift Miles high above his head by his hoodie.

They are both wet and dirty. I squeeze myself out of the basement window and run to my little brother.

"Who does this belong to?" the man asks, holding Miles up like a dirty diaper.

"Put him down!" I shout. "Who are you and why do you have my brother?"

He drops Miles to the ground, and I help him up.

"I'm Darrious Evens. I'm sure you've heard of me," he says with a smug smile as he clears his throat. Miles and I exchange a confused look. The stranger's face slides to the ground. "You don't know who I am?"

Miles and I reply in unison, "No."

The man's jaw drops.

"I'm Darrious Evens. Grammy Award–winning choir director . . . My records sold millions . . . I'm a member of the National Endowments for the Arts . . . Darrious Evens!" he insists. We look back at him blankly. This guy is so weird.

He snorts. "It's obvious you two are philistines."

"Philip? No, my name is Miles. And that's my sister, Sunny."

The man rolls his eyes and shakes his head in disbelief. "Never mind. Just call me Mr. Evens. I'm the new music teacher. I'm also directing the chorus."

Mr. Evens is a black pencil; everything about him is straight and perfectly aligned. He takes a handkerchief from his pocket and frantically tries to wipe the mud from his dark suit.

"What happened?" I ask Miles.

"I was looking out the window, and I spotted something unbelievable—*Phyllocrania paradoxa*! I ran outside and
climbed the tree so I could get a better look," Miles says.

Mr. Evens says, "What happened is I went to get some
stuff out of my car, and your kid brother fell out of a tree and
crashed down on me. We both landed in a dirty slushy puddle
of water."

I glare at Miles. He shrugs and looks down at the ground.
He does that when he knows he's in trouble.

"You were supposed to wait for me inside," I remind him.

He pleads, "But it was a *Phyllocrania paradoxa*! How could
I let it get away?"

"Miles, I told you—"

"—I know, I know. You told me to stay inside. But, Sunny,
it was a ghost mantis, the king of insect camouflage. It dis-
guised its body to look like a dead leaf. That's how it's able to
survive. Its enemies never know where he's hiding because of
its camouflage abilities! I had to get closer, I just had to."

Mr. Evens sees something on his dark suit and groans
loudly. "Aw, man. There was some kind of oil in the puddle.
Do you know how hard it is to get oil stains out?"

"Do you know how hard it is to spot a ghost mantis?"
Miles replies with a deep frown.

"Actually, I do," Mr. Evens says.

"Really?" Miles asks.

"Yes," he snaps. "I also know that ghost mantises are
largely found in Madagascar. So in all likelihood, that is not
what you saw."

"I knew it was a long shot, but—wait a minute. You've seen one?" Miles says as his eyes go wide with excitement.

Miles is waiting for him to explain. But judging by the scowl on Mr. Evens's face, he's in no mood to talk. He folds his arms over his chest, signaling he is done. He thinks that will discourage Miles, but it won't. It never does.

"Where did you see one? When did you see it? Did you sneak up on it? How long was it? Was there more than one?" Miles spits out question after question. He can hardly catch his breath. "Was it tan or a darker sand color? Did you ever see the green ones, the ones that look like bright leaves? Did you get a chance to weigh it? Did it see you?"

Mr. Evens looks at me and says, "Is this kid for real?"

I reply, "Yup."

"Will he ever stop with the questions?"

"Nope."

"Okay! Okay!" Mr. Evens says, throwing his hands up in defeat. "I know about ghost mantises because my wife was an entomologist. She studied insects for a living. There, happy now?"

"Is she Black?" Miles says.

"What? Yes, she's African American."

Miles cranes his neck up to look the pencil in the eyes. Miles's face is full of wonder and, yes, more questions. He doesn't even know where to start. When he opens his mouth, all my little brother can manage to say is "Wow."

"What are you two doing here so late, anyway? Stop

loitering! Go home," he says. Miles follows Mr. Evens, his questions not far behind.

"Did you see anything else while you were in Madagascar? The Madagascar pochard? The tomato frog? The leaf-tailed gecko?"

Mr. Evens turns around sharply with a mean look on his face. "Look, kid, I don't have time for this. I have to get my classroom set up, look over sheet music, and call my dry cleaner to see if he can save this suit. You and your sister need to go home right now, or I will call your parents."

"No! You don't have to do that. We're going," I reply.

"But—but—" Miles says.

"Let's go!" I order. He pouts and huffs, but he follows me down the street.

Every car that drives by, I keep thinking they are here for us. We need to be inside. Also, the sun is setting. It's freezing outside. I scold Miles for leaving the basement and make him promise never to do that again! He grumbles, and I can tell he's tired and wants to be home—our real home.

"Hey, want some hot chocolate?" I ask.

"YES!" he replies.

We've had an awful day, and we miss Nanna so much. We need something to make us feel better. Plus, it'll keep us warm. We quickly walk to the store. It's two blocks away, but that might be a good thing—maybe by the time we come back, Mr. Evens will be gone.

We reach the store and buy two cups of hot chocolate with extra whipped cream. We each take a long sip; it's rich and creamy, just the way we like it. We make our way back to school.

"I think Mr. Evens is gonna be my best friend," Miles says with confidence.

"You don't really know him," I point out.

"Not yet, but I will."

"What if he does something that annoys you?"

"Like what?" Miles asks.

"Like dig into the peanut butter jar with the same knife he used for the jelly jar. You hate that."

Miles nods thoughtfully. "Yeah, I do. That's gross. It gets mixed up. And I know that peanut butter and jelly go together but only between the bread. They should not mix before then."

"Will he still be your friend if he does that?"

Miles thinks hard before he responds, "Yes. I think our friendship can survive it."

"Okay, what if he likes a different kind of milk than you do?"

"Shine, friends don't have to like the same things. If Mr. Evens wants regular milk while I have strawberry milk, it's okay."

I suppress a smile and call him the nickname that Nanna gave him. "Wait a minute, Bug. What if Mr. Evens only likes skim milk?"

Miles stops dead in his tracks. "Then there's no hope for

us. Our friendship is over before it even really began."

I laugh and playfully squeeze him. "Don't worry. I'm sure he isn't a skim milk guy."

Miles breathes a sigh of relief, and we begin to walk again.

"I can't wait to meet his wife when he brings her to school concerts and stuff. I'm going to ask her about her pet lion in Africa. I think his name is Kong—Kong the lion. Because he's so big and bad," Miles says, unable to hold back his excitement. "I can't wait to meet Kong."

"How do you know she even has a lion or that his name is Kong?"

"Everyone has one over there. And what else would you call a lion?"

I smile to myself but don't say anything. Miles squeals, "I can't wait to meet her—a Black entomologist. So cool!"

Once we get back, we see Mr. Evens's car is still parked outside. We could have gone around to the back entrance, where there's a hole in the fence, but Miles wants to get a look at what his new best friend is doing. The truth is I'm kind of curious, too. So we hide in the bushes outside his classroom.

Mr. Evens walks around the room, talking. And although he's all over the place, his main focus always comes back to the teacher's desk. The only trouble is there's no one sitting there. Mr. Evens is talking to himself.

Miles and I exchange a look. We're both puzzled by what we see. We duck down into the bushes and speak in soft whispers.

"Did you see anyone seated at the teacher's desk?" I ask,

although I already know the answer.

"No," Miles replies.

"So who is he talking to?"

"Maybe he has an imaginary friend," Miles suggests.

"Grown-ups don't have imaginary friends."

"That's true," he admits.

I signal for Miles to stop talking, and together we take another peek. I take a chance and slowly slide the window up, just a crack. It's enough to overhear what Mr. Evens is saying, if we are very quiet.

"I'm here, Maya, just like you wanted and, well . . . it's a disaster!" he says, throwing his hands up in defeat.

Who is Maya and why is he the only one who can see her? I look at Miles, and without saying a word, I know he's thinking the same thing.

Mr. Evens stops pacing and folds his arms across his chest in dismay. "Yeah, yeah. I know what you're gonna say—this is only my first day—but I don't need to have a second day to know that this arrangement won't work out."

What arrangement?

"You should have told me that it would be like this. I had no idea. Did you know this school is full of . . . kids? I mean, I knew there would be a few, but not this many. They are everywhere, Maya!" he says as he starts pacing again.

"Did you know how sticky kids are? Yeah, that's right, they stick to everything. They also sneeze, cough, and touch. Oh, Maya, they touch *everything*. They're a breeding ground for germs. You know how I feel about germs." Mr. Evens falls silent, like he's waiting for this "Maya" to finish talking.

"I knew you were going to bring that up! And, yes, you're right. I said I would give it a try, but I'm no good at this. Do you have any idea how many questions they ask? A million. And that is not an exaggeration. I met this kid just now, and, babe, I think if you take a drop of his blood and put it under a microscope, you'd find teeny-tiny question marks."

Miles grins proudly and mouths the words "He's talking about me!"

"The kid has a big sister, and, yes, she looked adorable with her Afro pigtails, but don't let that fool you. When she thought I was gonna do something to her little brother, she got 'elementary-school gangster' on me."

I don't know why that makes me smile, but it does. Mr. Evens shakes his head and points at the person standing in front of him—the person who is not there. "Don't you dare laugh at me, Maya! Don't you do it! This is serious."

I think "Maya" is still laughing because Mr. Evens's frown deepens. "Okay, you think this is funny, huh? Well, it's not. I am no good at this. So it's time we call it off. I'm done. I'll tell the principal in the morning."

He waits for a reply. I don't think "Maya" gives him one. "C'mon, don't give me that look," he says. Slowly his stone face softens, his lips tremble, and he lets out a soft, pained moan. "I can't do this without you, honey. I don't know how," he says, sobbing into his hands.

My chest hurts and there's a lump in my throat. Plump teardrops spill from Miles's eyes and down his cheeks.

"We have to go inside and make him feel better. He's really sad," Miles says.

"Yeah, I know he's sad. But it's a private sad. We shouldn't have been listening, okay?" I reply, wiping the tears from his face. He nods reluctantly. We go around back and leave Mr. Evens alone.

"Shine?" Miles says.

"Yeah?"

"I won't get to meet Mr. Evens's wife, will I?"

"No, Bug. You won't."

Chapter Four
Luna

WHEN WE GET BACK to the basement, we look out the window and watch as Mr. Evens's car drives away. Miles asks if we're going to sleep on the floor. I promise him we won't.

"There has to be something here we can use as a bed . . ." I say out loud but mostly to myself. The two of us look around. We find a gym mat buried under a small mountain of junk and drag it to the center of the room. It's hard and cold like stone, but it's better than the floor. We sit on the mat and take a look inside the bag that Folake gave us. We eat the snacks but are smart enough not to touch the sandwich. (Cauliflower Courage turns out to be cauliflower, fried eggs, and honey.)

I thought Miles would ask a bunch of questions about how long we have to stay in the basement. But all he wants to talk about is Mr. Evens.

"You think Mr. Evens is coming back to teach tomorrow?" he asks.

"Probably not. I think he's gonna quit."

"Oh." And then out of nowhere, Miles looks at me and

says, "I'm sorry I didn't stay in the basement like you told me to, Shine."

"I know. But promise next time, Bug, you have to listen to me."

"Okay. I promise."

I take his little hands in mine and hold on tight. "Guess what book we're reading tonight?" I ask.

He smiles. "Really? We haven't read it in a whole week!" He's talking about our favorite fantasy. The one Nanna would read to us a hundred times.

"Well, maybe not. It's kind of late," I tease.

"Please! Please!"

I laugh. "Okay, okay." I take the book out of my backpack, sit on the edge of Miles's mat, and begin to read.

The Girl of Fire and Light

In the small village of Atar, perched on a hill, sits a mystical tree that's older than time itself. Its leaves are engulfed in a bright reddish-orange glow, as if it's on fire. This tree is known as Annora: the Tree of Fire and Light. Inside the base of Annora, there are immense treasures. People come from far and wide to beg her to grant them access to her riches.

If Annora took pity on them, she'd create an opening and allow them to enter. Once inside, they'd gaze upon a sea of treasures. Everyone that entered would quickly stack the trunks of treasures, one on top of the other, until it was sky-high. Then they would ask Annora to let them out.

But Annora had a rule: many could enter, but only the pure of heart could leave. Many people thought they fit that description. Unfortunately, they were wrong. And they were then transformed into branches of the illustrious tree.

One day, a brown-skinned girl with big eyes and even bigger hair named Luna kneeled down at the base of the tree. She asked Annora to allow her to enter. She explained that her family was poor and this year's crop was bad. And now they had nothing to live on. Annora opened up and allowed her to enter.

Once inside, Luna could not believe the vast treasure trove that lay out before her. There were countless chests filled with gemstones, coins, and jewelry. When it was time to take what she wanted, Luna selected a simple gold necklace. She knew she could trade it for enough money to keep her family fed for at least this year and the next. When it was time to go, she closed her eyes and prayed that the tree would permit her to leave—and it did! Once outside, she asked Annora why she was permitted to go and the others weren't.

Annora replied in a deep, gravelly voice: "Many have come believing that they are pure of heart: humble servants, beggars, fair maidens, and even holy men. But unlike them, you only took what you needed. That is the true sign of a good heart."

Luna thanked Annora and was on her way. However, she returned the next day.

"Are you seeking more riches?" Annora asked.

"No, my family has what they need. They thank you."

"Then why have you returned?" Annora asked.

"You are the only one of your kind. I wondered if you might be lonely. In that case, I could keep you company."

"I am older than the rivers, the valleys, and the sky itself. And no one has ever offered to spend time with me. And never has anyone inquired about how this old tree feels. Thank you. Yes, I would like your company." And from that moment on, every day after her chores were done, Luna would come to visit Annora.

One day, Luna was late for their daily meeting, and Annora worried that something might be wrong. Later that day, when Luna came to see her, she had tears in her eyes. Luna explained that her family had fallen into a deep sleep and could not wake up.

"I tried everything, Annora, and nothing worked!" Luna said. Annora thought and thought. Finally, she remembered a remedy that was almost as old as she was.

"It's called Loom. It's a potion that guarantees to cure whatever ails you."

"Great, where can I get it?"

Annora sighed. "That's just it, Luna, you can't get it. You have to make it. There are lots of herbs and oils that need to be combined to make Loom."

"That's okay! I'm pretty good at making soup for my family. A potion shouldn't be that much harder," Luna replied.

"No, it won't be hard to make. But there are three main ingredients in Loom that are very difficult to acquire."

"It doesn't matter, Annora. Whatever I have to get, I will get it."

"You will need a seashell kissed by a mermaid, a single hair from a manticore, and a tear from a Gorgon. Once you have these three things, add them to the mixture and your potion will be complete."

"What happens once the potion is done?"

"You spill one drop on your family's foreheads, and within minutes, they will be healed. I promise."

Luna wanted to start her quest to make Loom right away. However, Annora made her wait until she was able to find Luna a guide; someone or something that could help her along the way.

"Luna, meet your guide and protector, Wynn," Annora said.

A crimson red dragon swooped down and landed in front of them. It had large nostrils and exhaled thick puffs of smoke. Its massive wings spread wide and covered much of the area. When it opened its mouth, a sea of flames leaped out. Luna was frightened and jumped back. Annora assured her that Wynn was a friend.

Luna carefully stepped forward and tried to pet Wynn. Wynn playfully bounced his head from side to side. It was only then that Luna realized how gentle the dragon was. And together, the two set off to find what they needed to save Luna's family.

First, Wynn landed on the shores of the Baltic Sea with Luna on his back. He hovered above the water, where he had last seen a mermaid. It took a while, but eventually, they saw a beautiful mermaid, leaping from the depths below and breaking through the surface of the water. They shouted down to the creature and begged her to kiss the seashell they had brought with them. The mermaid kindly agreed so long as they vowed not to reveal the mermaid's location to any more humans. Wynn and Luna had gotten the first item they needed.

The second item would not be as easy to acquire. Most manticores do not like humans, and they don't play nice. Luna and Wynn weren't sure they could get one to give them a strand of its hair, but they were determined to try. They flew over the Black Forest, and from the air they spotted a manticore—a colossal half lion, half man—roaming among the trees.

It was hunting something, a creature that was too small for them to make out from the air. Luna told

Wynn to fly down as fast as he could so they could save whatever poor being the manticore was chasing. They came closer and realized the creature was a fairy. They swooped down and landed just in time to save it. The fairy scurried toward an opening in a nearby log. This made the manticore so angry, he turned his focus on Wynn and Luna.

"You interfered in my affairs, dragon! And you brought a human to my forest. Now you will pay!" the manticore vowed. He charged at them. Wynn was about to unleash a wave of flames, but Luna stopped him.

"No, Wynn, don't! You'll singe all his hair off!" Luna warned.

Wynn swallowed the flames back down and let out a smoke-filled burp. Luna slid off Wynn's back and addressed the manticore. She told him what they needed from him. The manticore agreed—but only if Luna was willing to give up Wynn and allow him to be the manticore's pet.

"No! I won't trade Wynn. He's my friend!" Luna shouted.

"Then you will fail your mission. I will never give you one single hair from my head," the manticore replied.

"It's okay, Luna. I will stay and be the manticore's pet," Wynn said. "It's the only way to help your family."

Luna thought about it and replied, "Manticore—"

"Relic." The creature snorted rudely. "My name is Relic."

"Fine. Relic, I challenge you to a battle. If I win, you will belong to me and must do as I say. If I lose, then I will stay here with you and do your bidding," Luna said.

"Forever?" Relic dared.

"Yes, forever."

Relic let out a wicked, thunderous laugh. "You think you can take me on?"

"Probably not. But my family is worth the risk," Luna replied.

"Fine. But if your dragon interferes, the deal is off! This is just between us, human," Relic said. Luna agreed. Relic shook his human head in disbelief. How could this human be so naive as to think she could beat him?

Relic scoffed. "This will be a foolish endeavor for you. And for what? What's so great about family?"

"Well, sometimes they aren't so great. Sometimes my little sister sings too loudly in the morning and wakes me up. Sometimes my dad makes me eat everything on my plate even if it tastes awful. And my mom won't let me swim in the lake until I do my chores. But they always love and take care of me. They would never give up a quest to heal me. Now, neither will I."

The manticore charged toward Luna. She quickly got out of the way and reached for a large branch from a nearby tree. She snapped it in half and used it as a makeshift sword, but her weapon could not compare to the manticore's talons. They cut through the air and came within inches of shredding Luna in half!

The fairy hiding in the log yelled, "This is the last of my magic!" She waved her hand and silver strands filled the air and molded itself into a glowing sword. It loomed just above Luna's head.

"Luna, get the sword!" Wynn roared.

Luna jumped into the air and grabbed the sword just as the manticore came toward her. Luna, whose mom had taught her to wield a sword, was able to go head-to-head with Relic, much to the manticore's surprise. Soon, Luna was able to pin him down. She pointed the sword at him and dared him to move an inch.

"Fine. You win, human. I will do what you say. I will be your pet," Relic conceded.

"No, all I want is for you to give me a single hair. Then we will leave you in peace."

Wynn and Luna got the second item on the list. And with the help of the fairy, they found the location of the very last creature they needed—the Gorgon.

Luna had heard about Gorgons—they were three sisters with hair made of venomous snakes. She was told that when they looked her in the eye, they would turn her to stone. So she made sure the two of them had a plan.

She tore off two small pieces of fabric from the sleeves of her shirt. She wrapped Wynn's eyes so he didn't have to look at the snakes. Luna hid behind a nearby tree and signaled to Wynn to knock on the door. When the door opened, she saw the shadow of three sisters standing with snakes on their heads. The triplets finished each other's sentences and demanded to know why a dragon had dared to knock on their door. Wynn began a long story about how he had gotten lost.

While the Gorgons were distracted, Luna entered the creepy home through the back window. She quietly moved the furniture around. Soon the Gorgons grew tired of Wynn and warned him that he had only a second to fly away or they would make the snakes on their head attack. Wynn thanked them for their time and took off.

The Gorgons slammed the door, and Luna heard the snakes hiss from behind the wall of the kitchen, where she was hiding. The sisters scolded the snakes and demanded that they "settle down and take a nap!" The snakes suddenly stopped hissing. Luna took a deep breath and poked her head out; the snakes were fast asleep. Luna breathed a sigh of relief, now that she didn't have to cover her eyes. But since she had no idea when the snakes would wake up, she held the fabric in her hand, ready in case she had to place it over her eyes.

The sisters began to argue about whose turn it was to clean the cauldron. They were so busy arguing, they tripped over a large chest that had mysteriously appeared in the middle of the room.

"Ouch!" all three of them yelled, as big plump tears sprung to their eyes. Luna quickly scooped up the drops with the small vial she brought with her and then scurried under the table. The sisters had been hurt in battle before, but that was nothing compared to the pain of stubbing their toes. It was odd, but that pain was worse than any other pain in the world.

"My poor toe!" the first one yelled.

"It hurts! It hurts!" the second one yelled.

"Who put that there?!" the third one said. One of them accused the other. And soon, all three of them were arguing. They didn't notice the little girl run out from under the table and climb out the window. When Luna and Wynn got back to Atar, they made the potion and administered it to her family members. Within minutes, her family was well again, just like Annora promised.

In the weeks that followed, the three friends spent a lot of time together. One bright, early morning, Annora announced to Wynn that her time on earth was coming to an end. She asked Wynn to whom she should gift the last of her powers. Wynn knew exactly who should get them and he told her so. Annora agreed. Later that day, the crowd gathered on the hilltop to watch as Annora transferred her powers to Luna.

Many people had looked at Luna's brown skin, big eyes, and even bigger hair, and thought she was just an ordinary girl. However, to her family, Luna was a good daughter and brave older sister. And to her two best friends, Wynn and Annora, she was a hero. But now Luna had power and could protect not just her family, but her entire village. And from that day, throughout the land, she would forever be known as Luna, the Girl of Fire and Light.

By the time I get to the end and close the book, Miles is so sleepy, he can hardly keep his eyes open. That doesn't stop him from asking me to read it again. I tell him we can tomorrow. He mumbles something about not being sleepy as his eyes roll to the back of his head. I get up and stretch just as Miles sinks deeper into sleep. I settle down beside him, and he mutters something.

"What is it, Miles?" I ask as sleep makes my eyes heavy.

"Luna."

"I'll read it again tomorrow, now go to bed," I reply, seconds away from deep, deep sleep.

"No, Shine. I said, Luna sounds like you. You have the same hair; you're both trying to save your families. It's like she's you." And just like that, he was snoring lightly and off to dreamland.

But as Miles falls asleep, a sudden realization jolts me awake. I sit bolt upright, eyes bugging out of my head. Oh. My. Goodness! That's it! That's why Nanna has read this story to us over and over again. She knew that I would have to save her one day, and she was telling me exactly how to do that: I have to go on Luna's quest!

Chapter Five
The Beast

WE HAVE BEEN HIDING for a whole night. It was hard to sleep because of the draft in the room and also because it was way too quiet. But it's morning now; we made it through the night. Miles asked if we could come out and I said yes. I figure the officers and the social workers have given up looking for us. Besides, I have to meet up with Folake and tell her the news!

There should be a rule: If you discover something awesome, your body should instantly be teleported to your best friend's house so you can share the news. But since I can't do that, I have to wait until school starts to share my news with Folake. The wait is torture! It's not as bad as when I have to wait to open my Christmas gifts, but still, it's pretty bad.

After getting ready, Miles and I sneak out of our hiding place and enter the yard where some of the kids have already started to gather. Folake is usually here by now. She only lives a few blocks from the school, and she likes getting here early.

"If Folake doesn't show up in the next ten minutes, she'll be late," I tell Miles, who's checking out his hair in the reflection in one of the classroom windows. He always checks his reflection when he's about to see Folake.

"She's never late," Miles says. "Unless . . ."

We look at each other with eyes as big as headlights. We shout at the same time: "The Beast!"

We race down the street, hoping we're not too late. The wind howls in our ears and the cold whips our faces, but we don't stop running. Two blocks later, we find my best friend standing in the middle of the sidewalk; even her braids are shaking. She's clutching her backpack to her chest, hoping it will shield her from the Beast that stands in front of her.

I remember the first time Folake told us about the Beast. She came running into the schoolyard. The handles of her glasses could hardly hang on to her ears. She was going so fast, her braids didn't show up until a few seconds later. When she was finally able to catch her breath, she told us the story.

"I was walking down the street, thinking of new recipes. One minute it was bright and sunny, and the next, a shadow appeared and blocked out the sun. I couldn't make out what it was yet; it was too far away. But I heard it make a sound. It sounded like the earth was burping. Burping so deep, it shook the pavement under my feet.

"It came closer. I could make out its long, thick, shiny claws. It had four powerful legs and fangs sharper than any of my pencils. The creature's nostrils flared and pumped out puffs of angry smoke.

"And its eyes. Its eyes were the reddest red. It took a step toward me. And another. Then, before I could get my feet to move, the Beast opened up its mouth and roared like thunder! I screamed and started running in the other direction, as fast as I could!"

After she told her story, we knew we couldn't just let the Beast run wild in the neighborhood, so we went to take a look. We were hoping to find it and figure out a way to stop it, or at least tell a grown-up where it was located. Folake wasn't too happy about going back, but she agreed that it would be bad to let the Beast go after someone else.

When we got to the spot where Folake first saw the massive monster, Miles and I exchanged a confused look. "The Beast" was a Pomeranian dog named Brownie who could fit in my pocket. Miles and I tried not to laugh because we didn't want to hurt Folake's feelings. We found the owners of the dog a few houses away and returned Brownie. Folake was so relieved; she hugged both of us so tight our eyeballs almost popped out!

Most of the time Folake can get to school without encountering the dog, but every once in a while, when the owners forget to lock the gate, Brownie gets out. And that's exactly what had happened just now.

"It's okay. He just wanted to play," Miles tells Folake as he goofs off with the dog. Folake scrunches her face, suspicious of the animal's wagging tail. I tell Miles to hurry or we'll be late for school. Brownie licks his face as Miles puts him back behind his owners' gate.

Folake is quiet as we make our way back to school. I want to tell her about last night, but I don't think now is the time.

She walks with her head down. I ask her what's wrong, and she slumps her shoulders.

"I don't think I'll ever stop being afraid of dogs. Little Miles can face them. He even plays with them! Why can't I?"

"It's okay, everybody is afraid of something," I reply.

"Shine is right, Folake. I'm afraid of some animals, too," Miles says.

"Really, like what?" she asks. "Sharks?"

He laughs. "Oh, no, Selachimorpha?! Those guys are super cool and very misunderstood. I'm afraid of animals with nice names that make people *think* they are friendly but they aren't—like the 'kissing bug.' See, it has a sweet name, but it's actually a bloodsucking—"

"Miles!" I scold.

"What?" he says, clueless.

I shake my head and wonder why I didn't get a brother who was into video games or comic books. I love Miles, but that little boy knows too much.

"I'm a coward, Sunny," she whispers as we make it back to the schoolyard.

I put my arm around her shoulders. "No, you're not."

"Yes, I am. I can't even face a dog that's named after my favorite dessert!"

"Folake, you're strong, smart, and you're also a chef! Did you forget that you're the queen of sandwiches?!" I remind her. I didn't lie to Folake. She is the queen of sandwiches. (Bad-tasting sandwiches, but I left that last part out.) The bell rings to start class. Miles says goodbye and runs off to the annex building next door.

Folake and I enter the main building on our way to class. Just as we take our seats, I whisper, "Who is the genius that thought to put bacon and PB and J together? Who thought to add grapes to a grilled cheese sandwich?"

She shrugs. "Me, I guess."

"That's right! You're a genius."

"In the kitchen, yes. But in the real world, let's face it: I'm a coward! Just admit it, you think the same thing," she says miserably.

"If I thought you were a coward, why would I be taking you with me on a quest?!"

Her eyes light up.

It's lunchtime, and Folake apologizes because she didn't have enough time to create a masterpiece. She said I would have to settle for a plain old PB and J. I try to hide my smile as I take my first big bite. We eat quickly and get down to business. I tell Folake what happened the night before. I don't leave anything out. I tell her about us almost getting caught by the new music teacher, Mr. Evens. How we saw him talking to someone who wasn't there, and, most importantly, I told her what I realized about the fantasy Nanna read to us every night.

"I think Luna is me! Nanna told me the story so that I could go on the quest and save her!"

She asks me to tell her Luna's story again and I do.

"So what do you think?" I ask once I'm done.

She bites her lower lip and tilts her head to the side. She's thinking hard about it. "Well, she does sound a lot like you . . . Yes! I think you might be right!" she says.

I fold my arms across my chest triumphantly. "I knew it!"

"Wait, I have an idea," Folake says, taking a notepad out from her backpack. "We have to make a list of all the things that Luna has in the story and make sure we find them in real life."

"Good idea!" I reply. "Okay, let's start at the beginning. Luna has to find a seashell kissed by a mermaid, a single hair from a manticore, and a tear from a Gorgon," I recite by heart.

"Yes, but before she goes out on her quest, the tree Annora gives her a guide: a red dragon. We can't start our quest until we see a red dragon," Folake replies.

"Oh, you're right!" I sigh and place my hand under my chin. Where are we going to find a red dragon?

"Do you think maybe we can start the quest without a dragon?" Folake asks.

I shake my head. "If Luna's quest is really our quest, first we have to find the one who's supposed to be our guide, the same way it happened in the story."

"Wait, in the story, Luna didn't bring anyone along. Are you sure it's okay to bring me?" she asks.

"Yes! If Luna had a best friend, she'd take her along too. I know she would. So you're coming and we're doing this together," I reply.

"Okay. Now, where do we find our red dragon?" We look around the cafeteria, expecting a giant winged dragon to enter, but nothing happens.

"Okay, well, the school day is not over. Let's just keep an eye out," Folake says.

I nod in agreement, but my stomach gets all twisty. What if we never see a red dragon? What if I made this whole thing up in my head and there's no quest to go on? How will I ever save Nanna?

Throughout the school day, Folake and I are on high alert for the red dragon, and there's no sign of it. It's the end of the day, we only have one more class left, and I'm starting to really worry. My last class is chorus.

I thought we would not be seeing Mr. Evens again. He didn't seem to like being around kids. I figured he quit this morning and was already off hanging out with adults, doing adult things like food shopping or paying taxes. But I was wrong. When we enter the music room, guess who is standing at the whiteboard? Mr. Pencil himself, looking even straighter than before. When he sees me, he quickly looks behind me in a panic. I smile to myself.

"Miles is not here," I promise him.

He lets out a big sigh of relief. "Good. That kid . . . How many questions can one child have?"

"I don't know. But I can ask him to come see you after class and help you figure it out," I tease.

His eyes narrow, and he folds his arms across his chest. "You will do no such thing. Now take your seat."

I do as he says. I sit down next to Folake. We both cover our mouths to hide our smiles. Folake whispers, "Looks like your little brother is making friends." We laugh. Mr. Evens clears his throat, and we quickly stop.

He goes over to the whiteboard and writes his name. "I'm Mr. Evens, your new teacher. Now, this is a learning institution, not a concert hall, so naturally there will be no autographs."

All the kids in the class look at him like he's got little green aliens oozing out of his ears. No one in the class knows who he is or why they should ask for his autograph.

He takes attendance while sitting on the edge of his desk, his feet dangling over the side. He talks forever about all the awards and stuff he has. The class is mostly sleeping with their eyes open. But Mr. Evens doesn't notice because he's not really looking at us. He's mostly gazing above our heads. He starts to laugh at something he thinks is funny. But no one else laughs.

"So, I said to him, I said, 'Mr. Jones, your arrangement is wrong!' Well, actually, I said 'Quincy' because he lets me call him that. Other people have to call him Mr. Jones, but since I'm a brilliant composer, just like him, I get to call him Quincy. In fact—and I don't want to brag—but he told me to call him Q." Then Mr. Evens laughs again.

Troy Woodson raises his hand. Troy has bright freckles and sandy, kinky hair, and he hums all the time. I mean all the time. It drives the rest of the class crazy, but he does have a really nice voice.

"Yes, how can I help you, young pupil?" Mr. Evens asks.

"I heard that there is going to be a big concert, is that true?" he asks. There's chatter among the class.

Mr. Evens tells them to quiet down. "I was going to announce that at the end of class, but since you brought it up . . ." Mr. Evens goes behind his desk and reveals a large movie poster. But instead of a movie, it's a picture of musical notes, autumn leaves, and a class picture of all of us in chorus.

"This school has been chosen to perform at the Fall Music Festival! We'll be representing all the other schools in our district. In the past, this school has applied to take part in this event, but that honor went to other schools. Fortunately for you, this year, you have me," he says proudly.

"Will we be singing in front of the whole school?" someone asks behind me.

"No. You'll be singing in front of this school and three other schools! Not to mention all your friends and family. This is the biggest musical event of the school year! And while there'll be parts for everyone, some talented and skilled singer will get a solo part! That's right, one of you will get to have the stage all to yourself!"

The class goes wild. They start talking all at once, and everyone thinks that they'll be the one to get the solo part.

"Now we're going to do this just like they do it in a professional environment. If you want the solo part, you are going to have to audition for it. There's a sign-up sheet posted on the door. Auditions are Friday."

"Are you going to be the one who picks the soloist?" Folake asks.

"It's not just me. There are two other music teachers from other grades—Mr. Hawk and Mrs. Hall. They'll help me select who the soloist will be. Now, take this show very seriously. This is how stars are made, people!"

Mr. Evens has a hard time getting the class to stop talking about the concert and focus on the lesson. Folake doesn't like singing, but she knows I do, and she tells me that I should sign up.

"No, I can't. Nanna won't be there," I reply.

"But you can sing without her. She'd be okay with it. She'd want you to sing—you always sound so good!"

"That's when I sing in church. And this isn't church. What if I get nervous or my voice cracks? And when I look out at the audience, Nanna won't be there to make the sign that she always makes before I sing."

"I didn't know you two had a sign. What is it?" she asks.

"In our church, whenever someone sings really, really well, the old ladies always fan themselves. It's their way of saying the singer onstage sang so good, they almost fainted. The first time I was going to sing solo in church, I told Nanna that I was scared. What if no one waves their fans? Nanna said, 'Baby, I'll always be there to wave my fan for you.'

"And ever since then, every time I'm about to sing a solo, I look in the audience, and there she is, waving her fan. Sometimes she brings a real fan and other times she uses her hands. But no matter what, she's always waving for me. That's our signal. I can't go onstage without it."

Folake says she understands, but she tells me to at least think about it. But there's no use. I can't sing without Nanna in the audience. When class is over, almost everyone rushes to go write their name on the sign-up sheet. Folake and I are the last ones to leave the class. We walk by Mr. Evens, and he stops us.

"I trust you and your rumbustious sibling won't be loafing around after school today, Ms. Williams?" he says.

Why does he talk like that?

"No, we won't be hanging out—I mean loafing," I reply.

He clears his throat. "Well, good. And as for that little brother of yours . . . make sure to warn him to watch where he goes. He can't just run out into the street. It's not safe."

"Okay," I reply.

"Oh, and, um . . . there are some animal documentaries that I thought he should consider viewing. Since he's into that sort of thing," he says, handing me a list on a bright yellow Post-it Note. I smile.

Maybe Mr. Evens isn't so bad?

Chapter Six
The Rules

I CAN'T TAKE THE chance that Mr. Evens might spot us again, so this time, we stay inside and don't leave the school at all.

"It's really cold outside. And Mr. Evens might see us, so we have to stay here," I say.

"You saw Mr. Evens today? Did he ask about me?" Miles wonders with big eyes.

"Well . . . yeah, he did."

"What did he say?" Miles asks, growing more and more excited. I hand him the Post-it Note with the list of documentaries Mr. Evens gave me. Miles reads it and shakes his head.

"What is it?" I ask.

"These are really . . . basic. For Mr. Evens and me to be best friends, I'm gonna have to teach him a thing or two. But that's okay. That's what best friends do."

"Well, you can make him your own list after you eat," I say as I take out the bag Folake handed off to me before she went home. I peek inside it and then look up at Miles.

"Oh no. Should I even ask?" Miles says.

I smile. "She said she didn't have all the stuff she needed to create anything for us, so she gave us leftovers from dinner the night before."

"Really? What is it?"

I take out two small plastic bowls and show it to him. He knows what it is even before I open the containers.

"Jollof rice! Yes!" Miles says, digging in with the plastic spoon I got from the cafeteria. Jollof rice is good, even cold. It's traditional Nigerian rice made with tomato, onion, pepper, and lots of yummy spices. I open my bowl and begin to eat. It makes me feel better, but not by much.

"What's wrong?" Miles asks in between bites.

"Folake agrees that we're right about having to go on a quest. But in the story, Luna had a red dragon to guide her. I looked all over the place today and not one dragon in sight. But that's okay. I'm sure we'll see a dragon—soon! Right?"

He looks like he's about to say something but then he just nods and gives me a sad smile. We eat in silence for a while, and then Miles sighs deeply and scrunches his face up; he does that when he's thinking really hard about something. "Shine?" he says.

"Yeah?"

"Do you think Nanna is okay at the home? What if she's hungry or cold? You know she gets really cold at night. She always needs extra thick socks."

A picture of Nanna flashes in my head. She's sitting alone in a gray-colored room, and she doesn't have any of the things she needs to make her smile. No pictures of animals made by

Miles and no family photos by her bed. Nanna loves to watch people walking by out the window. We would make a game out of it. What if she doesn't even have a window?

I can't tell Miles what I'm thinking; it'll only make him worry. So I try to hide my worry under my smile. "Nope, Nanna is warm and sleeping in a big bed with fluffy pillows. She has on two extra socks, and she's humming her favorite Stevie Wonder song. What song is that?"

"'As,'" Miles replies. Nanna sang that song all the time. It's a song about loving someone forever, until the end of time. She said that song was perfect because that's how much she loved us. I start to sing, even though Miles is already on his way to dreamland. It makes me feel better, like Nanna is somewhere out there singing the same song too.

I can see the notes come to life as I sing them. They start out looking like music notes but then turn to shimmering black birds that soar into the sky. When I'm singing with other people, I turn their notes into red birds. We harmonize together, causing the red and black birds to perform a beautiful dance in the air. Music is basically magic!

The more I sing, the more into it I get. I watch "the birds" soaring above my head and out the window. I didn't realize I had started to sing louder, but I guess I did because a few moments later . . .

"What are you doing here?!" someone says behind me. I turn around and come face-to-face with a very unhappy pencil!

For the next few minutes, Mr. Evens rants about reckless kids, safety protocol, and how us kids will cause him to age quickly. I think that's weird since he looks to be the same age he was earlier in class. When he finally starts to make sense, he orders us to get our stuff and come with him to his classroom. Miles and I look at each other, in a panic. I try to come up with a plan, but it's hard to think when your heart is stuck at the top of a roller coaster and won't come back down.

Mr. Evens helps us take all of our stuff to the music room. And of course we grab Noodle as well. On Mr. Evens's desk are Chinese take-out boxes, plastic forks, and napkins. Why is he having dinner here at school? Why didn't he just go home? I would ask him, but it might be better to wait until he starts blinking again.

"Do you have any idea how worried your parents are? What's their phone number? I need to call them right now!" Mr. Evens says. His eyebrows form a serious V shape, and his lips look the same way mine do when I bite into a Sour Patch Kids candy.

I feel my heart jump off the roller coaster and slide down between my toes. There's a lump in my throat, and I'm hoping that I don't have to say the words out loud. "Where are your parents?" is my least favorite question of all time. I turn to Miles; he hates that question, too. I don't want him to have to reply. I'm the older sister; it's my job to do the hard stuff.

"Our parents died in a car accident," I reply. "It was really bad weather and the car hit black ice. Do you know anything about black ice?"

"It's really slippery, and it makes it hard for cars to stop," Mr. Evens says.

"It's not black, you know," I mutter, looking out the window. "They call it black ice, but really it's clear. It just looks black because the road is black."

"That's it exactly. I'm impressed," he says.

I shrug. "I know everything about black ice."

In my head, I can see my parents, driving off down the road. I know it's not real, but it feels like it's real.

"I think they were laughing," I tell him.

"Who?" Mr. Evens asks.

"Our parents. I think they were sitting in the car, laughing, just before they died. Maybe our dad told a joke. Or maybe our mom saw a funny sign. I don't really have a way to prove it, but . . . I think they were laughing and happy just before . . ."

Miles turns to Mr. Evens. "I was a baby then. I don't remember Nanna telling us what happened. I don't remember their faces. But I look at their photo all the time, so I won't forget them."

Mr. Evens looks off in the distance, like he's watching a movie only he can see. "Pictures help. Sometimes," he says in a gloomy voice.

All three of us go silent. Mr. Evens is the first to speak. He asks who we stay with, and I tell him my nanna. I tell him that she was taken to a home, and we do not want to go anywhere without her.

"Why was she taken to a home?"

"She forgets things a lot," Miles says with a small, sad voice.

Mr. Evens nods slowly. "Okay. I'm gonna step out into the hall and call the principal. She'll have to come down here."

Before Mr. Evens leaves the room, I call out to him, "You have winter tires on your car, right?"

Mr. Evens smiles a little and then nods. "Yes, I have very good winter tires." That makes me smile too. I'm not really sure why.

After he makes the call, Mr. Evens tells us the principal will be here soon. When he sees the looks on our faces, he lies to us. He says everything is going to be okay. I'm not mad at him for lying. I think it's a nice lie. The kind of lie grown-ups say to try and make things better. But what happens now? Can a quest be over before it even starts?

We take a seat. Miles puts his head on my shoulder, and I squeeze him tightly. Mr. Evens watches as we huddle together. I whisper, "I'm sorry I got us caught." I try not to cry, but I can feel the tears run down my face.

"Hey, hey, now. Don't . . . don't do the water thing," Mr. Evens orders as he comes close.

"You mean cry?" I ask.

"Yeah, it's . . . You don't have to do that. We'll get this all sorted out. I'm sure there's a place for you and your brother to go."

"But there's nowhere for us to go. They're gonna send us to foster care. We're never gonna see our friends or our nanna again!" Miles says as he starts to cry.

Mr. Evens comes toward us. He's thinking so hard about what to say next; it almost looks painful. In my mind, I picture his brain at the gym, lifting weights way too heavy for it to pick up.

Finally, Mr. Evens gives up on words and comes over to Miles. He gives his shoulder two quick, short taps—like he's tapping the side of a music stand with his baton. Then he says, "There, there."

"I'm sorry, Miles, this is all my fault. I must have been singing too loudly," I reply, adding my tears to his.

Mr. Evens replies, "It wasn't how loud your voice was, it was—"

I don't mean to interrupt him, but my words just can't wait. They have to come tumbling out of my mouth, right this second!

"Where are we gonna go? How awful is the place they are going to take us?" I beg.

"Well, the foster system is notoriously underfunded. They have subpar housing and social services, and often a large section of kids are neglected." He stops himself once he sees the looks of horror on our faces. But it's too late.

Miles runs screaming into the instrument closet. He's sobbing now and won't get out from behind the door so we can open it. "I'm not going to foster care!" he declares.

"Miles, come out! Bug, please come out," I beg.

"No! I hate this! I hate this!" he yells. His cries make my stomach ache and my heart twist inside me.

I look at Mr. Evens; he's blurry because of the tears in my

eyes. But I can see him clearly enough to know he's worried too.

"I'm sorry. I didn't mean to say—Miles. It won't be that bad. It won't be bad at all. There is lots of fun stuff to do," Mr. Evens says.

"Like what?" Miles asks.

Mr. Evens thinks really hard and says, "Pudding. You kids like that stuff, right? Yeah, there's lots of pudding."

I look over at him, my eyes bulging out of my head. "Pudding?" I repeat in disbelief. Mr. Evens shrugs helplessly.

"Miles, please come out!" Miles doesn't reply. "If you come out, I will take you to the park."

"No," he says stubbornly.

"And Folake will be there, too," I add.

"Well . . . No! I won't come out. Ever!" Miles insists.

"I wish Nanna were here, she can solve anything. I'm not good at this. I'm not a good big sister," I admit to Mr. Evens as I try really hard to hold back tears.

Mr. Evens looks around the room like there's some huge sign somewhere that will tell him what to do. Mr. Evens's face suddenly lights up. "Maya . . ." he says.

I look back at him, confused. He looks at the closet and speaks to Miles from behind the door. "Okay, Miles, you stay in there. In the meantime, I will be out here telling your sister about the time my wife, Maya, found the rarest insect in the world—the land lobster!"

"The *Dryococelus australis*?! That's impossible!" Miles snorts.

"No, it's not! And I have pictures from when she worked with them at the Australian museum," Mr. Evens says. "But if you don't want to see it . . ."

Mr. Evens and I look at each other and hold our breath. Miles has stopped crying, but he hasn't made a move to come out. We wait. It feels like an eternity. We wait. We wait. And then . . .

"Where is this picture?" Miles says, peeking his head out slowly. His eyebrows are raised suspiciously. He's letting us know, if this is a trick, he's going right back inside the closet.

I hope that Mr. Evens isn't telling a lie and that he really does have a picture of this lobster insect or else we're in big trouble. Mr. Evens goes over to his computer bag, resting on a small table near the entrance. He takes out his laptop.

"It's right in here. I have Maya's drive with all her research papers and photos," he says proudly.

"C'mon, Miles, go see!" I urge him. It only takes a few seconds for Miles to make up his mind. As soon as the screen glows, Miles rushes to Mr. Evens's side.

"There, you see! The land lobster!" Mr. Evens says, just as excited. The two of them pull up chairs and sit in front of the laptop. They start talking about all the things that Maya saw and did while she was at the Australian museum; I have never seen Miles so happy. And the strange thing is Mr. Evens, the world's most perfect pencil, is a little less straight. I even hear what might be a chuckle!

Suddenly Miles's eyes light up with excitement. "I know, why don't we stay with you?" he says to Mr. Evens.

Mr. Evens's mouth drops to the floor, and his tongue rolls out like a carpet. He's too shocked to form words. I know Mr. Evens won't take us in; he's not very good with kids. It's like those old alien movies where humans meet the alien for the first time and don't understand them. Mr. Evens is the human, and to him, we're the aliens. He has no idea how to take care of us.

I'm pretty much almost a grown-up and can take care of myself, but Miles is a handful. There's no way Mr. Evens is ready for that. Also, I'm not sure he likes us. And even if he did, who takes in kids they've only known for a few hours? I don't need to wait for Mr. Evens to reply because I am old enough to know what the answer will be.

What will happen when we go to foster care? What if they don't have any zoos nearby for Miles to go to? What if they don't even have a park for him to study insects? What will he write in his insect journal? They might not let him keep a pet hamster. We'd have to give Noodle away. How would Miles feel about giving up his favorite pet?

Do zoos have basements? Maybe we could sneak in there and stay without being found out. Miles would love to live in a zoo. I still have the money from Nanna's coffee can. Maybe I can give the security guard some money so they would let us stay there. How much would that cost? And how long before we run out of money? I'd have to get a job. But what kind of job?

"What do you think, Mr. Evens? Can we stay with you?" Miles asks again.

Mr. Evens starts doing something really odd—he's saying words, but they don't form a sentence. They are just random words followed by nervous laughter.

"Ah—kids—sticky—questions—mud."

Miles and I look over at each other, not sure what to make of the words coming out of Mr. Evens's mouth. But the expression on his face is pretty clear—he is not happy with the idea of taking us. He just doesn't want to say that out loud and hurt Miles's feelings. And mine too, I guess.

"Miles, I don't think Mr. Evens can take us because it's a school rule," I reply. Mr. Evens exhales, relieved.

"Really?" Miles replies, confused.

The pencil nods quickly. "Yup, yup, that's it. It's exactly like your sister said. It's against the rules . . . Teachers can't . . . um . . . yeah. Sorry."

Miles nods his head and softly says, "Okay." I don't think we fooled him. He knows a lot about rules—rules in the animal kingdom and rules in the human world. He knows Mr. Evens does not want us. They both watch pictures of animals flash on the screen, but it's not like before.

I suggest to Miles that maybe before the other grown-ups come, we can write a note and they will pass it on to Nanna. Miles give me a small smile.

Mr. Evens makes his way over to me and says, "Honestly . . . I'm not the right person to . . . I mean, there's much better . . . I can't—"

"It's fine," I reply as my chest tightens. I look away. It

really shouldn't matter that he doesn't want us. I mean, we don't want him either. He'd probably demand that everything be nice and straight, even the curl in my lashes. He'd be no fun at all.

I go over to Mr. Evens's desk, looking for something to write our letter. I don't see anything. I move the food containers off to the side, hoping to find a pen or pencil. My brother starts waving his arms at me.

"What?" I mouth, not sure why he's saying what I think he's saying.

He rolls his eyes and points to the containers on the table. Is he saying he's hungry and wants some? I wonder how can he be hungry at a time like this? Well, it doesn't matter because the containers have no more food inside. I mouth the words, "It's empty." He signals for me to look on the *outside* of the containers. The restaurant's name is printed in big bold red letters: "Szechuan Palace." And below that is their logo: a big red dragon!

Chapter Seven
Glass Kingdoms

MR. EVENS IS OUR guide?! Out of all the people in the world, it can't be him! He's too serious, too grumpy, and talks way too much about himself. He has no idea how to have any fun; he's all about following the rules. He'd be a good guide if we had to go on a quest to find the straightest line or the most serious expression. But he's absolutely the wrong person for this adventure.

I'm about to take Miles aside and tell him what I think. But then I see an umbrella with a wooden handle in the corner. I remember the time we were supposed to go to the beach, but it rained all weekend. I pouted the whole time, and finally on Sunday, Nanna said, "Sunny, it's not about what the world gives you, it's about what you do with it."

I didn't understand at first, but then she made us put on our rain boots and coats. We had a raincoat fashion show and then went outside and played our first-ever game of "puddle wars." That's when we get to jump into puddles and see who can make the biggest splash. When we got back, she made us peppermint tea and let us add as much sugar as we wanted. (Well, almost as much as we wanted. Miles had to be stopped when he went for his fourth scoop.)

I think Nanna wanted me to know that I had to find the good parts even in bad things. That means I have to find the good parts about having Mr. Evens as our guide. And that's exactly what I will do. Now that I know he's our guide, I have to find a way to make him take us in.

I take Noodle's cage by the handle and bring it over to the window. "Noodle, how do I convince Mr. Evens to take us in?" I whisper. Noodle just looks back at me with a blank stare.

"I should have gotten a parrot," I mutter to myself. Noodle does not appreciate the comment and turns his back on me. Hamsters do not like sarcasm. Miles makes his way over to me while Mr. Evens is busy on his laptop.

"So what do we do now?" Miles asks.

"We have to stay with Mr. Evens. He's the red dragon. Our quest has started!"

"But what about the school rule?" he teases.

"Okay, okay. There's no rule," I admit.

Miles stares at Mr. Evens and says, "It's not just about him being our guide, Sunny. I looked at some of the files on his laptop. He put lizards in the same file as salamanders. Poor guy, he doesn't even know he needs my help."

"Wait! That might be it—maybe he needs help." I quickly make my way back to the table where Mr. Evens is sitting.

"Mr. Evens, step out into my office," I offer, walking over

to the window. He's surprised by my request, but still he comes along.

"What is it, Sundae?"

"Sunny."

"Right—Sunny. What is it I can do for you?"

I put on my best and brightest smile and cross my fingers that my plan works.

"Mr. Evens, it's not what you can do for me but what I can do for you!" I announce smugly.

"Oh, and what is that?"

"If you agree to take Miles and me—for just a little while—I will make you dinner every night!"

"You can cook?"

"Of course! And every night you will have a home-cooked meal, just like my nanna used to make. Red beans and rice, collard greens and red velvet cupcakes . . ."

"You know how to make all those things?" he says, his voice filled with doubt.

"I've watched my nanna make them, and I'm sure I can too. Although the last time I tried to cook anything other than tea and grits, I almost burned the place down. But what's the chances of something like that happening twice?" I say, laughing to myself. Mr. Evens isn't amused.

"Well, as delightful as it is to think about my home being engulfed in flames, I'm going to have to pass on that."

"Are you sure?"

"Very," he says, heading back across the room. I scan the

music room, trying to find something that might help. All I see are empty chairs, instruments, and the whiteboard. There has to be something here that I can use. I take a nice, big breath, close my eyes, and try to focus on finding something.

I exhale slowly and open my eyes. And right away I spot the minor details I missed in the room the first time. The trumpet case near the window has a sticker on it with a ghost playfully sticking its tongue out. On the other side of the room near the door, there's a coat rack with a bright, shiny scarf hanging on it. And on the whiteboard is an eraser with the company name on the back: "O-Shay."

So this is what I have to work with: a ghost sticker, a bright scarf, and an eraser.

I think for a moment, and suddenly a plan pops into my head. I look down at Miles and smile; he knows that I have a plan, even without me telling him. I walk over to Mr. Evens, who is putting his laptop away.

"Mr. Evens, I have a confession to make."

"I'm not the person for that kind of thing, young lady," he replies.

"But my confession is about you. I should have told you since meeting you yesterday, but I wasn't sure you'd be able to handle it. Adults can be so fragile."

He twists his face in disapproval. "I assure you I'm not fragile."

"Well, you sort of freaked out about a little mud on your suit," Miles reminds him.

"It wasn't *a little* mud and that suits costs—never mind."

Mr. Evens closes his eyes and pinches the bridge of his nose. "Go ahead, what is your confession, Sunny? I think I can take it."

"I'm not just Sunny. I go by another name."

"And what name would that be?" he asks.

I walk over to the silky scarf hanging off the coat rack and drape it over my head. I go to Mr. Evens's desk and signal for him to make room so I can take over. He's suspicious but lets me have his desk. I motion for Miles to come and stand next to me.

I announce in a big, loud voice: "I am also Madame O-Shay, the best medium in South Side Chicago! And this is my assistant, Mr. Bugsy. Together we can connect with dark spirits and stop them from hurting anyone. And since the first time I met you, I sensed a dark spirit around you. Let me see if I can still feel them." I close my eyes and wave my hands in the air in random circles. I scrunch my face, concentrating really hard.

"Oh no!" I say in a sudden panic. "There are even more dark spirits around you now. I'm looking out into a sea of them." I get up and walk around the room. Mr. Evens tries to get in front of me. I put my hands out and stop him from going farther. "Stay behind me!" I warn.

I swing my arms wildly at the air, swatting away dark forces. "No, you can't have Mr. Evens! No! I will fight to protect him. Go away, bad spirit, go!"

I secretly pinch Miles on his side and whisper, "Help me out here."

"Ah . . . yeah, get out of here, you *very* real ghosts!" Miles says.

I breathlessly clap my hands to my chest. "They are too strong. It's getting so hard to hold them back. But I'll try . . ." I slowly fall to my knees. I yank on Miles's jeans and signal for him to get on the ground with me.

"I'm sorry, I'm overcome with exhaustion," I gasp as I put my hand on my forehead and wither onto the floor. Miles follows my lead.

I sneak a peek at Mr. Evens between my fingers to see his reaction. He groans.

"Are you done?" he says.

Miles and I sit up. "Yes, it's over—but only for now. They will be back again for you. If only there was a way to protect you all the time . . ." I reply, thinking really hard.

"Any ideas, Mr. Evens?" Miles says with a grin.

Before he can reply, I jump up with excitement. "Wait, I got it! We can protect you by coming to stay with you!"

"Oh, really, you would do that for me?" Mr. Evens says.

"Well, Madame O-Shay doesn't normally do house visits, but since you and Miles are friends—"

"—not just friends, best friends. Right, Mr. Evens?" Miles says, glowing.

Mr. Evens stammers. "Ah . . . w-well . . . uh—um . . ."

I reach out and pat him on the back. "Don't worry, Miles and I agree to move in with you—for your own protection."

"Yup! We got your back!" Miles promises.

There's a knock on the classroom door. On the other side,

through the glass window, we see Principal Bishop. She's short, only five feet four inches, but the way she walks you'd think she was ten feet tall. Her eyes are huge and move robotically side to side, like the eyes of the kitty cat clock on Nanna's wall.

Behind Ms. Bishop is a small army of adults, wearing very serious-looking clothes, to match their very serious expressions. They signal for Mr. Evens to step outside and meet with them.

"Okay, stay here, I'll be right back," Mr. Evens says.

"Hey, buddy? What's the snack situation at our new house?" Miles asks.

"He's right. We can't battle dark forces without proper snacks," I add.

Mr. Evens holds out his hand and firmly replies, "Both of you stop. You aren't going home with me."

"But the spirits—" I plead.

"I will brave the spirits by myself, thank you. You two get your things ready to go with the social services lady," he orders.

We start to argue with him, both of us at the same time. He whistles, loudly, and we stop cold. "That's enough. I mean it," he scolds. "You two are not going to my place. Understand? You. Are. Not. Going. With. Me."

Mr. Evens marches out to the hallway and closes the door behind him.

The grown-ups start talking, and we get closer to the door to listen. But the door is really thick, and I can't make out everything.

"You and your wife were planning to adopt? Isn't that right? You two took the mandatory training for fostering a child, correct?" Ms. Bishop says.

Mr. Evens grumbles something I can't make out.

"Oh, okay. If you can't do it . . ." Ms. Bishop replies.

They both start speaking at once, and all I can catch are random words.

"Unfortunately . . ."

"Separation . . ."

"Several months . . ."

Suddenly, Mr. Evens comes back into the room and says, "Get your stuff. You're going home with me."

"Yes!" Miles and I shout as we give each other a high five. Mr. Evens groans . . .

Mr. Evens's car looks more like a spaceship than a car. It's black, has smooth curves, and the door handles are hidden. Miles and I look at each other, not sure how to get the door open. Mr. Evens has to come around and do it for us. We ask what the car is called and he says, "Tesla." And now I know what I'm gonna get when I learn to drive. But my Tesla will be bright pink and gold. We get inside the car, and Mr. Evens drives off.

"You kids know that running away was a bad idea, right?" he asks. Miles and I both shrug. "The social worker has been looking for you two. There was some mix-up with the paperwork, and . . . it's their fault for not being more organized. Maya warned me the system was flawed. I just didn't know how much. But that still doesn't mean it's okay to run away."

"So how come you're taking us?" I ask.

"Well, here's the situation," he starts. "The social worker—Mrs. Henry—couldn't find an emergency foster home that could take both of you. But she assured me that they would have a spot for you both in the same home soon."

"Okay," I reply softly.

He starts mumbling to himself in total disbelief. "It's only for a month. That's just four weeks . . . Twenty-eight days . . . A mere six hundred and seventy-two hours . . ."

Miles tugs on my coat and whispers, "Should we remind him that it's October first and that there's thirty-one days in October?"

I look over at Mr. Evens; he has the same dazed look on his face that I do when I realize how much math homework I have left to do.

"Let's give him some time," I whisper back. Miles nods in agreement.

Mr. Evens drives us to his neighborhood; it's nothing like the one we lived in with Nanna. The streets are clean and full of fancy spaceships. And above our heads are tall towers of glass and metal. It's too beautiful for words.

We get out of the car and make our way to the front of Mr. Evens's apartment building. There's an old Black man in a dark red uniform and a hat standing in front. He has a name tag that says "Hawkins." His big smile and bright white teeth remind me of Mr. Willis, an old man in our neighborhood. He lives above the corner store and calls all us kids "Li'l Bit."

"Good evening, Mr. Evens," he says in a deep, booming voice.

"Good evening, Hawkins. These are my . . . guests. Sunny and Miles."

Mr. Hawkins tips his hat toward me and says, "Good evening, mademoiselle."

He does the same thing to Miles. "Good evening, monsieur."

Miles and I wave awkwardly and reply in union, "Hi . . ."

We walk into the lobby, and I realize I was wrong. This isn't a building. It's more like the halls of a castle; a castle made of white and gray marble.

The ceiling is so sky-high, it would take ten ladders stacked one on top of the other to reach it. The floors are so polished, I can see my reflection. This really isn't the best I've looked. My hair is frizzy, my face is ashy, and I'm pretty sure my elbows are too. We didn't think to bring lotion with us. Nanna would be shaking her head right now.

We enter the elevator at the end of the lobby. Mr. Evens doesn't even push a button. Instead, he takes out a small plastic card and taps it on the button that has the number fourteen. The elevator begins to move. The ride is quiet, smooth, and over too quickly. I'd like to do it again and again, but I know Mr. Evens wouldn't like that.

We get out of the elevator. Mr. Evens turns right and enters his apartment. Our whole apartment can fit into his living room. There's a wall of windows that are twice as tall as Mr. Evens. They look out onto Lake Michigan. The floors are just as shiny as the ones in the lobby. There's a long hall-way with framed pictures of him playing and directing choirs. There are statues, vases, and artwork all around.

Everything looks too fancy to breath on, let alone touch. The more off-limits the things look, the more Miles longs to touch them. He reaches out to touch one of the statues. I quickly grab his hand before he can make contact. He looks at me and silently begs me to let him explore. I shake my head and he pouts. He goes back to just looking, but he trades touching for asking Mr. Evens questions—lots of questions.

"How did you get the floors so shiny? It looks so smooth. Do you ever slide on them? Can I slide on them?" he asks.

"Absolutely not," Mr. Evens replies.

"Are you sure I can't slide on the floor, even with socks on?" Miles says, raising his eyebrows.

Mr. Evens grumbles. "Yes, even with socks on you're not allowed to slide or slip or glide or anything that would damage these floors. There is no playing on these floors, no rough-housing or amusement of any kind. These floors are to walk on—slowly and carefully. Is that perfectly clear, young man?"

Miles lets Mr. Evens's words sink in, and then he nods and says, "So . . . two pairs of socks? Can I slide on the floor if I wear two pairs?" Mr. Evens mumbles something under his breath and continues to show us around.

"What's with the skull painting next to the window?" Miles asks.

"It's a replica of Jean-Michel Basquiat's *Untitled*," Mr. Evens says.

"Who's that?" Miles replies.

"He's a famous painter," I add. Mr. Evens looks at me, surprised. "I read about it in class. Miles, he's Black and his paintings sell for one hundred million dollars!"

Miles's eyes pop out of his head as he steps closer to the painting. "Sunny, we're rich! I can paint better than that! This Basquiat guy painted a skull, but it's all out of shape and messy. I'm gonna paint a better skull, and we're rich!"

Mr. Evens's face does something I didn't think it could do. The corners of his mouth stretch out to the side and form a smile! An actual smile! Well, it's more like a smirk, but that's something.

"Do you have anything to eat?" Miles asks. Mr. Evens takes us to the kitchen and tells us to take what we want. The only problem is we don't see a refrigerator anywhere.

"It's right there. It's built into the wall," Mr. Evens says.

Miles goes over to where he pointed and, sure enough, there's a refrigerator that blends into the white wall! Miles opens it and his jaw drops down to the floor, right next to mine. I have never seen a refrigerator that full before. It has *everything*.

"Mr. Evens, what's hemp milk?" Miles asks.

"Well, it's—"

"—and goat milk? Whew. What does it taste like? And what about this? Oat milk. Does it taste like oatmeal? I don't like oatmeal. You have water in a box? Why do you need it in a box? You know it comes from the faucet right there. Or you can put it in a pitcher like Nanna does. Why don't you just do that?" Miles is spitting out a million words every five seconds. I think if he keeps going, his head will explode.

"It's bad manners to go into people's refrigerators and judge what they bought," Mr. Evens informs us.

"We're sorry. We won't say anything about all the weird things you brought home from the market," I reply.

"Yeah, everyone does that sometimes. Once, I got coffee ice cream because I wanted to be grown-up. Do you know what coffee ice cream tastes like?" Miles asks.

Mr. Evens sighs softly. "Coffee?"

"Yup. Gross," Miles replies.

"If it was so gross, why did you finish the whole thing?" I remind him.

Miles shrugs and says, "Duh, it's still ice cream."

"Okay, you two are taking too long. Pick something and settle in for the night," Mr. Evens says, pinching the bridge of his nose.

We pick cornflakes so that way we can try it with the strange milks. I try the goat milk, and Miles tries the hemp. Miles spits it out, and the milk splashes all over the floor. I hold mine in and rush to the bathroom and spit it out. Disgusting! Only cows should make milk, no one else.

On my way back from the bathroom, I can't help but make dreamy eyes at the full-size, glossy white piano. I can imagine a beautiful, elegant woman in a gown standing by it, singing rich people music—opera! Yeah, she's singing opera, and Mr. Evens is accompanying her on the piano.

Wait, the roses are for me. It's me! I'm standing beside the piano wearing a huge sparkling gown that flows down to the floor; *a graceful waterfall of sequins. The small but passionate crowd* *gets up on their feet and claps loudly for my performance.*

"Bravo! Bravo! Bravo!" they shout as they throw roses toward *me. I want to blow them kisses, but I don't want to smudge my* *cherry-berry Hello Kitty lip gloss. So I blow my adoring fans air* *kisses.*

"What are you doing?" Miles asks me.

Uh-oh. It turns out the air kisses weren't just in my head; I was actually blowing them in real life. That's why both Mr. Evens and Miles are looking at me like I have lost my mind.

"Your piano is beautiful. It's even bigger than the one at Nanna's church," I say as I walk over to it. There's panic in my music teacher's eyes. He thinks I'm about to touch the instrument. I get close enough to give him a small heart attack, but then I don't touch it. "I know, I know, a piano is not a toy," I say before he has a chance to lecture me.

Miles wanders off down the hallway. "Hey, there's a big trunk in here. What's inside it, Mr. Evens?"

Mr. Evens turns to see Miles about to touch the trunk in the closet. He runs so fast he almost leaves his socks and shoes behind.

"No, don't touch that!" he shouts. He gently pulls Miles away from the trunk and shuts the closet door. "Don't ever go inside that trunk!"

"What's in it? Is it a secret?" Miles asks.

"Don't worry about that. Let me show you to your rooms."

"Rooms?" I reply.

"We have our own rooms?" Miles asks, certain he had misheard him.

"Yes, down this hallway."

He starts walking toward the room, but we stand still.

"Are you two coming?" he asks.

We shake our heads.

"What's the problem?" Mr. Evens says.

"We would rather have the sofa," I say.

"Why?" he asks.

"In case you change your mind about wanting us around anymore. We will be close to the door, and we can get up and go right away," I reply.

He furrows his brows. "I'm not gonna—you don't have to worry about that," he says.

I look over at him. "Can you promise you won't send us away?"

He can't look me in the eye. It's not a good sign when adults avoid eye contact. It means something bad is coming. "We're going to sleep on the sofa," I tell him.

He doesn't argue.

Miles and I snuggle up together under the comforter that Mr. Evens gives us. It's wide, fluffy, and smells like spring.

Mr. Evens mumbles, "Good night."

Miles smiles back at him. "Good night. And if you get scared, you can come out here with us."

Mr. Evens is about to say something, but then at the last minute, he changes his mind and turns out the light. Miles puts his head on my shoulder.

"This is a really nice place, right, Sunny?"

"Yeah."

"And Mr. Evens, he's like a Hystricidae—a porcupine. Sure, it *looks* all mean and stuff with spikes on its back, but really it's just a little mammal looking for berries and friends."

I turn toward him and warn, "Miles, we can't stay with Mr. Evens forever. That's why we have to complete this quest as quickly as we can and make Nanna well again. Don't lose focus. We have four weeks to get all the items we need to make the potion that will fix Nanna. If we can't complete this quest in four weeks, all hope of helping Nanna is lost."

"I'll be focused. But first, I have a question."

"No more questions. Sleep."

"Just one, please!" he pleads.

I groan. "Fine—one question."

"What's in the trunk?"

Chapter Eight
For Science (Mostly)

I WAKE UP TO the sound of laughter. Miles is still asleep, and as usual, he has kicked most of the covers off him. I cover him back up, and he mumbles something in his sleep—I'm pretty sure it's a question. I quietly get off the sofa and follow the sound of the laughter to the kitchen.

I stick my head out just enough to get a peek without being seen. Mr. Evens is at the stove making something, but I can't make out what. A lady sits at the table laughing at him. The woman radiates like a bright rainbow; a rainbow with a "take no mess" Afro.

She's wearing blue jeans with images painted on them: a bright rainbow and a Black hand in a fist. There's also a red heart painted on the left pocket of her jeans and music notes on the right. The bottoms of her jeans have big, bold wildflowers that sprout up and out. She wears silver rings on almost every finger and has on a necklace with the peace sign. Her curly, thick hair makes the biggest Afro I've ever seen.

She's eating fruit from the bowl in front of her and almost

chokes on a strawberry from laughing so much.

"Stop laughing, Rue! This isn't funny. What am I going to do with them?" Mr. Evens asks.

"I can't believe it. My all-knowing big brother doesn't have the answers to something? Wow, that has to be the very first time!"

"Are you going to be helpful or not?" Mr. Evens demands.

"If you didn't think you were ready for this, why did you agree to take them in?" Rue asks.

"It all happened so fast! One minute I was saying they could not come with me, and then the next thing I know, their sticky, curious little fingers were all over my car." Frustrated, Mr. Evens leans on the wall and shakes his head.

"Darrious, be easy. They're just kids."

Suddenly, Mr. Evens's eyes light up, and he rushes over to his sister. "Rue, why don't you take them?"

"Heck no!"

"Why?"

"Because I have a full load this semester. And because unlike you and Maya, I didn't take the classes needed to be a foster parent."

"Well, things have changed since we took those classes. Maya isn't here anymore, is she?" he snaps.

"I know . . ." Rue replies sadly. "But even if I wanted to take them, don't forget I live in a studio apartment. There's no room."

"I'll trade places with you. You can live here, and I will move to your place."

She rolls her eyes and scoffs. "Ha! You, Darrious Evens, move back to the South Side of Chicago? Boy, please! You wouldn't last a day in my hood."

"For the record, Rue, I offered to have you come stay with me."

"No thanks. You and that couple downstairs are the only Black people on this block."

"That's not true!" he says with certainty.

Rue folds her arms across her chest and raises one eyebrow suspiciously. "Darrious . . ."

"What? There are other Black people around here besides that couple and myself."

"Okay, who?"

He mumbles softly, "Hawkins."

"The doorman!"

"He's Black! It counts!"

"Hmph!" Rue snorts.

He says, growing more irritated, "Sis, I love you, but I need you to be more helpful."

She stares him down. "C'mon, man, those kids are cute and harmless."

"Yeah, that's what they want you to think—they use that cuteness to fool you! The younger one, Miles . . . that kid just knows too much. I'm usually a fan of education, but someone needs to take his library card away. He had the nerve to correct the way I organized Maya's files."

"Was he right?"

". . . That's not the point, Rue! That kid rubs me the wrong way. Even his questions have questions. And Sunny, his older sister, well . . ." He grunts.

"What's wrong with the sister?"

"Well, for one thing, she's an outright hustler. She actually tried to con me into taking them in. I tell you, that kind of charlatanism doesn't just happen. It takes years of practice. It's only a matter of time before that kid tries to sell me a used car or a sinking plot of land in a Florida swamp."

"Yo, that li'l mama hustled you?! I respect that!" she says, smiling proudly.

He groans. "You would. Both of you are little hooligans."

"When you say words like that, it makes we wonder if we really are related. But since we are, let me borrow a hundred bucks."

"'Borrow' implies giving it back, which you never seem to do," Mr. Evens points out to his sister.

"Okay, okay. I can see you're stressed, so . . . make it fifty."

He grumbles but goes into his back pocket and gets her a hundred-dollar bill. She kisses him on the cheek. He wipes her lipstick off the side of his face. She opens the refrigerator and shoves a bunch of snacks into her colorful cloth knapsack.

"Really? You're taking money and food?" Mr. Evens says.

"If I didn't take both, that would be unlike me, right? So really you should be grateful that I am consistent."

"Yeah, yeah," he says, waving her off. He turns his attention back to the stove. That's when she notices the food he's making.

"*That's* what you're making them for breakfast?" she asks.

"It's classic morning food."

"They won't eat it," she warns.

"Why not?"

"Because they aren't eighty-year-old ladies having brunch at the Plaza."

"They'll eat it!" he says firmly.

She shrugs. "Whatever."

She starts to head my way; I quickly pull back so she won't see me. But she stops when Mr. Evens call out her name.

"Rue . . ."

She turns to face him. He doesn't say anything, but his expression is gloomy.

She gently puts a hand on his shoulder. "Don't back out now. You took them in because you knew it was the right thing to do."

"I took them in because the social worker said she didn't have enough space in the emergency foster home to take them both. And that she would have to split them up. I couldn't let that happen. I remembered how much it hurt Maya when . . ."

Rue nods slowly and says to herself, "That's right. Maya was separated from her sister when they first got into foster care."

"She never got over it. And those two hustlers out there are trouble, but they take care of each other. Separating them would be wrong."

Rue makes her brother promise to introduce us to her the next time she comes by. Then she says goodbye and walks out of the kitchen. I have just enough time to run back to the sofa and pretend to be sleeping. When Rue is gone, Mr. Evens wakes us up.

"Good morning. Did you two find your sleeping arrangement satisfactory?" Miles and I just shrug. "Okay, well good. Perhaps tonight you can sleep in the room that's actually dedicated to sleeping?" I look over at my brother, and together we both shake our heads.

Mr. Evens grumbles. "This morning, I spoke to the nursing home where your nanna was taken. Right now, she's still adjusting to being somewhere new. But they assure me that once she's settled in, we can go see her. But for now, we can call your nanna on the phone."

Miles is beaming and pumps his fist in the air. I'm so excited, I can hardly stay still. Mr. Evens gets his phone and dials the number. He asks the nurse if now is a good time for Nanna to talk, and I guess she says yes because Mr. Evens puts the phone on speaker. And soon, we hear Nanna's voice fill the room.

"Hello?! Nanna?" I call out into the phone.

"There's my sunshine! How are you?" she asks, excitedly. When I hear her voice, I feel the same way I do after she makes us chicken noodle soup. I feel warm and happy; like everything is okay.

"I'm good! I miss you so much!" I tell her.

"Bet I miss you more! Are you behaving?" she says.

"Um . . . mostly," I reply, looking over at Mr. Evens. He doesn't look all that convinced, but he doesn't disagree with me, so I guess I'm behaving just enough.

"Go on, tell me: are you and Jell-O behaving?" she asks again.

Oh my gosh! Nanna remembered calling Miles Jell-O! That's the nickname she gave him because he used to jiggle like a bowl of Jell-O to make Nanna laugh. And she remembered that!

"Your Jell-O is right here! I'm here, Nanna!" Miles says.

"Is that really you? You sound so grown-up!" Nanna replies.

"Yeah, I'm basically a man now," he says proudly. Mr. Evens and I look at each other and silently agree not to correct Miles.

"I hear you two are staying with a nice teacher until I can get back home and we can be together," Nanna says.

"Yes! He's really nice. He really needs our help though. He doesn't know what the good snacks are, and he buys the wrong kind of milk. But he's really nice to us. Right, Sunny?" Miles says.

"Yeah, we put up with him," I tease. Mr. Evens rolls his eyes, but I can see the small smile he's trying to hide.

"Nanna, when are you coming to get us?" Miles asks.

"I'll get in my car right now and come get you two," she says.

My heart sinks. "Nanna, you don't drive anymore. Remember?" I ask, looking at Mr. Evens.

"Oh, yes. I forgot. And, dear, what was your name again? You know I am just not as good with names as I was back in the day," she says, sounding a little upset.

Mr. Evens takes over the call. "Nanna, can you please put the nurse back on the phone? Kids, say goodbye to Nanna."

"Bye, Nanna! We love you!" I shout.

Miles adds, "Yup! We both love you, and Noodle—he loves you too!"

Mr. Evens takes the phone off speaker and lowers his voice as he talks to the nurse. When he's done, he hangs up.

"The nurse said your nanna is a little tired, and she's gonna get some rest. Okay?" he says.

"She was better—for a few minutes. Maybe the next time she'll be better for longer, and soon she'll be all better, all the time! Don't you think so, Sunny?" Miles says.

"I know she's gonna get better!" I reply.

I'm gonna make sure of it!

"I think hearing your voices helped put her in a good mood. The nurse said as soon as Nanna is up to it, we can talk to her again." We cheer and thank Mr. Evens for calling her for us.

Soon we're all ready for school. The only thing left to do is have breakfast. Miles and I go sit at the kitchen table, and right away there's a problem. "Come on, start eating. We have to get going soon," Mr. Evens says.

We look down at our meal; neither of us says anything. Mr. Evens has already started eating and only stops when he realizes we aren't going to join him. His eyes go back and forth between the two us.

"What's wrong?" he asks.

Miles turns his nose up at the food on his plate. An

English muffin cut in half. And on each side, there's a flat slab of something pink. It's the same shade of pink as my big flat eraser, the one I use for art class. On top of that, there's a boiled egg drowning in thick yellow goop. On top of the goop, Mr. Evens placed little green specks.

"What is that?" I ask.

"It's chives. It's a great garnish for poached eggs," he says. We look at him, confused.

He explains, "We're having lightly poached eggs Benedict with hollandaise sauce."

"Lightly poked? Who poked it?" Miles says.

"Poached. It's a way of making eggs," he adds.

"It's not cooked all the way," I warn Miles.

"It isn't supposed to be," he replies.

Miles inserts his fork into the egg; a yellow, slimy ooze leaks out of it. Miles's face twists with disgust.

"Are you mad at us or something?" Miles asks.

"What? No, why?" Mr. Evens says.

"This looks like something you make someone eat as a punishment," Miles replies.

I nod in agreement. I lean over and whisper in Miles's ear. "I never thought I would say this, but I think I miss Folake's Cauliflower Courage."

Mr. Evens sighs. "Okay, get your stuff. We'll stop off at a drive-through."

On the way to the car, Mr. Evens says, "I didn't see you sign up to audition for the fall concert. Are you planning on putting your name down today?"

"Nope," I reply.

"Oh. It's a shame. Sunny, you have a lovely voice. I didn't come down the steps of the school basement because I heard a loud voice. I came because I heard a beautiful voice. You have real talent. It would be a shame to waste it."

I'm not going to audition because I have a very grown-up quest to go on. And I have never sung without Nanna. Still, I can't believe Mr. Evens likes my voice!

When we get to school, I can't wait to tell Folake everything that's happened. She won't believe that we don't live in the basement anymore and that we now live with Mr. Evens. Although I'm sure he's gonna send us away soon, it's still better than the basement. And now that I know he's my guide, I know the quest can begin. And there is no one better to help me with my quest than Folake. I search the playground but can't find her. I hope she didn't run into the Beast again.

Miles is the first one to see her. "Look, she's right over there!" he says.

I look across the street and see my best friend coming toward me. I am so excited to tell her everything, I almost shout it out for everyone to hear. But my update will have to wait because something is wrong with Folake.

She's squinting as she steps off the sidewalk and into the street. She has her hands out in front of her, like she's not sure what she's about to bump into. We wave to her, but she doesn't wave back. It's like she can't even really see us.

"Where are her glasses?" Miles asks. That's it; she's not wearing her glasses.

There's a guy on a bike coming straight for her. She should have stopped walking, but she doesn't.

"Folake!" I shout.

It's too late. She collides with the biker, and they both fall to the ground. I take Miles's hand and carefully cross over to them. They aren't hurt, but the biker had a brown bag of groceries with eggs and honey, which spilled everywhere.

"Hey, why don't you look where you're going, kid?!" the biker shouts.

"I'm sorry," Folake replies. We help her up, and together we try to put as much of the biker's food back in the bag. We would have helped more, but one of the teachers orders us to come back inside.

"Where are your glasses?" Miles asks once we're back in the yard.

"Were you using them to play hide-and-seek with your cat again?" I ask.

"That was one time. And Galileo was very sorry about what happened. Also, only a really clever cat would think to bury glasses in the litter box," Folake informs us.

She goes on to tell us that her glasses slipped between the sofa cushions and down to the carpet. Her dad then accidentally sucked them up with the vacuum. He's going to get them repaired this afternoon. We ask her about her backup pair, and she starts to fidget and twirl her fingers.

"Folake, where are your backup glasses?" I ask again as we head inside the school building.

"You know how much I love science, right?" she begins. Miles and I sigh at the same time. Whenever Folake begins a sentence reminding us about her love of science, it's usually because she's about to come up with a really bad idea.

The truth is she really does love science. She named her cat after one of the most famous scientists who ever lived—Galileo. Also, she places first in the science fair every year. But sometimes her love of experimenting goes too far. Sometimes things go horribly wrong, even more wrong than the strange sandwiches she makes us.

One time, Folake thought it would be a good idea to experiment with glue and discover which brand was the strongest. So she glued her bike to the wall of her room using different types of glue. When the bike fell off, so did a large chunk of the wall. Her parents were so mad, they grounded her for a whole month.

Another time Miles told her all about the world of bees and how they behave. Folake was fascinated and posed a question: "How close do you have to get to a beehive for the bees to feel threatened and start chasing you?"

So she went to the beehive that they had found in a tree a few days before and got closer and closer to it. We told her not to do it, but she said, "This is for science!"

It turns out bees don't like to be played with, even for science. And she didn't need to get too close. The moment she came near the hive, a swarm of bees leaped out of their nest and made an actual beeline for Folake.

She ran screaming down the street with her arms up in the air and her eyes popping out of their sockets. She got stung a dozen times, and her mom vowed if she did anything like that again, they would ship her back to Nigeria to live with her super-strict grandparents.

"You didn't go near the bees again, did you?" Miles scolds.

"No! Never again," she promises. "I'm not doing anything odd. I am just experimenting."

"With what?" I ask.

"My life," she explains.

"Huh?" Miles says.

"My dad had taken my glasses to get them fixed, and I was about to go look for my backup pair, but then a miracle happened. One of the Ha-Ha Girls was walking past my house, saw me in the window, and she said hi!" Folake says, thrilled.

The Ha-Ha Girls are a group of friends who love teasing other kids just because they aren't as popular. There are three of them, and they all walk the same, talk the same, and even laugh the same. They have the best outfits, the best birthday parties, and, of course, everyone tries to be their friend.

"What does that have to do with your glasses?" Miles asks.

"She thinks that not wearing glasses is the reason why the Ha-Ha Girl said hi to her," I reply.

"I don't *think* so, I *know* so," Folake says excitedly. "I did a quick experiment. I left the house without my glasses, and it was like a whole new world! I was someone else, someone . . . cool!" she says with a big grin.

"What happens when your dad gets your glasses fixed?" Miles says.

"I'll pretend to wear them. But as soon as I get outside, I'll take them off."

"Can you see anything without them?" I ask.

"I see shapes and stuff," she replies.

"Folake . . ." I moan.

"Oh, c'mon, Sunny, help me. This is what they call in the science world a social experiment. It's like the bees thing. I need to get close to see how they behave. What's it really like to be a Ha-Ha Girl? Deep inside are they just like us? Do they hate having a bedtime like the rest of us? Do they really like to dress up all the time, or is there a picture out there of one of the Ha-Ha Girls in a Bugs Bunny nightshirt with chocolate stains on it? I need to know these things—I'm a scientist. All I need to be happy is to study the Ha-Ha Girls. Get to know their ways."

"Last week all you needed was to study Doris, the lunch lady," Miles reminds her.

"Yes, and I learned that lunch ladies don't like it when you tell them how to 'fix' the meals they make. A very important lesson," Folake replies.

"And the week before that you wanted to study the crossing guard," I add.

She puts her hand on her hip and says, "And I'm glad I did. Oscar is a very complicated guy. Yes, he's the crossing guard, but he's also left-handed, a pet owner, and plays the clarinet."

"Oscar and Doris may be okay to study, but the Ha-Ha Girls? You sure this is a good idea?" I ask.

"Absolutely! What could go wrong with wanting to learn and do everything the popular girls do?"

Chapter Nine
Tornado Season

I TOLD FOLAKE THAT I had big news for her, but we had to wait until lunchtime to talk because we didn't want to get in trouble. I've never lived with a teacher before, but I'm sure if you get in trouble at school, they remind you about it when you get home. So we waited until lunch, and when it finally came, Folake was dying with curiosity. We sit down in the cafeteria and pretty much ignore the lunch tray in front of us.

"So last night in the basement, I was singing to Miles, and you won't believe who heard me." I give Folake all the details, and she's really into it. She says she wishes she was there in person to see the kingdom of glass and the white piano.

"I can't believe Mr. Evens is your guide. And now, you and Miles are living with him!" she says.

"I overheard him talking to his sister, Rue, this morning, and I think we better get started on the quest. Mr. Evens is really fragile. He might not last another round of 'a thousand questions' with Miles." She asks what Rue is like, and I tell her all about Mr. Evens's sister.

"Do you think I can meet her too?" Folake asks. "She sounds like fun."

"Maybe, but right now, let's figure out how to get our first item on the list: a seashell. And once we get that seashell, we have to find a mermaid to kiss it," I remind her.

"Do you think any seashell will work? Or does it have to be a special one?"

I think really hard and try to remember how these things go in all the stories I have read. "I don't think it's ever just any item. It can't be. We have to seek out a seashell that's special in some way."

"All right, I'm on it! For the rest of the day, I'll keep my eyes open for a seashell," Folake says as she dips her fish sticks in the thick white sauce next to her, thinking it's tartar sauce.

"Folake, that's yogurt."

"Yeah, I knew that," she says, laughing nervously. She slowly puts the yogurt-dipped fish stick in her mouth. She makes a face like she's chewing on a dirty rag and spits it out right away. And before I can say anything, she stops me. "I'm fine. It's good to try new food combinations. I'm also a chef, remember?"

"Okay, but I'm not sure you should be doing this. C'mon, the Ha-Ha Girls love watching other kids mess up and teasing them. Do you really want to be a part of that?"

"Well, maybe when I become one of them, I can help them change and be nicer," Folake says.

Honestly, I don't think things are going to go the way Folake thinks they will. But she looks happy, so I don't say anything. The bell rings, lunch is over, and because the wind outside is so harsh, we never get to go out to the yard. But I don't have time to play. My only focus is the seashell.

We line up to leave the cafeteria, and who is standing behind us? That's right—the Ha-Ha Girls, all three of them. They have nearly matching outfits, glitter in their hair, and attitude in their eyes. The only thing they enjoy showing off more than their perfect smiles is whatever new items their parents bought for them the night before.

"Folake, I hear you don't wear glasses anymore. Is that true or is it just for, like, one day?" the Ha-Ha leader, Tiffany, says.

"Me? No, I don't need glasses anymore. Right, Sunny?" Folake says, desperately poking me in the rib.

"Ah, yup. She can see very clearly now," I reply.

"I've never heard of someone's vision being bad one day and then suddenly being better. Doesn't that take, like . . . years?" Taylor asks. Yes, every one of the Ha-Ha Girls' names start with a "T." But so do the words "trouble" and "terror."

"What I mean to say is that I have contacts," Folake says with a smug expression.

"Wow, I wanted to get contacts—the color ones—but my mom wouldn't let me. She's so . . . argh!" Tamar adds. Then they all start talking at once. I try my best to drown them out. Folake whispers in my ear, "See? They noticed me!"

On our way back to class, Folake points to the sign-up sheet and says she knows I want to sign up. I remind her that we are on a serious quest, and I just don't have time for singing.

"Sunny, I know your nanna won't be there like she usually is when you sing in church, but that doesn't mean you can't still sing."

Maybe I can sing without Nanna. But I don't want to do that. I don't want to get up there, look down at the audience, and not see her face. It would break my heart into small pieces—pieces way too small to put back together.

Later, when school is over, I dread going to the car. What if Mr. Evens brings up the auditions? What if he tries to change my mind about singing? I hold my breath as we get ready for the ride back to Mr. Evens's apartment. I'm relieved when he makes an announcement that has nothing to do with singing.

"I have a pushy sister, Rue—you'll meet her soon, so no need to ask a hundred questions, Miles. She thinks I need to take you two food shopping so you can get more kid-friendly items. I'm told that does not include goat milk. So should we head to the market?"

"Yes, please!" Miles replies. I agree.

"Phew! I was worried about what you might try to feed us for dinner tonight. Probably frogs or something," Miles jokes.

"It's called cuisses de grenouilles. It's a French dish of frog legs. And for the record, it's delicious when paired with olive oil and a squeeze of lemon."

"You're funny, Mr. Evens," Miles says.

He looks back at us in the rearview mirror. He's not joking. Miles and I have the very same thought: *Yuck.*

The supermarket is smaller than the ones Nanna and I

usually go to. It's also a lot cleaner. All the vegetables look like new, and they're piled up neatly in a row. I don't think a person did it; it's just too neat. I think they probably have veggie robots. Like machines that come and pile up all the vegetables and make sure that it's perfect.

I notice hand-painted signs all around the market that say "Organic."

"Mr. Evens, what does 'organic' mean?" Miles asks as we go down the aisle.

"It means food that is grown without any added chemicals," he replies.

"I think it means 'pay more,'" I add.

"Well, yes. Organic products cost more than non-organic. But it's better for you. And how do you know about the price of things? You have a job?" he jokes as he picks out avocados.

"I know exactly how much money Nanna spends at the market because she would make us write it down. That way we would know how expensive food was and not waste it," I reply.

"Nanna started doing that after Sunny threw mashed potatoes at me from across the table," Miles says.

"Hey, I only did that because you threw yams!" I remind him.

"I didn't start it, Mr. Evens," Miles swears.

"Oh, really? Then how did green peas get in my hair?" I ask, folding my arms in front of me.

Miles smirks and says, "Anyone could have put them there. You have no proof it was me."

"Yes, it was," I reply.

"No, it wasn't," Miles says.

We go back and forth until Mr. Evens demands we stop or he will make us sit in the car. We agree not to argue anymore. Then we make our way down to the lemon aisle.

"Was your grandmother mad that you two were fighting?"

"Yeah, she was so mad, she had to take extra pills that night. She said, 'Y'all done raise my pressure up!'" Miles says, impersonating Nanna's voice. I hear a small noise come out of Mr. Evens; it almost sounded like a laugh! It was soft, but I heard it.

"We'd also help Nanna cut out coupons. Where are your coupons, Mr. Evens?" I ask.

"Oh no, you don't have one for goat milk, do you?" Miles says with dread.

Mr. Evens smiles. "No, I don't, Miles. You're safe."

Mr. Evens doesn't clip coupons. He says he downloaded an app that helps him save money, but most of the time he forgets to use it. We are almost done shopping when he tells me to go pick up an item he forgot—potato chips! Miles and I get really excited, but then Mr. Evens says, "Get the organic, no-salt, no-preservatives kind."

"Aw, man!" my brother and I moan at the same time. I don't know what preservatives are, but I'm sure they are the part that makes chips taste good. So, without it, it might as well be goat milk.

We go down the snack aisle and try to find the brand that Mr. Evens wants. There's an old white lady, about Nanna's age, in our aisle. She's talking on her cell, trying to make room for more stuff in her cart, while balancing three cans in her hand.

Miles and I face a wall of potato chips and try hard to find one that has everything Mr. Evens wants but still looks delicious. It's an impossible mission. We are trying to choose between two different bags of chips when the old lady starts shouting.

"MY WALLET IS GONE! MY WALLET IS GONE!"

My brother and I start looking around at the floor to see if maybe she dropped it somewhere in the aisle, but there's nothing there. We go back to the chips. Miles makes the final decision—we're going with the blue bag because the writing looks more fun than the red bag. It's sad that it's come to this. I really miss the corner store. So much junk food! Oh, well. I grab the bag of chips, and we start to walk away.

"Hey, stop them! They got my wallet! STOP THEM!" she says as she comes toward us like a tornado. Her eyes twitch, and her lips curl with rage. My heart is pounding in rhythm to her heavy footsteps. Miles latches on to my coat. I put him safely behind me. My fingers are too frozen to grip anything; I drop the bag of chips.

"Just give it back to me! Right now!" The lady yells so loud, people from other aisles are coming to see what's going on. Everyone starts to talk all at once around me. A chill runs all along my arms, leaving me with big, fat goose bumps. But I'm also hot, so hot; drops of sweat run down my back.

"I—I—we—we—didn't take anything," I stutter.

"I had my purse in my cart. I turned away and took a call.

And when I turned back, my purse was there but my wallet wasn't inside it. There was no one else in this aisle but you! GIVE ME BACK MY WALLET!"

The lady's anger is so strong, I think it can summon lightning; it could strike us in the chest. Then Miles and I will disappear into a puff of black smoke.

I try to find my voice, but my throat is dry, and it doesn't get better no matter how many times I swallow. "I didn't take anything," I reply as my voice cracks.

"Liar! You're a liar! Get the manager over here!"

"Don't call my sister a liar!" Miles shouts from behind me. He tries to come out front, but I won't let him. One guy enters the aisle wearing a green-and-white uniform. He says he's the manager and asks what's going on. The old lady tells him that we stole from her, and she won't let us leave the store until we show her what's in our backpacks.

"We didn't take anything from her!" Miles shouts back.

"Yes, they did, little thieves! Make them show me what's in their backpacks! NOW!"

The manager is sweating, and the color in his face is fading quickly. He, too, looks like he's about to pass out. He says in a whisper, "Um . . . can you two . . . um . . . can you please show us what's in your backpacks?"

"Why are you *asking*? Just take it from them," the old lady says, coming around to rip our backpacks off our backs.

"Don't you dare lay a finger on them!" Mr. Evens says, rushing over to us.

The old lady replies, "These kids took—"

"I don't care what you *think* they took. You don't talk to my kids like that," Mr. Evens informs her in a hard tone.

"They aren't leaving this store until I look inside their backpacks. Or I will call the authorities," the lady says, her jaw ready to detach and swallow us whole.

Mr. Evens says, "You want to call the cops, lady? We will stay right here and wait for them. But you will not address these children again." He puts his arm around Miles and me, and his eyes dare anyone to come closer.

Everyone in the market seems to be standing still. And then an old man with thinning hair, thick glasses, and gentle eyes enters the aisle. He talks to the tornado.

"Milliard, honey, you left this in the car. I called you to come back and get it, but you didn't hear me." The old man walks over and hands her a small black-and-white wallet.

We leave all the food behind and walk out of the store. We enter the parking lot in silence. Even Miles is speechless. Before we get in the car, Mr. Evens makes sure to get a good look at both of us. He kneels down so that we are all at eye level.

"Are you two okay?"

We both nod. There's concern in Mr. Evens's face. The same kind Nanna gets when we are sick or when she doesn't know where we are. I didn't plan to give him a hug; it just happens. I hold on to him tightly. Miles joins in. Mr. Evens hugs us back, just as tightly. The words he said a few minutes ago replay in my head:

You don't talk to my kids like that.

My kids . . .

Chapter Ten
Frankie

WHEN WE GET HOME, we do our homework and Mr. Evens helps. When it's time for dinner, we still don't feel like eating, but Mr. Evens says we should at least try. He lets us order pizza but has one rule: there should be some vegetables on it. Miles and I have a rule, too—Mr. Evens can't put anything on the pizza that's hard to pronounce. We end up sitting at the dinner table eating a mushroom and pepperoni pizza.

"What that lady did in the store—did it bother you, Miles?" he asks.

Miles lowers his head and shrugs. Mr. Evens nods and then asks me the same thing. I look away, not sure what the right answer is supposed to be.

"It bothered me. It made me upset," Mr. Evens admits. "Were you upset, Sunny?"

"No. I was scared," I reply.

He reaches across the table and puts his hand on top of mine. "You know what, kid? I was scared, too."

"You were?" Miles asks.

"Oh, yeah. There was a lot of yelling, everyone looking, feeling like you did something wrong when you didn't. It's a very scary thing. And you know what else? I get accused of doing things I didn't do, too."

"Really? Like when you were a kid?" I ask.

Mr. Evens gives us a sad smile. "Not just as a kid. Even now. Some people look at me and think really bad things about me before they even get to know me." Mr. Evens looks us in the eye. "Some people do that—they judge other people by their skin color, their hair, or even how big or small they are. It's important to remember that you are the ones who get to decide what kind of person you are. Don't let some random lady in the market make you feel bad or enter any room with a lowered head. Do you understand? Every room you and Miles enter, you enter it with your head up. Show the world what a great job your nanna did raising you two."

We both nod and say, "Yes."

"But what about the old lady? Is she going to be nicer when she talks to other kids like us?" Miles asks.

"Maybe," Mr. Evens says, nodding slightly. But honestly, he doesn't sound all that convinced.

The week is almost over; the good part is we have talked to Nanna three times this week. It's best to call in the early morning, right before we go to school. She doesn't stay on long, but that's okay. Miles and I are just happy to hear her voice. The bad part is we're no closer to finding the seashell. The seashell is the very first item; we can't do anything until we find it. Also, Mr. Evens has been playing some of the music from the concert on the piano in the living room. When he gets to the solo song, I can feel him waiting for me to sing along.

He thinks I won't be able to resist the music and I'll end up trying out for the solo part. I try to stay strong, but the music is pretty and impossible to resist. He even caught me softly singing it one day this week. He didn't say anything. He just smiled knowingly. He thinks he's so sneaky!

And to make things worse, Miles keeps looking at the trunk in the hall closet. It's like it's calling his name. He isn't the only one drawn to the trunk. I have walked in on Mr. Evens opening the closet to look at it. He slides his hand on top of the trunk gently. It makes him really sad. But then later that same day, he'll go back to the trunk and make the same gesture, but this time, it makes him smile!

That makes no sense to me.

Miles sees it, too. "Sunny, how can the trunk make Mr. Evens sad and happy at the same time? What's inside?"

I don't know what is inside, but I know that I am tired of trying to keep Miles away.

Because of everything that's going on, I wake up really grumpy this morning. When I open my eyes, I quickly shut them again and put the blanket over my head. Argh! Why are quests so hard? They didn't seem that hard when I was reading about them.

I hear Miles in the kitchen. He calls out, "Breakfast is coming soon, Noodle! Hang on."

"You don't have to yell, Miles," Mr. Evens says from his bedroom.

"I don't have to, but it's fun!" Miles yells back. "Didn't you have fun yelling just now? I did!" Miles giggles.

Hearing him giggle makes me smile. He's a pretty cool kid when he's not talking a billion miles a minute. I get up and go over to Miles, not to check on Noodle's food, but to check on the best pet owner in the world. The quest is very important, but so is making sure that I'm being a good big sister. And pretty much all I've said to him this week is to warn him away from the trunk. That's not really checking up on him. I enter the kitchen, where he's adding small pieces of fruit to the hamster mix.

"I thought you only added fruit for special occasions."

"Yeah, it's not good to give hamsters too much fruit. But Noodle has been very good. He deserves a treat," Miles says.

"Can I help?"

"Yeah, can you get more pellets?"

I do what my brother says, and together we prepare Noodle's treat. Miles can talk for hours about everything, but if I ask him about himself, he just shrugs and doesn't say anything. That's why I usually ask him about Noodle. Most of the time, whatever Noodle feels is really close to what his owner feels, too.

"So . . . does Noodle like this new place?" I ask.

"Oh, yeah, he loves it!"

I nod and look him straight in the eye. "If Noodle ever gets sad or doesn't like being here anymore, you let me know and I'll fix it," I promise him.

"I will. But I think he really loves it here," Miles says.

"Good. Did you finish your homework?" I ask.

"I only have one left. My English teacher, Mrs. Randall, says we have to do a presentation on our favorite thing—an animal, a person, or a place. And we have to tell the class what we like about them."

"You know all about animals. You should do something about animals," I remind him.

"Yeah, but that's the problem, Shine. How can I pick which animal I love the best? That's like asking me to pick which *Toy Story* movie is the best or asking which Slurpee flavor is the best—cherry or blue raspberry? Like I said to Mrs. Randall, this is the kind of decision that a guy has to think carefully about."

"Oh, okay, but try and make up your mind. You don't want to get in trouble for not handing in homework. When Nanna comes back, she won't be happy if you don't do well in school."

He looks at me with a serious expression. "Shine, remember I told you about Noodle's new friend?"

Mr. Evens put Noodle's cage on a stand in the hallway, just outside the room where Miles and I are supposed to sleep. Right across from Noodle's stand is a big mirror with a black border. Every time we walk by, we see Noodle playing with his new friend. He doesn't know that his new friend is really just his own reflection.

"It makes Noodle very happy to think he has a new friend, but I know he doesn't. Should I tell him the truth? Or is it better to let him keep thinking that because it makes him happy?" Miles asks.

"Well, I think you better have a talk with him. He needs to know the truth."

"Okay, then. Sunny . . . ?" he begins.

"Yeah?"

"About the quest . . ."

I smile at him. "I know, I know. You want to help. And when Folake and I need you, I promise we'll come get you."

I let out a big sigh. "This quest is huge, Miles, huge! But Nanna gave it to me—to us—because she knew we could handle it. And once we get everything we need, all of Nanna's memories will come back! She'll remember how much she loves us, how much fun we used to have. She'll never forget anything ever again! Aren't you excited, Miles? Soon, we'll all be together again!"

He nods. "Yeah, I am." He picks up the container of hamster food from the counter and starts to leave the kitchen.

"Are you going to tell Noodle the truth right now?" I ask.

He faces me and says, "Nah, I don't think Noodle is ready for the truth yet."

Miles really does like Mr. Evens a lot. He's started to imitate him. When he saw Mr. Evens carefully laying out his ties for work the next day, Miles started to do the same. But instead of ties, Miles lays out his socks. He chooses which pair to wear by how closely they match Mr. Evens's tie.

In the beginning, Miles had to convince Mr. Evens to show

him the tie he would be wearing the next day. But it wasn't long before it became their routine. Mr. Evens will come out to the sofa when we are getting ready to sleep and say, "I'm thinking dark blue with black polka dots." And Miles will go and lay out the socks that match.

Yesterday, Mr. Evens said, "I'm thinking of going with a sage-colored pin-striped." Miles asked me what sage looked like, and I said it's kind of light green.

Miles looked through his backpack and his shoulders slumped. "I don't have any green socks."

I looked over at Mr. Evens. He shook his head and said, "What am I thinking? Sage is the wrong color for this season. I think I'll wear a solid red tie. There, that's much better."

Miles's eyes grew wide as he dug inside his backpack and took out a pair of bright red socks. "I got it!"

Mr. Evens and I smiled at each other.

It's not just dressing alike; Miles sits up straight like Mr. Evens and even eats his chicken nuggets with a knife and fork.

I told Miles about Rue, but he had yet to meet her—that is, until this morning. Rue introduced herself in a very "Rue" way. She entered the apartment and started jumping on the sofa like a kid, shouting in a joyful tone, "Everyone get up, up, up!"

Miles pops one eye open and groans, "What's going on?"

"I'm Rue. And you two are young, gifted, and Black. Let's not waste all of that sleeping. Get up!" she calls out again.

"Who are you?" Miles says, still groggy.

"I'm the one who knows where Maya hid all the best candy around here. You wouldn't be interested in that, would you, Miles?" she teases.

He gives her a goofy smile and nods. She laughs. "Yeah, I thought you would be. Go wash up and get dressed. Auntie Rue is paying for breakfast." Miles runs off to the bathroom.

"Hold on, you're paying for a meal? Since when?" Mr. Evens says, in complete shock.

"Since I memorized your credit card number," she replies. And then she turns to me.

"And you—wow. My brother was right—you are giving me rebel vibes. I like it!"

I like being called a rebel, so I smile back at her. "Hi. I'm Sunny."

"Yes, you are, baby! Come here, give me hugs." She pulls me in and rocks me from side to side. Her hugs are different from Nanna's. Nanna's hugs are like falling into a fluffy, gooey marshmallow; the kind you melt in hot chocolate. Rue's hugs remind me of the chains that hold up the swings at the park. They're strong, sturdy, and so long as I hold on to them, I know I will be safe and I won't fly away. I like both types of hugs.

Rue holds me at arm's length. "Sunny, if that one gives you any trouble, just let me know."

"Thanks, but Miles is a pretty good kid," I reply.

She scoffs. "I'm talking about *my* brother. He can be so extra sometimes!"

I look over at Mr. Evens. He's rolling his eyes. "Mr. Evens, can we go for pancakes?" I ask.

"Mr. Evens? Why you make them call you that?" Rue asks her brother.

"I don't make them call me anything. It's just the way things—"

"You should call him by the nickname the kids on our block gave him growing up. They called him Scoop!"

"Scoop? Why did they call him that?" I ask her.

He glares at Rue. She smirks and says, "Well, it all started with—"

"Don't you dare!" Mr. Evens scolds.

Rue looks at me and mouths the words "Tell you later." We exchange a smile.

Later, we all pile in a booth at a diner and order pancakes. Miles brings up the market. He asks Rue if she ever shops there and tells her to be careful. Rue has no idea what he's talking about. Mr. Evens didn't tell her. When she asks him about it, he says, "It happened, let's just move on." That only makes Rue more curious. She hounds him until he tells her what happened.

She is furious! She wants to stage a protest and boycott the market. By the end of breakfast, she's already called the store and demanded to have a meeting with the head manager.

I lean in close and whisper to Mr. Evens, "Is she really going to meet with him?"

He nods slowly. "That's my little sister. Never a battle she won't confront. Even when she should let it go," he adds loud enough for her to hear.

"I'm not letting anything go. What would have happened if you weren't there to defend them? Nope, we need to fix this."

"You want to schedule an appointment to fix racism?" Mr. Evens asks.

"Yeah, I've got some time later," she says casually.

"Rue . . ." he warns.

"Look, I'm just reaching out to talk to them and let them know that it's not cool to behave like that. That's all."

"That's it?" he says suspiciously.

"And I may or may not egg their store."

"RUE!" he snaps.

She laughs. "You're so easy to torment, big brother."

I like seeing the two of them together. I think Miles does, too. They pretend to argue, but, really, I think they enjoy hanging out. I hope Rue comes by the apartment a lot. She's fun. And also, I really want to know how Mr. Evens got the nickname "Scoop."

I check out all the stalls in the girls' bathroom and they are all empty. Earlier, I ran into Folake in the hallway and she told me to meet her here. She said she thinks she found what we've been trying to get our hands on—a special seashell. My stomach ties itself into a bunch of knots. I start pacing just like Mr. Evens does when he's worried. What if Folake is wrong and it's not the seashell we have been looking for? What if we never find it? What happens to a quest if it's incomplete?

"Sunny!" Folake says in a hushed voice.

I pop out of the stall I was hiding in. "I'm here. What's the update? Is it good news? I could really use some good news." I speak almost as fast as Miles does when he's excited.

"Yes, it's good news. This morning when I was headed to class, I overheard Frankie the janitor say he was having a bad day. And Mrs. Woods, the new art teacher, she asked him what was wrong. And he said he lost something, something so important to him, he'll never be the same again."

"Okay, what did he lose?" I ask.

"A seashell! He lost it somewhere in this area a few hours ago. He's sad and can't wait for his shift to be over so he can go and try to find it again."

"That has to be it! That has to be our seashell!" My joy doesn't last long. "Wait, Folake, he's a grown-up. Why would he care about a little seashell?"

She shrugs. "It could be his good-luck charm. On my dad's first day of teaching at a new school, he always wears his good-luck tie."

"That's true! And Nanna always uses her good-luck pen when it's time to pick her lotto numbers! You're right, that could be it—his good-luck charm. But if he lost it, how will we find it? We don't even know the exact spot where he dropped it," I reply.

"Now comes even better news: on my way to meet you, I saw Mrs. Woods and asked her if by chance the janitor found his seashell and she said yes."

"He found it?!" I gasp.

"Yup, and now all we have to do is get him to let us borrow it for a little while so we can find a mermaid to kiss it."

I hug Folake so hard I almost knock her over. She laughs and hugs me back. I pull away, and we jet off to find our now-favorite janitor.

We start on the third floor and work our way down. We're

in the stairwell on the first floor, and still there is no sign of Frankie. The thing is, we don't have all day to look for him. We both told our teachers we were going to the nurse's office because we didn't feel well. It's only a matter of time before they realize we never showed up. Then they will come find us, and we'll get in trouble.

Thankfully, just as we are about to give up, we hear music—rap music. Frankie loves rap music!

"Where's it coming from?" I ask.

"Shhh," Folake says. We both stand very still and listen to where the sound might be coming from.

"Auditorium!" we announce at the same time.

We take off like speed racers and don't stop until we reach the double doors of the auditorium. We could get in trouble for running, but since we are already breaking the rules by being out of class, what could a little running hurt?

We enter to see Frankie spinning around in the middle aisle, showing off his dance moves like he's onstage. Frankie doesn't get to play his music as loud as he would like, but he bops his head so hard, the volume doesn't matter. He gets lost in the music no matter what. He starts using the mop as his microphone. I do that, too. I think the two of us would have an epic imaginary concert tour.

"Frankie, did you find it—the seashell?" I ask.

"My little seashell? I sure did! It's mad cool the way y'all students helped me out. I appreciate that," he says, going back to the music and head bopping.

I tap him on his arm and signal for him to turn down the music.

"What's up? Someone spill something? Oh no, it's chili day. Did someone throw up? Argh! I keep telling the school board it's a bad idea to have gym on the same day as chili day. You're just asking for trouble," he says, getting ready to go clean up the mess that doesn't exist.

"No, Frankie, it's not that," I reply.

"We were hoping that you would let us borrow your seashell—we'll give it back, we promise," Folake says.

He eyes her suspiciously. "Wait, you want Seashell? You, out of all the kids?" he says to Folake.

"Uh, yeah. I do. Please," she replies.

"I read about this somewhere: admitting your fears and facing up to them. And I'm going to look in on Seashell right now. Wait, what am I saying? Man, I must have lost my head. You kids can't come with me. It's not a good idea. That would be against school rules. I'm sorry," Frankie says.

He takes off, and I signal to Folake that we should follow him. Maybe there's a chance he's going to get the seashell from wherever he's hiding it. If we find it, we can borrow it. We follow Frankie out to the hallway and into the school-yard. He almost catches us, but thankfully we're really fast and hide behind a tree. I hate to think what would happen if Mr. Evens caught me. He'd be more than upset; he'd be disappointed. But this is something I have to do. Frankie is about to enter the shed, but then his cell phone rings.

"This is Frankie . . . What? The freezer's down? Already melting? Do you know how many pounds of mystery meat will go bad? Okay, I'm on my way." He looks toward the shed and says, "I'll be back, Seashell. Duty calls!"

We watch from behind the tree as Frankie runs back inside the school.

We make it to the supply shed and enter. The room is small and has very little light. It's hard to see anything. I can just make out a thick white string dangling above us.

"I think this turns on the light," I tell my best friend.

"Good, pull it."

I yank on the string, and the shed floods with light. Standing only a few feet away is the biggest rottweiler I have ever seen. Folake is checking the shelves behind me and doesn't see the rottweiler yet.

Miles made Nanna and me watch a whole season of *Dog Whisperer*. The host said when faced with a dog about to attack, make no sudden moves or loud noises. So as much as I want to run screaming, I try to take deep breaths and stay calm. Besides, no matter how scared I am, it's nothing compared to how Folake will feel. She will totally lose it. I'm hoping that if I'm relaxed, then she will be, too. But my plan doesn't exactly work out because, right at that moment, Folake turns to me with something in her hand.

"All I found was this ball," she says.

Folake is frozen in terror as she comes face-to-face with the animal she fears the most.

"I don't have my glasses, so maybe I'm not seeing clearly,

because that kind of looks like the outline of a dog."

"Folake, stay very still."

"Oh. My. Gosh!" she says as her jaw drops. I can hear her knees knocking together.

"I think Frankie likes to name his pets after things—things like seashells," I say, thinking out loud.

Seashell is wagging her stub little tail, excited and barking. But so far Folake is doing a good job at staying still. Phew!

"You can do this, Folake! Let's back out very slowly."

Folake nods but doesn't say a word. I think my plan to leave quietly would have worked had it not been for one tiny little thing: the ball that Folake found isn't just any ball—it's Seashell's ball. She thinks that Folake is asking her to play. So she rushes over to her at full speed. Folake bolts out of the shed and runs for her life. I follow.

"Folake, drop the ball!"

But Folake is too scared to do anything but run. We blow through the school doors and zoom down the halls, yelling at the top of our lungs. Seashell is only a breath away from catching us. Folake is running so hard, she loses a shoe. I don't lose my shoe, but I think somewhere along the way I drop my lungs; I can hardly breathe.

"Seashell, no!" we hear Frankie shout behind us. Seashell isn't in the mood to listen. She's too excited with what she thinks is a game. She runs even faster. We zip down the corridor just in time to smash right into Principal Bishop!

She was coming from the cafeteria, carrying a stack of lunch trays for her and her staff. We slam into her at top speed. It wouldn't have been so bad if it had been sandwich day, but it wasn't. Today is chili day. We look on helplessly as ground beef and beans rain down on the three of us.

Frankie manages to get to Seashell, but not before he licks the chili off the side of our faces. I think the worst is over until I look at the harsh expression on Principal Bishop's face. Uh-oh.

"Frankie, you know the rules: Seashell is not allowed inside the school! She can come to work with you, but she must stay outside!"

"That's just it, she was outside. I left her in the shed with all her favorite toys," Frankie replies.

"Then what is she doing inside?" Principal Bishop asks.

"Um, we kind of . . . went inside the shed, and she followed us out," I mumble.

"Instead of being in class where you two belong, you went outside? Alone? Without any adult supervision?" Principal Bishop demands.

"A little," Folake says in a small whisper.

"Folake Musa and Sundae Williams, my office. Now!" Principal Bishop roars as big chunks of beef slide down her cheek. Her eyes are wider than oceans, and she is not blinking—at all.

Folake and I look at each other. It was nice to be alive for ten years. And we would have loved to see eleven and maybe even twelve. But we both know we'll never live that long. We drag ourselves off the ground and enter her office. We're soaked in chili and shame.

Principal Bishop does her best to dry herself off with a roll of paper towels. When she's done, she hands us the rest of the roll. It turns out she didn't really need the paper towels to get dry; the heat from her anger could have dried all three of us off.

"I can't believe you two—ARGH! How could—what were you thinking? You can't go outside without an adult! Do you know what could have happened? No one knew where you were! How could—ARGHHHHH!" No one is more shocked about Principal Bishop's outburst than Principal Bishop herself. She takes a deep breath and finally starts blinking again.

"They have to invent a new word to describe just how much trouble you two are in! I'm gonna call your parents, Folake. And, Sunny, you can bet Mr. Evens will be notified. You two could very well be suspended for being out of class without permission, not to mention wandering outside without an adult present."

Principal Bishop launches into a lecture that I should have been listening to, but I'm not. I'm too distracted by the bookshelf behind her. On the top shelf, she has her much-beloved objects: a glass triangle-shaped award for Principal of the Year, a framed gold-trimmed certificate from the school where she graduated. And over on the far left is a photo of her and her family, vacationing on an island. The photo is inside a frame with the word "Caribbean" written on top. There are three tiny objects glued to the bottom of the frame: sandals, a beach chair, and a seashell . . .

Chapter Eleven
Saaaaaaang!

I POKE FOLAKE IN her side and signal for her to look at the shelf behind Principal Bishop. She sees it, too. But how are we going to get to it? Thankfully, right then, the principal's office phone rings. She stops her lecture long enough to answer it. I lean over and tell Folake my plan. She quickly agrees. Principal Bishop ends her call and comes back to us.

"Now, where was I? Oh, yes—do you know long it will take to clean up the mess you two made?" she demands.

"You're absolutely right, Principal Bishop. I think Folake and I should start by giving you and the school an official apology. But not just any old apology, right, Folake?"

"Oh, yeah, we need to do a lot more than that. We need to write you an official sorry note, Principal Bishop," Folake offers.

"Oh, well . . . yes. That would be a start—but just the start!" she warns us. "Lucky for you school is almost over, but tomorrow morning—"

"Oh no! We can't wait until tomorrow. Don't you know that saying?" Folake asks Principal Bishop.

"Saying? What saying?" Principal Bishop replies. Folake looks at me.

"Uh—yeah, the saying goes: If it's an apology you seek, best get it said before the sun peeks," I reply.

"I've never heard that saying," Principal Bishop says.

"I have! It's true," Folake adds.

"So you see, Principal Bishop, it's better if we write you a sorry letter now and not wait for the sun, in the morning."

Principal Bishop nods slowly and mumbles, "Okay . . ."

Before she can change her mind, I reach for the stray pencil across the desk and end up "accidentally" knocking over a stack of files. They fall to the floor, and Principal Bishop scrambles to gather them up.

"Oh no, I'm so sorry!" I shout.

"I'll help!" Folake says as she gets down on the floor alongside Principal Bishop.

While the two of them are busy gathering the files, I work my way around to her desk, get on the tips of my toes, and grab the frame from the shelf. I pluck off the seashell and shove it into my pocket. Folake and I look over at each other. At least one thing has gone right today!

Folake's parents were called and told they needed to come to the principal's office. When they got here, they yelled at her in their native language—Yoruba. I don't understand any of the words they're using, but when your mom puts her hand on her hip and wags her finger in your face, it means trouble—in any language.

The principal told us to go out into the waiting area of the main office while she talked to Folake's parents. We do as she says and take a seat on the bright orange plastic chairs.

"What did your mom say?" I ask Folake.

"I can't play outside, I can't have company over, and I can't use my new experiment kit."

"I'm sorry. I know how much you love your kit."

Folake's parents signed her up for a monthly delivery of science experiments in a box. That was her gift last year after she won first place in the science fair. I always know when she gets a new box in the mail because she gets this wild, crazed look in her eyes. I think, if given enough equipment, Folake could actually become a mad scientist.

"I'm sorry I got you in trouble. I know how much you love getting a new box in the mail, and now you can't even open it."

"Nope, they're making me wait a whole week. I can't even peek and see what the experiment is inside. A whole week! That's basically like a year in science. Who knows what amazing discoveries I could have made by then?" she groans.

"How about I go in there and tell your parents that I forced you to go along with me. Maybe then they won't punish you."

She shakes her head. "We're best friends, Sunny. I can't let you face punishment alone. Best friends stick together."

When Folake's parents come out of the office, they order

her to get her stuff and get into the car. We say our goodbyes, and her dad gives me a look of deep, utter disappointment. I know that look very well.

On their way out, her mom says in English, "Where are your glasses?"

Folake's eyes are actually bigger now than when she ran into Seashell. "I left them at home," Folake says carefully. Her mom shakes her head as they leave the main office.

Mr. Evens shows up not long after Folake's family leaves. Classes are over by now, and all the kids—the ones who didn't crash into the principal—are headed home.

Mr. Evens looks down at me and says, "What did you do?"

I look up and try to put on my best "I'm still cute" smile. It doesn't work. Mr. Evens's eyes narrow, and he frowns deeply. He signals for me to follow him into the principal's office. Once we are seated, Principal Bishop tells him what we've done. If Mr. Evens were a cartoon, there would be red smoke coming out of his nose and ears. He'd erupt like a fiery, angry volcano.

The principal says she didn't suspend Folake or me because we don't usually cause problems. She also pointed out that she didn't suspend us because she doesn't want us staying home for a week just to watch TV. She wants us in school so she can torment us. Okay, she didn't say the word "torment," but that's exactly what she means.

She hands Mr. Evens a list full of things we now have to do before, during, and after school. She also gave Folake's parents the same list.

I read from the list out loud. "Stack books at the school library before class, detention after class, and join the clean-up crew instead of going to recess?!"

I try to let the words sink in, but they don't. I look up at the two grown-ups, thinking surely this is a mistake. "But, Principal Bishop, I won't have any free time at all."

"That's just as well because it's obvious you're not mature enough to handle free time. You need structure to help you stay out of trouble. You have carts full of books to shelve."

I'm about to argue, but something tells me I've already lost this battle and am lucky to get out alive. So I nod and agree to the end of my freedom.

Mr. Evens doesn't say a word to me in the car. Miles is really the only one who talks. He heard about what happened at the school. The kids in his class thought it was cool to get chased and to smash into a grown-up. When Miles tells us that, Mr. Evens shoots him a warning look.

When we get home, he makes Miles go straight to the table in the corner of the living room to finish the homework he started in after-school Homework Help. Then he tells me to sit on the sofa and explain myself. I'd love to tell him about the quest, but what if he doesn't believe me? What if he tries to get me to stop searching? I can't take that chance.

"All right, I know we've only known each other for less than a week now, but I got the impression you were smart and mature for your age. And now you go and pull this stunt, and I'm at a loss. What were you thinking?"

"I need to find something, and I thought it would be in the shed. But it wasn't."

"What were you looking for?" Mr. Evens asks.

Oh, you know, the usual—a seashell that I can give to an enchanted mermaid, so she can kiss it and help me save my nanna.

But out loud, I say, "We were just . . . fooling around."

"That's it? That's all you have to say for yourself?"

"And I—I like your tie," I add with a smile. He does not smile back.

"I am extremely disappointed in you. And it seems to me that your nanna wouldn't be very happy with you right now."

"Hey, that's not fair!" I shout, not sure why my chest hurts when he mentions Nanna. My face grows hot, and tears spill from my eyes. I didn't know I was holding in tears until they slid down my cheeks.

"No, no, don't do the salty-water thing," he says, grabbing the box of tissues on the coffee table. I wipe my eyes and blow my nose.

"That's it, isn't it? The reason why you went on this ill-advised adventure, right? It has to do with your nanna?"

"Kind of . . ." I reply.

"Look, I know that you're worried about your grandmother. And talking to her on the phone isn't the same thing as seeing her in person. But don't worry; as soon as she's settled in, we will go see her. I promise. But you have to stop getting into trouble. I don't get to break the rules and act out, and neither will you. Is that clear?"

I nod. Mr. Evens hands me more tissues. "Don't do that

crying thing—it's not necessary or anything. However, I'm going to have to punish you for breaking so many rules."

Miles looks in my direction. I dry my eyes with a tissue and try to brighten up. I don't want him to worry.

I nod. "Okay."

He thinks for a minute and says, "You will write me a three-page report."

"A report?" I ask.

"Uh . . . yeah, yeah. That's right. A report on why it's important to follow the school rules. I expect it to be done by next week. I want it single-spaced, in pencil, and no spelling errors. Do you understand?"

I roll my eyes before I can stop myself.

"You do that again, and it will be five pages!" he warns.

"Sorry," I mumble. I'm not sure if Mr. Evens sounds more like a teacher or a dad. But either way, he's really mad!

"And just so you know, reports happen to be fun. I was in charge of writing all the reports whenever we had a class project back when I was in school."

Did he just say reports are *fun*?

ARGH!

Later that night, I give Miles an update on the quest, just before he falls asleep. I try my best to close my eyes, but I just keep thinking about how the first week is over and we're no closer to completing the first object. I overhear Mr. Evens on the phone in his room.

"Rue, I already told you I'm not going. . . . If you want to go, that's fine, but I won't. . . . No, I won't change my mind. . . .

I'm not going. Why? Why? Because Oz scares the heck out of me!" He then says goodbye and hangs up on her.

What's Oz? Why is it making him so angry? And what's happening there that he's so afraid of?

When I get to school the next day, some of the kids are making fun of Folake and me for what happened with Seashell the dog. It's a joke all over the school. I hoped it would end by the time lunch came around, but it doesn't. So instead of having lunch and being laughed at, Folake and I get permission to start stacking the books on the shelves in the library.

On our way back, we see the kids from music class practicing in the hallway. I forgot that today is the day of the auditions. I sigh longingly to myself.

"Just try out, Sunny!" Folake says. "And you know Mr. Evens would like it. I'm sure he's mad at you for getting in trouble. This could help. And you love the songs in the show. You hum them all the time."

"What? No, I don't."

She narrows her eyes and tilts her head to the side. She looks just like her mom when she does that. "Sunny, you hum. All. The. Time."

"Oh. Sorry."

"It's okay. You don't even know you're doing it. The point is you love the music and you're good at it. So go and try out already!"

"I can't. Nanna won't be there in the crowd if I get the part," I remind her.

"Do you believe you'll finish this quest and find everything you need to save your nanna?" she asks.

"Yes! There's no other choice. I am going to be a hero, just like Luna was in her story. I'll save Nanna. No matter what!"

"Then audition for the concert. By the time the show goes on, your quest will be completed, and Nanna will be in the audience."

"That's true! The concert isn't until November; I'll be done with my quest by then! But wait, what if I audition and get the role? What if rehearsing for the solo part distracts me from the quest?"

Folake rolls her eyes at me and then says in a very sweet voice, "First, get the part and then worry about that."

I look at her and shake my head. "You're so smart!"

"I know," she says, breaking out into a smile. She walks me down the hall to audition.

We stand in front of the sign-up sheet posted on the door of the music room. I sign up and wait with Folake.

"Are you going to be okay to sing in front of Mr. Evens?" she asks.

"Yeah, I can do it because it'll only be Mr. Evens and two other judges. So I'll be nervous, but not nervous enough to need Nanna. If I get the part and have to stand up in front of a huge crowd, yup—gonna need Nanna big-time!"

"Don't worry. You got this!" she says proudly.

Mr. Evens calls out from inside the classroom. "Next!"

I read the name on the sign-up sheet; up next is Shelia Sims. Shelia can hit notes that are so high, I'm sure they reach the mountains. She never runs out of air and knows how to follow along to the music. She could get the solo. The next three people Mr. Evens calls are also good—or even great—singers.

I start to panic that maybe I won't get the solo. Maybe my voice is not good enough. But then Nanna's voice comes back to me, from the last time I was nervous about auditioning: "You can go out there and sing. Or you can believe in yourself, like I do, and saaaaaaang! In the end, what matters is that you give it everything you have and that you find the joy in the song. Find the joy."

When Mr. Evens calls me next, Folake and I are the last ones standing out in the hall. She asks if I'm ready. I smile to myself.

I'm so ready! Get the part or not, this is my chance to sing out and find joy in the music. And that's just what I'm going to do.

I walk into the music room. Mr. Evens looks up. He smiles a little to himself. I thought he'd be surprised to see me, but he's not. Argh! It's like he knew I would come. He didn't push me to audition, but he knows I can't fight the urge to sing and hum along back at home. He knows how much I love singing.

Wait, did I just call Mr. Evens's place home?

"Sunny, are you all right?" one of the judges asks.

I nod.

"Whenever you're ready," the other judge says.

I look at Mr. Evens, and I can't find any doubt in his eyes. It's like he just knows that I can do it. Nanna is the same way . . .

"Sunny? We're waiting," Mr. Evens says.

I take a deep breath and remember not to sing but to saaaaaaang!

Later, Miles and I pile into the car. Before he starts driving, Mr. Evens says, "We'll announce who got the solo in the next few days. I'm not the only one who has to make the decision. And to be fair, I can't discuss the audition with you." Then he starts to drive.

"But did I sound okay?" I ask.

His face tells me the answer way before his mouth does. He lights up, but then he quickly catches himself and clears his throat. "You were fine."

I grin, feeling good. Even if I don't get the part, at least I know Mr. Evens is happy with my performance.

Chapter Twelve
The Artist

RUE COMES OVER AFTER dinner, and I overhear her in the kitchen with Mr. Evens. She's talking about Oz again and trying to get him to go.

"You're the only one in the family who hasn't gone yet, Darrious. That's not good. Look, it was hard for me, too! I loved her, too! But I went because it's the right thing to do."

"Why won't you just drop this, Rue? I told you already, I can't handle it. Just leave it alone. I have to look after the kids; I'm in charge of getting a concert done; and I have a thousand other things going on. Oz will have to wait!"

"Until when? Have you ever thought it might be good for you to go? Maybe take the kids with you."

"I'm not talking about this anymore," Mr. Evens says, storming out of the kitchen. I enter and ask Rue if everything is okay. She smiles sadly and says yes. But I don't think either of us believes that.

"What's Oz? Does it have anything to do with the trunk in the closet?" I ask.

"The trunk . . . Has Darrious been looking at it?" she says.

"Doesn't open it. He just touches it and stares at it for a long time. He told Miles not to touch it. Do you know what's inside?"

"It's for him to tell you. But maybe he will one day."

"What about Maya? How come there aren't any pictures of her here?" I ask.

She looks at me and says, "You are way too smart!"

Miles enters the kitchen, pouting like he just lost his favorite toy. We ask him what's wrong, and he tells us he has an art project and has no idea where to start. The project is called "My Happy," and Miles has to make a piece of art that shows everyone what makes him happy. He said his art teacher would not let him just bring in a catalog from the zoo.

"But the animals make me happy," he protests. Rue tells him to try to go deeper. He grumbles and says, "That's what my art teacher said, too. I don't get it."

Rue suddenly gets an idea. She tells Miles he needs to be exposed to art, so she's taking us all to her weekend art class. Mr. Evens says Miles can go with Rue and that he will stay home with me. I'm still on punishment; also he isn't in the mood to go anywhere. But Miles refuses to go without his best friend, so Mr. Evens has no choice but to come along and bring me, too.

When we get there, the place is wonderful. They have shelves that go all along the walls with artwork that other people have done. By the sink, there's a bin containing different colors of paint. There are cans full of brushes in the center of every table. The brushes are all different sizes—some are wide with thick bristles or medium with stubby bristles; others are needle thin. If I didn't have to worry about finding a magical creature, I'd be having a lot of fun.

"What are you thinking about over there? You hardly painted," Rue says after giving Miles his first art lesson.

I look down at my white mug. It's the biggest one I've ever seen. I could practically swim in it. It's a perfect canvas for a colorful painting. But I've only painted a few random, dull-colored strokes.

"Sorry," I reply.

"Are you worried about your audition? Darrious said you killed it!"

"Yeah, it was fun," I reply.

"So you're not worried about the audition, but something's up with you. What is it?" Rue asks. I look over at her and then at her mug. Wow! She painted a full forest with little birds soaring above a mountain peeking through the trees.

"That's really good!" I tell her.

"Aw, thank you. I'm an art major, have to rep my people," she says smugly as she smiles back at me.

"I didn't know you were an artist. That's really cool. I don't draw everything well, but I'm really good with houses, trees, and no one, *no one* makes a better sun than me."

"I like your confidence, sis. So where's this amazing sun you're supposed to paint?" she asks, studying my mug.

I sigh. "I'm really not in a sun-painting mood," I admit.

She looks toward the back of the class where Mr. Evens

and Miles have just finished cleaning off their brushes. They add new colors to put on their trays and walk toward us.

"Hey, you two mess around a little more over there. Sis and I are gonna need some girl time," Rue says.

Miles and Mr. Evens look at each other, and then they shrug and turn back around.

"Okay, now that we have a few minutes, talk to me," Rue says, putting down her paintbrush.

I chew on my bottom lip; it always helps me think. I don't think I should tell her everything, but maybe I can tell her just enough to get her advice.

"How do you find someone when you have no idea where they could be?" I confess.

"Okay, who is this person?"

"It's more like . . . a magical creature. Anyway, I need to find them. But I don't know how to do that."

"Remember I told you I take art in school?"

"I'm not sure art will help me here."

"Art is my minor. It's the second thing I'm learning. The first thing I'm studying in school is criminal psychology."

"What's that?" I ask.

"That's when you learn to think like criminals in order to catch them."

"Oh, well, this girl isn't a criminal," I reply.

"That doesn't matter. When you are trying to track someone down, you have to think like the person. For example, if Miles went missing while you two were in the park, and there were two places he could be, a nearby dance studio or a nearby zoo, where would Miles likely be found?"

"The zoo," I reply.

"Exactly! You have to put yourself into the person's head. Think about it: what does this magic girl like to do? What makes her happy? Is there something she can't live without?"

"Like Miles at the zoo?"

"Exactly!" she replies.

The mermaid can't live without doing her favorite thing— swimming! She needs to swim!

I jump up out of my seat and hug Rue. "Thank you! Thank you!"

My embrace surprises her, but she hugs me back. "You're welcome, sis. Anytime."

"I got it! I know what I'm gonna do for my art project— and it's not about animals!" Miles shouts from the back of the art studio.

He rushes to our table and sits down. He waves for Mr. Evens to hurry and join us. Mr. Evens comes to the table and puts a can of newly washed paintbrushes in the center. I can't help but notice that Mr. Evens's paintbrushes are the cleanest ones at our table. In fact, they are the cleanest brushes in the whole studio.

"What's your art project going to be?" I ask Miles.

Miles is about to reply, but then he looks over at Rue and says, "I'm an artist. And my new art teacher told me that when an idea is fresh in an artist's mind, they need to let it grow before they share it with the world. So for now, my project is a secret!"

"Wow, you won't even tell your favorite and only sister?" I tease.

"Nope!" he says, turning his attention back to Rue. "What's the thing you said to say when I'm not ready to talk about my project?"

"Respect my process," she replies.

Miles crosses his arms over his chest and nods firmly. We all agree not to push him into telling us exactly what his art project will be.

Mr. Evens asks how our girl talk went. Rue refuses to share info because she says it was between us girls. He says, "I will have you two know that Miles and I will be taking some guy time ourselves."

"We will?" Miles replies.

"Yes. We're going bowling," Mr. Evens says.

"I've never been bowling. I might not be good at it," Miles warns.

"Don't worry. I'll teach you," he says. Miles looks up at Mr. Evens with a big smile—so big I'm sure it hurts.

"Are you good at bowling?" I ask.

"I was on an award-winning championship team," Mr. Evens brags.

Rue presses her lips together tightly. She's trying really hard not to laugh. I'm not sure what's so funny.

"Rue, is Mr. Evens a good bowler?" I ask.

She can't hold it in anymore and chuckles loud enough for the people at the other table to look over at us.

"Don't listen to Rue. I *was* on an award-winning bowling

team," Mr. Evens says firmly.

Rue stops laughing just long enough to say, "Tell them what your role was on the team."

"Were you captain?" Miles asks.

"No . . ." Mr. Evens says carefully.

"Mr. Evens, were you co-captain?" I suggest.

Rue shakes her head, and again she smashes her lips together to trap in the laughter she's trying to hold back.

"Mr. Evens, what did you do on the bowling team?" Miles asks.

He clears his throat and proudly announces, "I was the hygiene marshal."

Rue is laughing so hard, tears come out of her eyes. And the more her brother tries to defend his title, the more she cackles.

"Bowling hygiene is critical to the sport and its players!" Mr. Evens says sternly.

We cannot help but laugh along with Rue. When we finally stop, Miles goes up to Mr. Evens and says, "I would be proud to learn from you, Marshal." Then he holds out his hand, and Mr. Evens shakes it.

"Ha! See?!" Mr. Evens gloats.

The rest of the night they talk about bowling and what fun they'll have. I start to focus on my mug and make the biggest and best sun of anyone else in the class. I'm happy because Miles is happy and also because, thanks to Rue, I know exactly where to find my mermaid.

Chapter Thirteen
The Mermaid

THE NEXT MORNING, WE get a surprise visit from Mrs. Henry, the social worker. Mr. Evens gave her a tour of the apartment and answered a bunch of questions about what we ate, where we slept, and how things were going. She seems happy with the answers Mr. Evens gave her. When she wasn't looking, I whisper to Mr. Evens that I think Mrs. Henry is being nosy. He told us she was just doing her job, making sure that we were in a safe environment.

Before the end of her visit, Mrs. Henry took us aside and asked us to tell her about living here. We promised Mr. Evens that we'd answer any questions she had and we did. But Miles naturally had a set of questions for her too. The moment she entered the apartment, he insisted Mrs. Henry meet Noodle. And going by the look on her face, Mrs. Henry isn't a big fan of rodents. That didn't stop Miles from asking her what her favorite rodent was.

He also asked her which video she liked better, the one he showed her with the rat feasting in a trash can or the one where a possum fakes its death and then springs back to life and hisses at its owner. That video almost gave Mrs. Henry a heart attack. Mrs. Henry said she planned on coming by more often, but now that she sees we are fine, she's going to check on us via video call. I'm pretty sure she just didn't want to run into Noodle or Miles again.

When we get to school on Monday, Miles bugs me to get him some hot chocolate from the corner store by our school. I say no at first because I don't want to miss Folake when she comes into school. I have so much to tell her. But he keeps begging and says he earned the hot chocolate because the night before he had eaten all his vegetables.

That's not exactly what happened. Mr. Evens said Miles couldn't play with Noodle until he ate his veggies. He choked down three little pieces of green beans.

"I'm sorry, I . . . just . . . can't," he said with a deep, dramatic sigh. He threw the top half of his body on the dinner table, like he had just battled a great evil and was exhausted.

But I didn't argue with him and, besides, hot chocolate is also one of my favorites, so I leave him in the schoolyard with some of his friends and run down the street to the corner store. I rush so that I can come back in time to see Folake before class starts. I would have made it, too, but when I get to the store, there's a line and it takes forever.

On my way back with two cups of hot chocolate, I can't walk as fast as I want to because I'm afraid it will spill. I guess it's my fault for asking the store clerk to fill it all the way to the top, but it's also their fault for making their hot chocolate so delicious. I walk slowly toward the school. I'm only a few yards away when someone appears from out of nowhere and blocks my way to the entrance.

Tessa.

"Hey, I checked it out and there's no such thing as a license to fight! You tried to trick me!" she spits out angrily.

"I didn't try, I actually did," I joke before I can stop myself. Tessa does not find that funny. Honestly, that girl needs to work on her humor.

"You think you're funny?!" she says, coming closer. I take a step back.

"Hey, you're right. Let's work this out. And I have been feeling really bad about tricking you—that's why I was going to surprise you with this yummy, hot, and creamy cup of hot chocolate. So you want some?" I offer with a smile.

"No. What I want is to beat the mess out of you!" she says, coming even closer.

"I don't know that drink. Is it from a tropical island? Tell me where they sell it, and I will buy it for you!"

"ARGH! I'm gonna get you!" she roars as she takes off after me at full speed. I drop the cups and run for my life.

The thing about running for your life is that you need all parts of your body to agree to the speed you should be running. My legs want to go as fast as they can. But my heart and my lungs disagree. They want me to stop running immediately, or they will burst open.

I picture them coming out of my chest and turning into

red-colored confetti once they hit the air. People will be walking on the sidewalk hours later and say, "Hey, what's with all the red-colored shiny confetti?" And someone will reply, "That's what's left of Sundae Williams. Her heart and lungs burst open. Yes, it's a tragedy, but look how pretty that red is."

C'mon, heart and lungs, work with me here!

Thankfully, both heart and lungs decide to stay in my chest. Phew! I run even faster. I hear the wind whipping by my ears as I jet down the street and into the back of the store. I look for a place to hide. I see the giant dumpster and look for any other place. There's no time—I hear Tessa calling my name and vowing to end me. I jump into the dumpster and pull the lid over my head. I hold my breath for as long as I can. The truth is if Tessa doesn't end me, the smell in this dumpster will.

"Where are you? I know you're in this alley. I saw you come in here. Where are you?! I'm gonna get both you and your little friend Folake. Trust me!" she swears.

I peek out of a small hole in the dumpster. I see Tessa turning over large boxes, crates, and containers. She's only a few feet from me, but she doesn't think to look in the dumpster because who would do such a crazy thing?

Something scurries across my feet.

Don't panic, it's just a butterfly. Yup, that's all it is.

Wait, do butterflies scurry?

"You better come out now!" Tessa says. I hear her turning things over in hopes of finding me.

"Gotcha!" she says, looking behind a large blue plastic bin

full of empty soda bottles. When she sees I'm not there, she curses at the sky. And just when the smell is about to make me gag and give up my location, someone else enters the alley. It's one of Tessa's friends—Mia. She's almost as tall as Tessa and has blond curls with pink clip-in highlights.

"Tess, I saw you running this way. What's up?" Mia asks.

"I'm looking for—"

"Leave it, whatever it is. The bell just rang, you're gonna be late. And you know that if you're late one more time, your parents will make you quit the team. And we need you. So let's go!" Mia insists.

Tessa looks around the alley one last time.

"Tess! Move it!"

Tessa groans and follows her friend back to the school. I don't know what team Tessa is on, but I'm grateful to them for saving my life. I jump out as fast as I can and thank my lungs and heart by getting as much clean air inside them as I can.

I look at myself and I look like . . . well, like a girl who jumped into the trash.

I scan the street, and Tessa and Mia are both gone. I run back to school, and the yard is empty. Wow, I am really late for class. But even if I were on time, I couldn't go in like this. I'm filthy, and I smell like gym socks, rotten eggs, and puke.

"Hey, what are you doing out there? Shouldn't you be inside?" someone shouts out the window on the second floor. I look up. It's the school nurse—Mrs. Throne. I've always liked her. She usually wears a friendly smile. She's slender and wears her brown locs pinned to her head in a high ponytail. The tips of it flare out like the feathers on a proud peacock.

Mrs. Throne is giving me her "no-nonsense" look. I know that look really well.

"How did you get so dirty? What happened to you?" she asks when she gets a good look at me.

I thought I would have to go into deep detail, but since she's the school nurse and knows everything and just about everyone in the school, I take a chance.

I simply reply, "Tessa."

"Got it. I'll have a talk with her. Come inside."

When I get back in the school, I take a shower in the girls' locker room, and Mrs. Throne gives me an extra set of uniform scrubs she keeps around in case a student might need it. She also gives me a hall pass so that I won't get in trouble for being late; all that for hot chocolate.

Then again, it really is good hot chocolate . . .

When I get to class, I show the teacher, Mrs. Free, my pass, and she tells me to sit and catch up on the work the class is doing.

Folake, who sits next to me, leans over and whispers, "Mr. Evens is never late. And I saw Miles this morning. So what happened? How come you're late?"

I quickly tell her everything and warn her to be on the lookout because she's on Tessa's list, too. I also tell her that I have an update on our quest to find a mermaid. But I don't get a chance to give Folake more details because just then,

Mrs. Free announces that she will be using the last few minutes of class to call out the name of the kid who won the biweekly essay contest.

The whole class perks up—we all want to win the essay contest because that means we can choose any prize we want from the game closet. Whenever Mrs. Free opens up that closet, we all try to sneak a peek. She has shelves after shelves of treasures that any kid would love to get their hands on.

After she opens the closet, only the essay winner gets to take a really good look inside as they pick what they want. When class is over, we form groups in the hallway and try to piece together the small bits of what we saw. One kid said he saw a video game set; another kid said there was a box with the picture of a drone on it—a real-life drone!

I would have won the essay contest many times, but there was always something standing in my way—time. I always hand in my essays late. It's not my fault. There are just so many things to talk about in this world, and asking me to choose just one topic—well, that is really hard.

Mrs. Free says she loves my writing and that I have flair! I'm not really sure what that means, but it sounds like a very good thing. I thought that meant I would win, but according to Mrs. Free, it's not enough to have a good essay with flair. That essay has to be on time.

The Ha-Ha Girls are in the same class as we are. They go on and on about wanting to win a makeup set thingy. But their essays never make the list because they always write about the same thing: their beauty routine.

Mrs. Free told the Ha-Ha Girls that while they look very nice, she wants them to dig deeper. The next time the Ha-Ha Girls wrote about an event that happened and changed their lives: their favorite influencer went through a really hard time and that affected the Ha-Ha Girls deeply. So deeply they started crying as they read from their essays.

But it wasn't until the end that they told us what actually happened to their idol that made them so upset. She misread an invite to a party and attended the party wearing the wrong kind of footwear. Mrs. Free rolled her eyes so far back in her head, they didn't come back until the next period.

Although we all want to win a prize, the person who wants it the most is Folake. When Mrs. Free first started having the contest, Folake wasn't really that into it. But one day she spotted a box with the words "Science VR & Chemistry Kit" and she lost it! She looked up the box online, and it was her dream kit! I'm not into science, and even I had to admit some of the stuff inside the box sounded really cool.

There are over eighty different types of experiments that can be performed with the kit. That's even more than the kits Folake already has at home. There are goggles, test tubes, and a bunch of miniature lab equipment. They even have a cut-out lab coat pattern that you can wear and pretend to be an actual, real scientist!

But the best part of all—the part that makes Folake so excited she can't stay in her seat—is the VR. There are virtual reality glasses in the box. You put them on, and you become part of a virtual science lab. It connects to other kids who are playing from different parts of the world. They compete to see who can run an experiment faster and who gets the most accurate results. So the VR box is basically science nerd paradise.

This month, Folake worked extra hard on her essay. Folake wrote about her family history. She didn't just write about it; she videotaped interviews with all the members of her family—including her grandparents and her great-aunt—who is, like, almost one hundred years old. Folake wrote and rewrote the essay about four hundred times. When she was done, I was tired just from watching her work so hard.

Mrs. Free stands in front of the class and announces that she has chosen the winner. She always wears palm trees and sunset button-down shirts. She puts them together with tan cargo pants with way too many pockets. She loves wearing Timberland ankle boots and has at least three different pairs. Her bottom half looks like she's going on safari, and her top half looks like she's going on a beach vacation. She shaved her hair, and now it's really short, like a boy haircut. It's very unusual. That's why I like it.

"All right, as usual all of you have done a terrific job with your essays and should be very proud of yourself. But this student went above and beyond. This student worked so hard, she added additional material to accompany her essay."

Folake is sitting across the aisle from me. We exchange a look. Could this be? Could Folake finally get her prize VR chemistry set?

"This student went out of her way to really tell a story with her essay and her added material," Mrs. Free teases.

Folake and I reach across the aisle and hold hands.

"This student I'm referring to is our one and only . . ."

Both of us hold our breath.

". . . Folake!" Mrs. Free shouts.

I am the first to jump up! I clap hard, and the class does the same. Folake zips up to the front of the class, and Mrs. Free hands her a certificate. She's so excited about getting to go to the game closet she's squirming like she really has to go to the bathroom. But she doesn't want to just say, "Open the closet and let me have my kit." She knows it would be rude, and her mom really doesn't like it when kids are rude.

Finally, Mrs. Free smiles says, "Yes, Folake, you can open the closet."

"YES!" Folake shouts as she makes a dash for the game closet. And just as she gets to the closet door, one of the Ha-Ha Girls calls out to her, "Good job, Folake. Pick carefully. . . ."

I scrunch my face. What does that mean?

I look over at Folake, and her smile slides down her face. She reaches into the closet and comes back out with a big box.

"Okay, let's have a look at what you decided on," Mrs. Free says.

Folake slowly turns the box around to reveal a starter makeup kit.

What the heck?!

When class is over, we walk down the stairs and into the

lunchroom. Once we take our seats, the first thing I do is check Folake's temperature by putting my hand on her forehead. Folake playfully swats my hand away.

"I just want to see if you're running a fever."

"I'm not sick. I'm fine," she says as she explores what's inside the makeup kit without having to open it, thanks to the see-through box.

"C'mon, Folake, why did you take the makeup set instead of the chemistry kit?"

"Tiffany, Taylor, and Tamar all love this kit. And they asked me to come hang out with them and try some of this stuff on together."

"You're gonna hang out with the Ha-Ha Girls?"

She sighs. "Don't call them that. They have names. And why not? Ever since I took my glasses off . . . they've started to like me. Besides it's a science experiment, remember? I'm studying people."

"You need your glasses!" I remind her again.

She shakes her head stubbornly. "I only need them to see shapes and stuff. Anyway, what about the mermaid? How will we find her?"

I'm not sure this new Folake is who she really wants to be, but I don't know how to say that to her without hurting her feelings. Maybe I should just leave it alone? Or should I say something? And what exactly can I say that won't upset her?

Folake waves her hand in front of my face to get my attention, "Hello?! Mermaid, remember?"

"Oh, yeah." I tell her about the idea Rue gave me about

thinking like a mermaid. She agrees with Rue and wonders if we should be looking for people who have pools in their backyard.

"I thought of that too, but no. If you were a mermaid and had to give up the sea, would you settle for some small little backyard pool? No, you'd want something big. You know, a pool that you can do tricks in and spread out."

"You're right! You would want to be in, like, an Olympic-size pool," Folake replies.

"Exactly. This morning I went online, and do you know what they have at the community center just a few blocks away?"

Folake nods and grins widely.

"It's not Olympic-size, but it's the biggest pool in the area. And lots of people swim there," I add.

I know we could get in trouble, but I can't help but be excited that we get to go on another adventure. It's only a matter of time before we have all three things we're looking for: a seashell kissed by a mermaid, a hair from a manticore, and a tear from a Gorgon.

"It sounds good to me. When do you want to go?" she asks.

"Right after school. Miles has to stay late to work on a project for art class, and Mr. Evens is busy doing the lesson plan for the week. He won't even know we're gone."

"Mom is working late, and Dad is teaching a class tonight. So if I come home a little late, they won't know."

I look at her and wonder for the first time if maybe I

should keep her out of this. I don't want her to get in any more trouble.

"Folake, maybe—"

"No, don't try and tell me to go home after school. We are doing this together. That's the whole point of being best friends."

Folake is really good at reading my mind. She's so good sometimes, I think it's her superpower. I nod and agree to let her come with me.

She holds up another clear tube with lip gloss and looks at it like she's looking at an alien inside. "Sunny, did you know there's a color named Strawberry Shortcake? How is cake a color?"

Chapter Fourteen
Find the Light

I ASK MR. EVENS if I can go to the community center after school to check out some classes and he agrees. It's not a lie. They have lots of stuff that I'm interested in—step classes, arts and crafts, and a rock-climbing wall. But I'm also going there to find a mermaid to kiss the magic seashell; I just left that part out.

Although he agrees to let me go, Mr. Evens says I have to wait until after rehearsal. I don't really mind since rehearsals are fun and going really well. Mr. Evens always starts out by saying, "Take a deep breath and let your lungs fill with air." I think it helps to be reminded. Sometimes I forget and run out of air in the middle of singing.

I'm not nearly as nervous as I was when we first got started. The class says I sound good, and Miles agrees. He comes to sit in the back of the auditorium when he's not working on his art project. I wish he would tell us what it is, but he insists that it has to remain a surprise until he's done with it.

After rehearsal, Folake and I head to the center. It's a

strange feeling to not have to sneak off somewhere. I like it. I wish I could tell Mr. Evens that I'm hunting for my quest, but I know that might not be a good idea. Maybe he'll be okay with me hunting down magical items, but what if he's not? Then he would make me stop, and this quest is just too important. But when this is all over, I promise to not lie to him—well, I promise to try really, really hard.

Folake and I enter the center just as a crowd of people, all different ages, comes out. We ask the redheaded guy at the front desk about classes, and he tells us that the last class just let out and that he's about to close up.

"There aren't any more classes at all?" I ask.

"No, sorry. Everybody's gone for the night," he says.

"Aw, man, we missed the swim class," Folake says, sounding just as disappointed as I am.

We're about to go when I get an idea.

"Excuse me, sir, is there anyone in the swim class that always comes, like every day? Someone who loves to be in the water and is an excellent swimmer?"

"Well, swim class has a lot of people, and some come more often than others. I can't really say if anyone in the classes is particularly good. I'm not in class with them. I'm here at the desk all day."

"Oh. Okay, thank you," I reply.

"Let's try again tomorrow but get here earlier," Folake says.

I try to cheer up, but I can't muster a smile. "I just hope the classes aren't too big and that it's easy to find the best swimmer here," I reply as we make our way to the door.

"Oh, that's easy—I can tell you who the best swimmer here is. Sure, I can do that!" the guy says, calling us back.

Folake says, "I thought you didn't know—"

"—in swim class, I have no idea," he admits. "But we also have a swim team. They compete with other community centers from the area. And well, there's only one girl who is so good, she might make it to the Olympics!"

Folake and I smile at each other and walk back over to the redhead, whose name tag says "Jay."

"Jay, how good is this woman?" I ask.

"That's just it, she's not a grown-up. She's just a girl. I would say she's about your age," he replies.

"Wow, okay. But exactly how good is she?" I ask.

He lets out a slow whistle. "Man, she's the best I've ever seen. Her coach thinks so, too. She's the captain of the team. When she's in the water, it's like she glides. I've seen it; she swims even better than most fish. That girl is gonna be big someday. In fact, everybody around here calls her "Light." Because that's just how fast she is."

"When does she practice? We'd love to see her," Folake says.

"Yes, can you tell us when the next swim practice is going to be?" I ask. "We'd love to meet her."

"Oh, well, the next swim meet is three days from now, but if you want to meet her, she's in the pool. She should be just finishing up."

"Really? I thought everybody was gone," Folake says.

"Everybody but Light. Light is always here, when she's not in school. She's the first one in on the weekends and the last one out. Like I said, she loves the water. I joke with her all the time. I say, 'Light, you just come on land to eat junk food from the vending machine. But your home, your *real* home, that's in the water.'"

We beg Jay to let us go to the pool and meet Light. He's about to say no, but then he looks at our faces and then says, "Okay, okay. Y'all can put those sad eyes away. Go ahead. But tell her it's time to wrap it up. I want all three of you out of here in ten minutes! I need to lock up. It's Dungeons and Dragons night!"

Jay directs us to the pool area, and we take off running.

"Hey, no running!" he shouts.

We walk—very quickly. My heart is racing, and I'm pretty sure Folake is feeling the same thing. We are only moments away from meeting a mermaid and, best of all, getting the very first item on our list. We see the light blue and white double doors that Jay told us to look out for. There's a large window panel on the doors. We look through it, and there it is—a massive pool with a girl standing with her back to us. She's wearing a bathing suit, and all her hair is tucked inside her swim cap. I wish we could see her face.

"You have the seashell?" Folake asks.

I pat my coat pocket to make sure I feel the hard shell inside. "Yup, it's right here. Let's go."

We open the double doors just in time to see the girl dive into the pool. We watch from a few feet away, our mouths open with awe. Jay was right; the moment the girl's body hits the water, she moves through it like she has fins. She's more than quick, more than graceful; she's mesmerizing. It's just not possible. No human can be this nimble and agile in the water. Yup, there's no doubt about it: we found our mermaid!

A few moments later, Light emerges from the water just as gracefully as she went in. The water slides off her face and body, allowing us to finally get a look at the mermaid's face—Tessa!

Folake and I quickly hide behind a rack of life jackets. Tessa walks right past us. We are weak with relief when she keeps going and disappears into the girls' locker room.

"Tessa! Really? How could she be—"

"Sunny, keep your voice down," Folake says, putting her index finger to her lips.

I lower my voice. "Sorry. I just can't believe . . . Tessa?!"

"I didn't even know she swam. Did you?"

"No!" I reply. My stomach begins to twist in tight little knots. There's a lump in my throat. The kind you get from trying really hard not to cry. I lean against the wall and curse my luck.

"Tessa is never gonna help us. She hates us," I moan.

"Maybe she's not the mermaid," Folake says.

I look at her, "Folake . . ."

"Yeah, okay. She's the mermaid. I know. Wow, who knew that bullies could be great swimmers?" she says.

"Who knew that they could also be mythical creatures? ARGH!" I reply, raising my voice again.

"Okay, so what should we do? I mean, besides run for our lives?" Folake asks.

I ball my hands into fists. I demand that the knots in my stomach untie themselves. They do—most of them. And although I'm still scared, I refuse to let being scared stop me.

"Well, I'm not giving up on helping Nanna. There's gotta be something that Tessa wants more than to beat the mess out of us. So let's get in there and figure out how to bargain with a mermaid."

We enter the girls' locker room. Tessa sits on the bench in front of her locker. She's finished putting on her street clothes and tying her sneakers. She hears us come in and looks up. She's just as shocked as we were when we first saw her.

"What are you two dorks doing here? Do you really want me to kick your butts that badly?" she shouts.

"Well, we thought first we'd start with a nice hello before we go to the butt-kicking part. Right, Folake?" I joke.

Folake laughs nervously. "Yup, she's right. So . . . hey, Tessa! How are you?"

"You two have ten seconds to tell me what you are doing here. And nine of them have already passed!" she sneers.

I dare to get a few steps closer. My nanna is the only reason I would ever take a risk this big. Folake comes closer, too, but she remains behind me.

"Look, I think we just have a misunderstanding. I really didn't mean to run into you. I was chasing Noodle—"

"You were chasing food?" she asks.

"No, my hamster Noodle. Anyway, I was chasing him because he got out and—"

"I don't care, Sunny. You are all out of time. And now I have to break something of yours."

"Oh, like a cell phone? Because you can have mine. It's really old and—" Folake begins.

"No, I mean break something like your face!" Tessa informs her.

I reply. "You could do that or . . . you could hear us out. And *then* decide if you want to make a deal or if you want to . . . you know . . ."

"Break your face?" Tessa adds.

I clear my throat and try my hardest not to throw up the tuna sandwich I had for lunch earlier. I should have just had dry toast. Next time I'm on the verge of getting beaten to a pulp, I will remember—light lunch.

I take a deep breath. Folake nods and whispers, "You can do this."

I sure hope so . . .

I speak to Tessa and try to keep my voice even and calm. "Okay, so here's the thing. Folake and I need for you to, um . . . well . . . kiss something for us. It's a seashell. I know it doesn't make a lot of sense, but we think that if you kiss the shell, it will help someone who is really important to us."

She looks back at us like we're from another planet—a planet we need to go back to now!

"It doesn't matter if it sounds crazy. We know that," Folake adds. "We just need to know if you are willing to do it—kiss a seashell."

"No," she says, glaring at us.

"That's what we thought you'd say. So we have an offer. If you kiss the seashell, we'll pay you for it. I have sixty-five bucks," I reply.

"Oh, and I have twenty from when my uncle came to visit last time," Folake says.

"That's eighty-five dollars. That's almost a hundred!" I tell her.

"Yeah, I know how to add, dork!" she snaps.

"So what do you think?" Folake says carefully.

Tessa is quiet for a few seconds. "I think I could mess you two up really badly. And then take your money," she says with a mischievous grin.

Whoops, didn't think of that . . .

She takes a step closer to us. We take one step back—a big step back. I signal to Folake that I have another idea. "Tessa, if you kiss the seashell, you'll get the money and I'll do your homework for a month!" I offer.

"That's a better deal coming from Folake. She's the smart one."

I reply before I can stop myself, "Hey, I do well in English. Once I finally hand in my assignments."

"It doesn't matter. The answer is still no," Tessa replies, her voicing growing cold.

Folake takes a turn. "All right, how about this: You get

the money, I will do your homework for two months, and you can have my brand-new makeup kit. Did you know that Strawberry Shortcake isn't just cake? Yup, it's a color. I learned that today."

"Are you saying I need makeup? You saying I'm ugly?"

Folake and I both fake a big laugh. "What? No! We would never say that. You're a very . . . special-looking young lady," I reply.

"That sounds like code for ugly," Tessa concludes.

"I promise you that's not what we're saying," I assure her.

"I'm done talking. Now I throw punches, and something on your body breaks in half."

She comes toward us. I block Folake so that Tessa gets to me first. She grabs me by my arms and picks me up in the air. I know it's only been a few seconds, but I really do miss the ground. Folake shouts at her to put me down.

"You should have known better than to come find me. And now I end you!" She's about to fling me across the globe—or in this case, a row of lockers over. Either way, I'm guessing it'll hurt.

But just before she does, we hear Jay calling from outside. "Okay, girls, time's up! I gotta get home. I'm going to check the locks on the back door, and by the time I get back, there better be no one left in this room. That means you, too, Light!"

We hear his footsteps as he walks away.

"Argh! You're so lucky," she says as she drops me down to the floor. "Get out of here now! Or face the consequences."

She turns her attention back to her locker. She takes out her gym bag and starts shoving stuff inside it. When she realizes we have not moved an inch, she's confused.

"Seriously, what is it with you two? Do you know what I could do to you?" she warns.

"Yeah, I do," I reply, picking myself up with Folake's help. "Here's the thing, Tessa. I really did bump into you by accident. But I think you already know that. I think you're just looking for a reason to fight. I don't know what your reason is, but the reason I'm willing to stand here and face you is because of a lady named Coretta Jolene Williams.

"When it's late at night and I'm coughing so hard, I can't sleep, she puts VapoRub on my chest and makes me honey-lemon tea. My brother outgrew his uniform and we couldn't afford new ones, so she went down to the pawnshop and sold her best purse. And when I come home crying because someone is trying to bully me, she reminds me that I'm special, I'm important, and I'm loved."

"Who is she?" Tessa asks.

"She's my nanna. She's quick to swat my behind if I disrespect her and quicker to hug me when I need it. She cheats when we play cards, bakes the best 7UP cake in the world, and calls me Li'l Bit, even though it embarrasses me."

"This is crazy. You are making no sense. You know that, right?" Tessa says.

"Yeah, I know it doesn't make sense to you. But she's sick and that seashell is going to fix her. You're the best swimmer in Chicago, and that's who needs to kiss the seashell. I'm not leaving here until you do. You can hit me if you want. Still not leaving."

"Count me in, too. I'm not leaving," Folake says, standing right beside me.

"Okay, go ahead. Start punching." I swallow hard and close my eyes. But the blows don't come. I wait another few seconds and still nothing. Where's the pain? The sound of bones breaking? I pop one eye open and see Tessa sink down onto the bench in front of her locker.

"I'm not gonna hit you," she mutters.

Folake and I look at each other, not sure we heard her right.

"You're not gonna beat us up?" Folake asks.

"No," she whispers as she rolls her eyes. Folake and I exhale. We're light-headed with relief and need to sit. We plop down on the bench a few lockers away from Tessa.

"What's wrong with your grandma?" she asks.

"She keeps forgetting things and people," Folake says.

"She even forgot us," I reply softly to myself.

"And this seashell thing is gonna fix her? That makes no sense," Tessa says.

"Maybe not, but it's something I have to try. I need to know that I tried everything," I confess. "She'd try everything to save us."

All three of us are quiet. The only sound is from the heating vent coming from above us.

Tessa is the first to speak. "Cocoa Num-Num." We both look at her, confused. She shrugs. "It's what my nanna calls me. When I was a kid, I used to say 'num, num' every time I tasted something I liked. And I really liked Cocoa Puffs cereal. So she started calling me . . ."

"Cocoa Num-Num," Folake and I say in unison. We both try not to laugh because something tells us Tessa would not appreciate it.

Then Tessa grumbles, "Oh, all right, fine. Give me the stupid seashell."

I take the seashell out of my pocket and place it in the palm of her hand. She looks at it and brings it up to her lips. And then, she gives the seashell a kiss and hands it back to me. It could be my imagination, but I swear the seashell sparkles right after she kisses it.

I say thank you, and then Folake and I head for the door.

Tessa calls after us, "Hey, hey, aren't you forgetting something?"

Folake and I stare blankly at each other. Tessa clears her throat and signals toward her palm. We both sigh and empty our pockets. We leave the community center minus eight-five bucks but super happy. We're one step closer to completing our quest!

Chapter Fifteen
Abeo

IT'S THE SECOND WEEK in October, and I'm trying to look on the bright side. We have one item, and maybe by the end of this week, we'll find item number two. But I don't get to think about the quest as much as I would like for the next few days because I have to wake up super early to continue stacking books in the library with Folake. When I'm done in the morning, I finally finish my report for Mr. Evens. It's boring and takes a lot of work. I try not to complain because I did break *a lot* of rules.

But my day gets much better when Mr. Evens announces to the whole music class that there was a unanimous vote among the judges and I get to sing the solo! Everyone claps. Folake is the first to congratulate me. Mr. Evens is beaming with pride. He says he's going to take us bowling to celebrate. He asked Miles if he was okay adding a few people to their bowling plans, and he said yes.

So this afternoon, we pick up Rue and go to a place called Lucky Duck Bowling. I know the place will be crowded because there are a lot of cars in the parking lot. It takes a really long time to find a parking spot, and once we finally do, we eagerly open the car doors, but Mr. Evens makes us get back in the car. He says we need to know the rules before we go inside.

"They can learn the rules as we play," Rue says.

"No, not bowling rules; my rules," he replies. Rue rolls her eyes and pretends that she's so bored, she fell asleep.

"What are the rules?" I ask.

"It's a pretty big place. Do not wander off without telling me. Do not talk to total strangers. And most importantly, never, ever interrupt me when I go up to bowl," he says. Miles and I laugh, thinking he's joking, but Rue flashes us a look that tells us, *Mr. Evens is very serious.*

"Ah, okay. We will not interrupt you while you're about to bowl. Can we go in now?" I ask.

"Yeah, can we?" Miles says.

"Yes, now we can go. Oh, and there's one more rule—this one is just for Rue," Mr. Evens says. She gives him a wicked smile that tells me she already knows what he's about to say. "Under no circumstances are you to bring food to the bowling area! We all know what happened last time."

"Excuse me? I have no idea what you're talking about," Rue says, still smirking.

"You know what I'm talking about—the sweet potato fry incident!" he says.

"What's that?" Miles asks.

"I'll never forget that night," he starts. "I was having the best game of my life. I was about to win and set my own personal record. It should have been easy; I was knocking 'em down all night. All I had to do was knock down the last three pins to win the game.

"I picked up my bowling ball. I was laser-focused—had my back straight, shoulders centered, and knees bent. I was ready to enter bowling glory. That's when it happened . . ." Mr. Evens takes a pause. It's like it's hard for him to go on because the memory is so terrible.

"Mr. Evens, what happened?" Miles asks. "Did you win?"

I can see Rue out of the corner of my eye. She puts her hand over her mouth to stop from laughing out loud, but it's not working. Her whole body is shaking from silent laughter.

"No, Miles, I didn't win. Do you know why? Because just when I was about to let go of the ball, I was assaulted."

"Tell them what assaulted you," Rue says, barely able to keep a straight face.

"A sweet potato fry," Mr. Evens says.

Rue loses it! She laughs so hard, she can't catch her breath. We don't want to make Mr. Evens feel bad, but it's hard not to join in.

"That fry came out of nowhere. It landed on the side of my face, and I lost all focus. My bowling game was never the same after that. And who threw that fry?" Mr. Evens looks over at Rue.

"You have no proof it was me."

"I know it was you, Rue, I just know it! And tonight my buddy Miles and I are going to band together and get revenge! Are you with me, Miles?"

"Yes! Tonight we revenge!" Miles shouts. They high-five and rush out of the car. We follow, and on our way to the entrance, I lean over and whisper to Rue, "Did you throw the sweet potato fry and make Mr. Evens lose the game?"

"Just between us, it was his wife, Maya." She smiles sweetly and puts her finger up to her lips and says, "Shhhhh."

Maya was the sweet potato fry bandit! Wow, I wish I'd gotten a chance to meet her. She sounds like a really fun person to get in trouble with!

The minute we enter, I know I'm going to like bowling. Each bowling lane has shiny wooden floors and colorful lights. The neon-bright bowling balls are all different sizes and weights. I try them out; some weigh as little as a grapefruit and some are as heavy as a boulder. The music is loud and makes it feel like the walls are vibrating. There's a counter where people are picking up bowling shoes and another counter where people are buying food. The menu has a lot of yummy things: pizza, wings, burgers, and sweet potato fries. The last item makes me smile.

Everyone is having so much fun. There are lights everywhere, people jumping up and down when they get the ball to hit all the pins. The grown-ups who are bowling get just as excited as the kids do when they knock down all the pins. After we get our bowling shoes on and pick a section to play in, Mr. Evens shows Miles and me how to bowl.

We don't get it right away. In the beginning, we send a lot of balls down the lane and hit nothing! We learn that's called a gutter ball. But after a while, we start to get it. We can't hit all of them in one try, but at least now we don't make as many gutter balls.

Rue is an excellent bowler, and so is Mr. Evens. They get super competitive, and twice Miles and I have to give them a time-out from each other. It's nice to watch Mr. Evens get so excited about something, aside from music. He jumps up and down whenever he gets a good score.

Miles gets better at the game and starts to dance when he does well. It isn't long before he and Mr. Evens have a whole routine. They call it "The Winner Two-Step." Rue and I come up with our own routine for when we do well, and it ends with us sticking our tongues out at the boys and flipping our hair.

When we get hungry, Mr. Evens gets us a huge tray of food. We sit down in the chairs in front of the lanes and stuff our faces. Mr. Evens eats everything except for the fries. He says he just can't face them. I ask when the last time the two of them went bowling was, and the siblings look at each other. Their eyes suddenly look dark and sad.

"We last came here with Maya," Rue says. This is the most serious I've ever heard her sound. Mr. Evens looks away.

"Was Maya a good bowler?" Miles asks.

Rue nods and puts down the burger she was eating. Mr. Evens clears his throat and announces, "Less talking and more playing. Let's go!" He rushes over to the lane and starts playing.

I look over at Rue. "Did we say something wrong?"

"No, baby girl. It's not you. Come on, let's go and show these two what real bowling looks like," Rue says with a new smile.

We throw away what's left of our food in the trash. But just before that, I spot Rue sneak a single fry off the tray and hide it behind her back. This is going to be so much fun . . .

When Folake joins us in the schoolyard the next day, Miles and I can tell right away that she's having a bad morning. We call that an "Alex" morning. It's from one of our favorite books back when we were little kids: *Alexander and the Terrible, Horrible, No Good, Very Bad Day.* It's a book about a kid who has everything go wrong from the moment he gets up until he is about to fall asleep. In the end, his mom reminds him that everyone has bad days and that tomorrow will be better. But that book was written a long time ago. Things have gotten so much more complicated for us kids.

We knew that Folake was having an "Alex" day because she's pouting and scrunching her face. She thinks she's giving a "stay away from me or else" look, but that expression just makes her look even cuter and more round than she normally does. She's like a puffy little chocolate storm cloud.

"Folake, what's wrong?" Miles asks before she can get the first words out of her mouth.

"Abeo!" she says, gritting her teeth. Miles and I should have known that would be her answer. Like I said before, including Folake, there are seven kids in the Musa family. Folake is the youngest, and they all get along pretty well. That is, except for the second-youngest member of the family: her fifteen-year-old brother, Abeo.

Abeo is almost six feet tall. I know that everyone grows

taller, but I think he's doing it just to spite his sister. I've seen him use his height to torture her. In the morning, if Abeo gets to the cereal first, he holds the box above her head so that she can't reach it. He waits until his parents aren't looking and eats all the meat off Folake's plate. Then he'll add the veggies from his plate and call out Folake for not eating all her veggies. He hides her stuff throughout the house and watches with glee as she desperately looks for them. And whenever he gets into trouble, he tries to blame it on her.

"What did your brother do this time?" I ask.

"Mom and Dad asked me to bring them some orange juice from the kitchen. I poured out two full glasses and made my way over to them. Then I saw something out the window that scared the life out of me—a devil mask with red eyes and fangs! I screamed and dropped the glasses I was holding. I saw Abeo laughing from the corner of my eye as he took off the mask. Then he disappeared before anyone knew he was there.

"I broke the glasses, and I spilled orange juice all over my clothes. I had to change, which meant I was gonna be late for school. So my dad had to drop me off. And he was annoyed about that because he had to be at work early today. ARGH! I wish Abeo was someone else's brother!" she says angrily.

Miles steps up to Folake and takes her hand. Folake and I exchange a look of confusion between us. Miles acts like I'm not even there.

"Folake, I have let this go on for too long. Your brother is chocolate to Sciuridae." Folake and I look back at him—blank.

We have no idea what he's talking about.

He sighs and rolls his eyes. "Your brother is chocolate to squirrels or dogs! He's very bad for you. He's always upsetting you and making your life harder. Well, it stops today! I am challenging Abeo to a fight. It's going to take place after school today."

"Miles, that's really nice of you, but—"

Miles puts his index finger on Folake's lips and speaks to her like he's Thor about to save the world. "Shhhh, it's okay. I know that you're worried about me because your brother is a little bigger and taller than I am."

"A little?" both Folake and I say in unison.

"Yes, a little!" Miles says, turning around to snap at me.

"Okay, yeah. Abeo is a little taller than you," Folake replies, trying to hide her growing smile.

"But that doesn't matter. My size is the very reason I am going to win this battle against your brother. When he looks at me, he sees a puny, short runt with no body mass and no chance of winning. But there's something he doesn't know, my love."

Did Miles just say "my love"? I roll my eyes. Oh brother!

"What doesn't Abeo know about you, Miles?" Folake asks.

Miles looks her in the eye and proudly proclaims, "Folake, I only *look* weak. I'm actually an African wild dog. I use my small frame and large ears to give my enemies a false sense of hope—hope that they can defeat me. But the truth is, I'm an apex predator. The kill rate is eighty-five percent! Eighty-five! That means I almost never lose when I set out to hunt. And today, I'm going to hunt your brother. I will make him apologize for all the wrongs he's done to you!"

"That sounds really nice, Miles, but African wild dogs are ten times more likely to lose prey once they've killed them to other predators like hyenas and lions."

Miles's mouth drops open. Mine does too. Folake shrugs. "Remember that book you gave me last year about sub-Saharan animals? The one you kept begging me to read, Miles? Well, I read it."

"You did?" Miles says breathlessly.

"Yeah," Folake replies.

Miles looks deep into her eyes and sighs as a goofy, odd smile appears on his face.

"Our children will be both smart and beautiful," he says in a dreamy voice.

"Miles, the bell rang. You have to go inside. Class is about to start," I remind him.

He's still looking into Folake's eyes and nowhere else. "It's art class. One of my favorites, but I will give it up and stay with you if you want, Folake. I choose you over molding clay!"

I cross my arms over my chest and glare at him with my eyebrows raised, just like Nanna when she gives us her "I ain't mess'n 'round" look.

"Miles Jamaal Williams, get your butt to class now!" I order.

He's about to protest, but then he looks into my face and decides he'd like to live to see lunchtime. "Okay, fine." Then he looks back at Folake. "I will return. And my offer to defend you against Abeo is still on. You just let me know when."

"Um, yeah. Sure. Thanks, Miles," she says, leaning over and giving him a kiss on the cheek. Miles floats out of his body and inside the school. My kid brother will never be the same again.

The key to getting Folake to feel better and forget about Abeo is to avoid using any of these three words: doll, backyard, and glue. Those words always bring her back to the worst thing Abeo ever did to her. And even though it was years ago, whenever that memory comes back, Folake spits out fire. It makes her so upset that all the calming down she did goes away.

And once she's that upset, she will tell the "Backyard Buddies" story. I have heard that story more than fifty times. But that doesn't stop Folake from getting angry and telling it all over again. She will start out in a normal voice, but by the end of the story, she erupts and it takes even longer for her to get back to being okay.

I am doing pretty well at keeping her mind off Abeo and not saying any of the three words. It also helps that we are both thinking really hard and brainstorming about where we can find a manticore. We were hoping that we would get to brainstorm outside. Maybe the fresh air would help us think better. But it's super-cold today so we all have to stay in for lunch.

"I never thought it would be so hard to find a manticore!" I confess while I poke at the cold french fries on my tray.

"Me too! Who knew that it would be hard to find a lion

with the head of a man? It seems like the kind of thing that you could just run into," Folake replies.

"Wait, what about the zoo? I know it sounds obvious, but maybe they are hiding in plain sight to trick us?" I ask.

"I looked online. Only lions with lion heads and bodies. No manticore."

"Argh!"

One of the lunch staff ladies comes to our table and tells me that Mr. Evens is looking for me. Folake glances at me with suspicion.

"What did you do?" she whispers as I get up to follow the lady out of the cafeteria.

I shrug. "I don't remember doing anything wrong."

"Good luck," she says.

When I return to my seat, Folake is shocked to see me with a big grin. She says, "That doesn't look like the face of someone in trouble."

"Nope! Guess what? Mr. Evens told me he has a meeting with your mom and the rest of the PTA tonight about the concert coming up. And he said that since I handed in my report and have been good, we can hang out at your house while the meeting is happening!"

"You're coming over after school?!"

"Yes!"

She reaches out and hugs me really tight. She asks about Miles, and I tell her what Mr. Evens told me: Miles is working on his art project again so that it will be ready for the big presentation the class is having. I am so excited to hang out with Folake that I forget about the three words I'm not supposed to say.

"I just wish it was warm enough that we could play in your backyard." The words come out of my mouth too fast for me to stop them. Folake's good mood is gone. She's flashing back to the worst memory she has of Abeo.

"Folake, don't—"

"Backyard. Sunny, did I ever tell you what Abeo did to the four best dolls in the world that I had?"

Now, she's going to say, *They were a collection. They were called "Backyard Buddies."*

Folake gets this faraway look on her face and says, "The four dolls were part of a collection I got for Christmas. It was called the 'Backyard Buddies' collection . . ."

I sigh deeply and let Folake tell the story. It's my fault for forgetting not to use the word "backyard." The story goes like this: When Folake was seven and Abeo was twelve, she hid her most precious gift far away where he would not be able to get his hands on them. The Backyard Buddies collection came with four dolls: Fossil Hunter Holly, Engineering Angie, Astronaut Ada, and Folake's favorite doll—Laboratory Lottie. She came with her own clipboard, beakers, and goggles.

Abeo was sick one day and got to stay home from school. Instead of using that time to watch cartoons, eat yummy junk food, and play video games, he decided to go on a hunt to find where Folake had hidden her precious dolls. He found them. And by the time Folake came home, her dolls had been experimented on by Abeo. He'd glued their hands together to see if he could pull them apart. He'd tried to melt the hair off their heads to see if fake hair burns. And then there was what he did to Lottie . . . She never did open her eyes again.

Once Folake is done, I promise her that I won't let her defend herself alone. If Abeo messes with her, he messes with me!

Today, luck is on our side because when we get to Folake's house, we find out that Abeo got stuck working late at his after-school job. He's a busboy at a restaurant owned by a friend of the family. It's a kid's theme restaurant. It has games, a play area, and the waiters dress up in costumes. Abeo doesn't like working there, but Folake's parents refuse to raise his allowance so he has no choice.

Folake and I have more fun than we've ever had before in her house. We make popcorn and watch a scary movie with Folake's twin older brothers, Akin and Azi. They are so nice. They don't even make fun of us when we scream at the scary parts.

Then Folake gets a video call from her two siblings who live in New York. They say she might be able to come and visit them in the summer. They say I can come too if Nanna says it's okay! Then Folake's oldest sibling, Funmi, comes home from the dorms where she lives so she can do her laundry. While we help her fold towels, she lets us play the new *Little Mermaid* soundtrack and sing as loud as we want. She laughs at us at first, but by the time we get to "Under the Sea," she's belting out right along with us! Then she helps us make

Rice Krispie treats with three different kinds of crushed-up cookies!

Mr. Evens calls the Musas' house phone and tells me the meeting is over and to get ready to leave. I quickly pack my backpack, and then Folake says I can take some treats for Miles and Mr. Evens. I'm in the kitchen loading treats into a sandwich bag when Abeo enters, wearing a long, thick, heavy winter coat.

Folake and I roll our eyes at the same time. This is the part where Abeo usually acts mean for no reason. We wait for him to tease us or say something mean. He doesn't. Instead, he slumps onto the nearest chair and groans.

"What's wrong with you?" Folake asks.

"It's not fair," Abeo says, sounding tired and frustrated.

"What happened?" I ask.

"What happened, Nosey, is that the host at the restaurant called in sick, so they made me wear his costume and greet people. This month the stupid theme is beloved children's books. I was so over it by the time the restaurant closed, I didn't even change. I just put on my sneakers, threw the mask off, and rushed here. I hope no one saw me. Thank goodness it's nighttime. Do you know how embarrassing it would have been if one of my friends saw me in this thing?!" he complains, taking off his coat. "I don't even like *The Wizard of Oz*. And there's nothing cowardly about me."

Folake and I are stunned. Standing in the kitchen, directly across from us, is a human head with a lion body! Abeo is the manticore!

Chapter Sixteen
Best Friends

THAT NIGHT, I UPDATE Miles on what we just learned about the second item. He's interested, but not nearly as much as he's interested in what's in the trunk. Mr. Evens has been going in the closet more and more to look at it. And it's still the same thing: one day the trunk makes him laugh softly, and the next time he looks like he's about to cry.

"What could be inside that thing, Shine? I need to know," he says.

"No, you don't," I scold as I tuck him in.

"It's too big a mystery. I have to know."

"You're supposed to be focusing on the quest. Remember?"

"Yeah and I am. But I can focus on two things at one time. I have a lot of brainpower," he informs me.

"Well, put all that power to rest. It's late. Good night."

"Shine?" he says.

"No more talk about the trunk, Miles. I mean it!" I reply.

"It's not about that."

"Then, what is it?"

"Do you think Mr. Evens's wife, Maya, would like me? I mean, if she were still . . . you know."

"I think so."

"Yeah, me too," he says with a big smile as he drifts off to sleep.

In the morning, as soon as Folake and I are done stacking more books onto the library shelves, we huddle together and try to work out the best way to get Abeo's hair without him knowing about it. We plan on getting a strand of it from his hairbrush, but Folake told me he brushes his hair in front of a mirror in his room. So the only way to get it is to go into his room. That sounds simple, but Abeo goes nuts if anyone goes into his room. We try to find other ways, but there just aren't any.

So after thinking it over, Folake finally tells me at lunch what she was hoping to never have to say: "Okay, okay. I'll go into Abeo's room," she says sadly.

"You sure?" I ask.

"Yeah, I just wish I had made it to age eleven. I was just about to be tall enough to go on all the rides at Great America," she adds as she throws the leftover food on her tray in the trash. We head outside. It's not as cold as it's been in the past few days, so all the kids rush to eat and go play. We don't play. We stand in the corner of the schoolyard; that's what happens when you are on a serious quest. There's no time for games.

"It's okay. I'll be brave. Go in. Get hair from brush. Get out," Folake says, mostly to herself.

"No, *we* will be in and out."

She looks at me, unsure. "Sunny, you don't have to go with me. No need for both of us to die."

"Nope, we're in this together, right?" I ask.

"Right! I think tomorrow is the best time because there's another PTA meeting with Mr. Evens. I'm sure he'll let you come over again. And the rest of my family has to help out at the youth fair the church is having. My mom knows I have a big science test, so she said I could stay home and study."

"So tomorrow we'll be at your house, all alone?"

"Well, except for Miles," she points out.

"Rue is taking him to the museum after school to help him get more inspiration for his secret art project."

Folake nods. "So we're all set. Tomorrow we get the manticore's hair!"

This afternoon at rehearsal, we're doing a full run-through. That means we rehearse the whole show from start to finish. I want to do my best so that both Mr. Evens and Nanna are proud of me. That means I have to put everything except the show out of my head—just for a little while. But my focus is a little off. I can't stop thinking about the manticore and our plan to get a hair from his head.

"All right, is everyone ready to begin?" Mr. Evens says as he stands in front of the class. Everyone says they are ready, and Mr. Evens picks a student to hand out the music sheets. He sections us off and gives us our parts so that we know what we're singing.

Mr. Evens looks like I did the first time I went to a water park—like I'd entered paradise. I knew he loved music, but I didn't realize just how much. Whether he's directing us, helping us with our parts, or just figuring out the order of the songs, Mr. Evens lights up with joy. I thought I would have to work really hard to stay focused, but it turns out, just watching Mr. Evens makes me want to concentrate and do my best.

We start singing one of the group songs, and the chorus sounds a little off. It doesn't take Mr. Evens long to find out which of us is off. When he finds the students who are on the wrong note, he picks me to help them get onto the right note. He picks me!

"Are you sure you want me to show them?" I ask.

"Of course. You have a great ear. In the next rehearsal, I'll have someone else take over and show the parts to anyone who is off. But for today, for our first rehearsal, that person is you," he replies. "Do you think you can handle it?"

I nod with confidence and, for the next half hour, help kids get on to the right note. And when it comes time for all of us to sing together again, we sound much better. The whole class is happy, and I can tell they are even more excited to be part of the show.

When rehearsal is over, so is the school day. Mr. Evens says he wants to work with me one on one. But instead of singing in the classroom, he has us go down to the auditorium.

He makes me get up on the stage.

"Wow . . ." is all I can say.

"Yes, it's a very large space. That's why I wanted you to get a feel for it, right from the beginning."

I look out at all the empty seats. I'm fine now, but I wonder how it'll be when it's full of people. I ask Mr. Evens how many people the auditorium fits, and he says over three hundred!

"Three hundred?!" I ask, just to make sure I heard him correctly.

"Yes, but it's going to be fine. We'll work on your performance, and by the time the show comes, you won't be nervous, you'll be excited."

I look out and picture all these seats now filled with people. I swallow hard, and before I let myself panic, I remember that, by that time, Nanna will be back and she'll be sitting in the front row.

"Are you ready to start?" he says.

"First, can I save a seat in the front row for someone?"

"Sure. Who is it?"

"Nanna."

He gets up onstage and puts his hand on my shoulder. "It would be great if your nanna could come. I hope she can. But in case she can't, you might have to be okay with that."

"She'll be here."

"Why are you so sure?" he asks.

I'll be done with the quest and she'll be all better.

But out loud I say, "I just get a feeling that she'll be able to make it."

"I hope so, Sunny. Now, let's start . . ."

The first part of the lesson is boring because it's all technical stuff like how to hold the microphone and how to have the best posture. But the second part, the part where I get to sing—that's fantastic!

Mr. Evens makes me stop and start, but every time he corrects me on something, it makes me sound even better. And just before our lesson is over, I mention that the solo could make a good duet, too.

He says, "Let's see. Just for fun. You sing the top part and I'll sing the bottom."

I start singing and he joins me; we sound incredible together. It's like our voices were destined to join together.

Nanna had a gift for knowing when we were up to something. It didn't matter how hard we tried to hide it, she somehow always knew. I think I have the same gift when it comes to Miles. I know when he is up to no good. I can tell because he goes out of his way to say nice things to me. So, after dinner, when he tells me how much he likes my hair, I know something is wrong.

"What did you do?" I ask.

"Nothing!" he says, laughing nervously as I gaze around the room to see what looks out of place.

"You did nothing wrong—nothing at all?" I ask again.

Miles twists his lips and stares up at the ceiling like the question requires him to think really hard. Then he does another thing that is always a dead giveaway—he sways from side to side with his hands behind his back.

"Miles, what happened?"

"I am wishing my favorite sister a very good morning. Are

these new pajamas? They look really pretty! You look like a superstar!"

"Oh no. It can't be that bad."

He looks down at the floor.

"Miles! Talk!"

"Shhhh," he pleads, putting his hand over my mouth. "You'll wake him up."

I sit up, wide awake now, and try to figure out just how bad Miles has messed up. "What you did—is it something we can fix easily?" I ask.

"Yup! Very easy!" he says proudly.

Phew, okay. That's something.

"Well, we can fix it if we get a handyman. Do you know any?" Miles says.

"A handyman? What did you break?" I ask, jumping off the sofa.

"Remember how I wasn't supposed to open the trunk in the closet?" he says carefully.

"Oh no. Tell me you didn't open the trunk."

"I didn't open the trunk."

"Phew!" I reply, relief washing over me.

"But I did *try* to get it open."

"What? How?"

"I found some keys in the drawer in the kitchen. I thought I would try them out—just to see if they *could* open the trunk. I was trying out the last key, and it broke inside the lock. Now, it won't come out!"

I go to the closet and pull out the trunk. I take a close look at the lock and see a chuck of metal jammed right in the center of it. I get down on my knees and use the rest of the jagged key to try to pluck out the broken piece. It's no use; the lock is jammed. There's no way to yank out the metal that's stuck inside.

"Miles, didn't I tell you not to touch the trunk?"

"Yes, but I forgot."

"How could you forget? I tell you that every day. Every single day, I say, 'Miles, do not touch the trunk.'"

"No! You don't say it every single day. You didn't say it yesterday!" he says.

"That's no excuse! You know better. How could you jam the lock? How are we supposed to fix this?"

"I'm sorry, Sunny, but it's not my fault. It's very hard to fight curiosity. You know how many cats get in trouble that way?"

"ARGH!" I shout before I can catch myself.

Mr. Evens grumbles from his bedroom, "What's going on out there?"

"Uh, nothing! Nothing is going on!" Miles says. "Oh, and your trunk is fine. There's nothing wrong with your trunk. The lock works very well."

"Miles!" I say in a harsh whisper.

"What? I said it works well!"

Mr. Evens rushes out of his room in his big black-and-gold bathrobe. He runs to the closet and inspects the trunk.

"You broke it! You broke the lock!" Mr. Evens says.

"Um . . . I can fix it. I think," Miles replies as he goes to take another look at the lock.

But Mr. Evens slides the trunk away from him, "No! You've done enough! I told you not to go in there and you didn't listen. This trunk is mine, not yours. You had no right to go into it without asking me!"

"I'm sorry, but it's hard not to. I just wanted to know what was in there. I wanted to know why the trunk made you sad sometimes and then happy other times. I was curious, and Nanna said there's nothing wrong with being curious," Miles says.

"That's not a reason, Miles! It doesn't matter how hard it is for you to stay away. When I said not to touch it, that should have been the end of it! Look at what you did!" Mr. Evens snaps.

I say, "Mr. Evens, I can fix it. And if I can't, I'll find a way to pay for a new lock. Don't be mad at Miles. He didn't mean it. It was an accident."

"No, this wasn't an accident." He starts pacing up and down the hallway. "Maybe it's my fault. I should have removed the trunk and put it in my room, had I known I couldn't trust you."

"What? But you can trust me. We're best friends!" Miles reminds him.

Mr. Evens shakes his head angrily. "No, we're not friends. Friends don't break each other's trust. And that's exactly what you did today. And I am so disappointed in you."

"You're not supposed to yell at your friend or make them feel bad. So I'm disappointed in you!"

"What? Me? I'm the problem?" Mr. Evens says, shocked.

"I did what I did because I was curious. You just yelled at me to be mean. That's different. That's worse! You're a mean friend."

"You're an untrustworthy friend!"

"ARGH!" they both shout at the same time. Mr. Evens storms off into his room. Miles storms off into the bathroom.

It's a good thing we're going to be back with Nanna soon. These two are impossible!

Chapter Seventeen
The Sneaker King

MY SCIENCE TEACHER TOLD me that a human being can hold their breath for maybe a minute or a minute and a half. She's wrong. I know because since we got into Folake's house, five minutes ago, she's been holding her breath. I want to get this done as quickly as we can because Folake can't handle being in Abeo's room. I understand why. We're standing just outside the door to his room, and in case there was any misunderstanding about Abeo and what he did and did not like, he left a sign on the door written in blood!

Okay, okay, it isn't actually blood; it's just a big traffic-like sign that says "Keep Out or Else." But he picked the design that was written in red splashes of pretend blood. That means he will likely actually kill us if he finds us in his room. I know that he will because there's another sign just below the "Keep Out" sign, and, yeah, it actually says "I will end you, if you enter!"

"There's no one home. He'll never know," I remind Folake, whose bottom lip is now trembling. I know she has seen that silly sign every day, but today I think it has a whole new meaning for her. Today that sign doesn't look like a warning; it's more like a creepy prophecy, a promise about what will happen next.

I slowly reach out and put my hand on the door handle. Folake lets out a small squeak. She swallows hard, and her eyes get wider and wider with worry. We enter Abeo's room, and even though we know he's not in there, we enter with caution and close the door behind us.

There are dirty clothes everywhere except the laundry basket. Textbooks are all over the room, and there's a video game console with socks thrown on top of it. I can see a laptop peeking out from a small mountain of junk food wrappers on Abeo's desk. I think there's carpet on the floor, but it's hard to see because so much of the floor is covered with empty soda cans and basketball jerseys.

"I saw a video once on YouTube where a tornado picked up a house with every single thing in it. It did that to all the houses on the road! I think this is where the tornado threw up the stuff it couldn't keep down," I say as I look around.

"Actually, it's neater than I thought," Folake replies.

"His hairbrush is probably on the dresser," I say as I head over to inspect it.

Out the corner of my eye, I catch a glimpse of the only other thing in Abeo's room. "Well, there's one thing he looks after really well," I reply as I walk over to the closet a few feet away to get a closer look. Folake follows me.

The only things that Abeo has taken good care of are his

sneakers. The ones he wears are placed neatly along the floor of the closet. He takes such good care of them that I would have sworn they were new had I not seen him wear them before.

On the top shelf of the closet are three clear, stacked-up plastic boxes; each one holds a shiny pair of kicks.

I don't know anything about sneakers, but the way Abeo separated them from the others, I know that they must be his three favorite ones. The sneakers on the bottom are purple suede and look gorgeous. The ones in the middle have two different shades of gray and are sleek, like they come from outer space. But the prize, the ones he most loves, has to be the white-and-black pair with a fire-red outline along the edge. There is white net paneling on the side, and the logo is drawn in flames. Again, I don't know anything about sneakers, but these are marvelous!

"When did he get those?" I ask Folake. "They look so cool! How come I've never seen him wear these?"

"Oh, no, he'd never wear them. These sneakers are his special ones. Since he was twelve, he's asked for sneakers as birthday presents. When he gets them, he puts them here."

"I know you don't like being in here, so let's get the hair from the hairbrush and go," I say as I start to make my way back to the dresser.

"Wait. Not yet . . ." Folake says, pulling me back. I look into her eyes. The look of fear and nervousness is gone. She is now wearing the same expression as the stray cat in our old neighborhood when he's outsmarted a dog. She's smug.

She comes closer to the open closet and leans her head back so she can get a good view of the sneakers in their protective cases. She eyes them like they're her enemies. It's like a scene from *Harry Potter*, when Harry faces off against Voldemort. The only trouble is I don't think Folake is Harry.

"Folake . . . ?" I say slowly.

She doesn't respond. Her thoughts are on the sneakers. I'm not sure she even remembers I'm in the room.

"Do you know what these are?" Folake says as the menacing look on her face grows.

"Really expensive sneakers that we should not touch," I reply.

"Don't you see, Sunny? Abeo loves these sneakers more than anything else in this whole world. Even more than video games. He's been collecting them forever. He never lets anyone touch them. Not even our parents. He bought these special cases so that the sneakers don't get dust on them. These sneakers are Abeo's Backyard Buddies!"

"Okay . . ." I reply as my stomach starts to twist. I'm not sure where Folake is going with this, but something tells me it's not good.

A sly smile spreads across her lips. "I've waited for this for a really long time . . ."

Okay, how do I get her to sound more like Halle Bailey in *The Little Mermaid* and less like Ursula?

"Whatever you're thinking, Folake, it's not a good idea," I warn.

Folake reaches up as high as she can. She even stands on

tiptoes. The tips of her fingers are able to reach just the edge of the first box.

"Okay, you touched it. Good. Let's go get the hair," I tell her as I motion toward the dresser.

Folake isn't interested in the dresser. Instead, she looks around the room for something she can step on to reach the top sneakers.

"Got it!" she says, her eyes lighting up. She drags the trash can out from the corner of the room and uses it as a make-shift stepladder. She steps on it and starts reaching as far as she can for the top box. Okay, so far Folake has been Ursula and Voldemort. Who else is she going to turn into before this is over? I try my best to reason with her.

"Folake, I know that the Backyard Buddies were super important to you and that Abeo was wrong for ruining them. But messing with his stuff is the fastest way for you to end up . . . dead. Did you read the sign on the door? Open your eyes and see what you're about to do," I suggest.

She turns back and looks at me. "Laboratory Lottie opened her eyes when I first got her. And she closed them too. Then Abeo came, glued her eyes back, and then they stayed open forever!"

"Folake! We don't have time for this."

"Then help me! All I want to do is reach the top sneakers and put my hand on them. It will be sweet justice. And he'll never know."

"So you just want to touch them, nothing else? You're not gonna glue the laces together or anything?" I ask.

"No, just one touch—for Lottie," she says.

Argh, being a best friend can be a lot of hard work. But then again, she is helping me break into her brother's room and risking her life so . . .

"Okay, okay. I will help you. But just one touch and nothing else. And you have to wipe your hands before you touch them so that there's no mark on the sneakers at all."

"Deal!" she says, excited.

We add some textbooks to the top of the trash can to give her more height. Folake announces that she is close to reaching them. But she needs something to hold her steady. I tell her to lean on me so she can keep her balance, and it works! Folake reaches the top box! But the weight put on one of the textbooks is too much. It slips out from under her feet and sends Folake tumbling backward toward the floor—and all three boxes come down with her!

"No!" I shout, trying to catch her before she falls. It's too late. Folake lands hard on the floor. The three boxes land a few feet away. "Ouch," she groans as she lies on her back and looks up at the ceiling.

"Are you okay?" I ask, rushing to help her up.

"It hurts, but I'll be okay," she says, taking my hand to get up from the floor. She gathers the boxes. "You were right, Sunny, let's just put these back and focus on getting the—" Folake freezes midsentence. I understand why—there are only two clear boxes.

"Where's the third box? The one that was on top? The

one with the sneakers that Abeo loves the most? Where is it?" Folake begs.

I see it before she does. The box containing the most favorite sneakers of all didn't fall on the soft carpet area. Instead it landed far away and hit two things: an open can of Mountain Dew Code Red soda and the wall.

The soda spilled onto the floor and seeped inside the clear box. Folake and I rush over to save it, but it's much too late. Abeo's favorite white sneakers are now swimming in a red sparkling sea of soda goodness.

The sign was right; we are dead.

Folake's mom scans me from the roots of my braids to the tips of my toes. She's suspicious. She puts both hands on her hips, narrows her eyes, and leans in, really close. I can feel her looming over me.

"So . . . you were here playing with Folake and then thought it would be fun to take a look at Abeo's sneakers. You went to his room, took the box of sneakers out, and accidentally dropped it. It hit a can of soda and then the wall?" she asks.

"Yeah . . . yup . . . yes," I reply. Okay, I didn't lie; I just didn't tell the whole truth. Besides, the only reason Folake was in Abeo's room was to help me get the next item. If anyone should get into trouble, it should be me.

Mrs. Musa looks over at Folake, who is standing next to me, and asks her if that is what happened. I try to help. "Mrs. Musa, it's all my fault. Please don't blame Folake."

I hear a car honking outside. That's Mr. Evens, wondering why I haven't gotten my stuff and come out to the car yet. Once we're done here, Mrs. Musa is going to take me outside and tell Mr. Evens what I did. Well, there might be another report headed my way. Or worse. Could this be the thing that makes him change his mind about taking us in? I feel dread zip down my body, and my fingers grow cold.

"Okay, Sunny, get your stuff. Mr. Evens is waiting. I'll walk you out," Mrs. Musa says.

Folake opens her mouth, and I can tell she's about to confess even before she starts talking.

"Mom, I—"

"Let's talk when I get back in, Folake. Mr. Evens is waiting for Sunny."

Mrs. Musa and I walk out of the house, and just before we get to the car, she stops me. She leans forward all the way so that we are both at eye level.

"Sunny, I know there's more to that story than you're telling me."

"But—"

"Let me finish!"

I nod and stay quiet.

"I'm letting this go for two reasons: One, you and Miles have had a rough time lately, and you two deserve kindness and understanding. Your nanna would appreciate that. Also, I'm letting you off the hook because I know that you're only telling part of the truth because the whole truth will in some way get my daughter in trouble. I think Folake is lucky to have a friend like you, who will go this far to protect her."

"I'd do anything for Folake. Anything!" I vow.

"Now, I'm letting you off this one time. And one time only. I do not condone lying. And I do not expect to be lied to again. Understood?" she says in a firm voice that scares me so much, my dimples jump off my checks and hide in my pockets.

"Yes, Mrs. Musa. I won't do that again. So you won't tell Mr. Evens?"

"Not this time. But you will stay out of Abeo's room from now on."

"Yes, I will," I reply. I leap into her arms and hug her, without thinking about it, "Thank you! Thank you!"

It's been a few days since the disaster at Folake's house. She keeps saying she's sorry about us not getting the hair. I promise her that I don't blame her. I tell her we'll find another way. The truth is, I don't have another way, but Folake already feels bad, so I don't bring that part up.

Miles and Mr. Evens are still not talking to each other, which just makes things even worse. Mr. Evens hired a guy to come and fix the lock; it only took him twenty minutes! The trunk now has a new lock. Mr. Evens moved the trunk to his bedroom. I thought because it was now safely in Mr. Evens's bedroom, the two would go back to how they were before, but they don't.

On Monday morning, Rue comes over for breakfast, and the first thing she notices is the tension at the table. Unlike most other mornings, no one is talking. Miles bites down angrily on the tip of his toast and glares at Mr. Evens from across the table. Mr. Evens is also pouting as he stabs his eggs with his fork.

"Everything okay with you two?" Rue asks.

"Yes," they both lie in unison.

Rue looks at me and I shrug. She signals for me to come meet her out in the living room. I follow her and when we are far enough away, she says, "Okay, what's the deal?"

I explain what happened to the trunk and how Miles couldn't fight it anymore and gave in to his curiosity. He opened the trunk.

"Mr. Evens reacted like—"

"I know what my big brother's reaction was," she says sadly.

"I'm sorry Miles opened it. But it was my fault too. I usually remember to check and make sure that he doesn't go in the closet."

"It's not your fault. The trunk is . . . important to Darrious. But that doesn't mean he should bite your heads off for touching it."

"I promised to keep Miles away. But now Miles is so mad at Mr. Evens, he won't touch anything of his. Not even breakfast! He only ate the toast this morning because I made it."

"It's that bad, huh?"

"Rue! They have to make up! All I know how to make is toast. Miles can't live off that."

"I'm sure the two of them will work it out."

"And what if they don't? Miles already has a plan—he calls

it the 'Find a new best friend' plan. It starts with him moving to the sub-Saharan desert and making friends with the owner of the largest zoo there."

"The desert?"

"Yes!"

Rue looks at me and sees the nervous expression on my face. "You know the two of them are friends, and friends sometimes don't get along. Don't worry, sis. They got this."

"Really? Look at them," I reply, tilting my head in the direction of the kitchen.

Rue looks and sees Miles and Mr. Evens now competing to see who can butter their toast using the most threatening strokes. It's like they're in a duel, and toast and butter are their weapons.

Rue groans. "I got this. You and Miles wait outside in the hall. I need to talk to my older brother, who has somehow become a toddler."

I tell Miles it's time to go. He gets up from the table and never takes his eyes off Mr. Evens. The two of them are still having an "evil glare" contest.

"Miles, let's go!" I insist. He comes into the living room and grabs his coat and backpack. Rue goes back in the kitchen and closes the door. I really want to hear what they are saying, but I know it's wrong to eavesdrop.

But is it eavesdropping if I happen to tie my sneakers near the kitchen door and overhear something? I'm thinking that should be okay. Miles must be thinking the same thing because he inches closer toward the kitchen door, too. I slowly push my weight into the door so I can take a peek—just a small peek.

Rue doesn't start talking right away. Instead she sits down, butters a piece of toast, and eats it slowly, like it's the best thing she's ever tasted. Mr. Evens rolls his eyes and looks really annoyed.

"What?!" he asks after a few moments. "What do you have to say?"

"Me?" Rue replies innocently.

"Argh, don't drag this out. I know you. You have something to say—you always have something to say. So just go ahead and say it!" Mr. Evens replies, crossing his arms in front of him.

"I'm just sitting here enjoying this nice breakfast and a show."

"There's no show!"

She laughs. "Oh, now that's a lie! There's a very funny comedy show right here."

"I don't know what you're taking about," he says.

"Oh, so I didn't just see you having a staring contest with a seven-year-old?"

"Well, he started it!" Mr. Evens blurts out before he can take it back.

Rue smiles and puts down the food. "Darrious, you just used the phrase 'he started it.'"

"Yeah, yeah, I heard it," he grumbles.

She laughs and shakes her head. "You have got to find a

better way to handle this, or these kids will eat you alive."

"I am doing the best I can. Is it my fault that the young one is impossible? I told him to stay away from that trunk. Then he tells me he was curious. He said he *needs* to open it. Well, I'm not gonna just let him do what he wants. He has to follow the rules."

"This isn't about the rules. Miles is a good kid. They both are. You're upset because of the trunk."

Mr. Evens's face grows hard, and his expression is dark and serious. "Miles had no right to open the trunk."

"Yes, but it was time someone did. And it was never going to be you."

Mr. Evens stands up and takes his plate to the sink. He scrapes the food off the plate loudly and says, "It's my home, it's my trunk. I make the rules."

Rue gets up and pours herself a glass of juice. "There's a lot of stuff here that Miles could have gotten into, but he got into the trunk because he sees that it's special to you. And he wants to know why. He wants to be close to you."

"He doesn't need to know why that trunk is so important."

"No, but you do. You have forgotten why that trunk matters, and maybe it's time you remembered." Rue makes him turn away from the sink and look at her. She puts both hands on either side of Mr. Evens's face and looks deep into his eyes, "Darrious, Miles isn't the only one who needs to open the trunk."

———

The next night, Miles mentions he has a toothache. Mr. Evens and I think it's just so he would not have to eat the brussels sprouts on his plate, but later, when he doesn't want any pie for dessert, we know he isn't faking it. It's already nine at night, and all the dentist offices are closed. I'm not sure what we are going to do. Nanna always has a way to fix these things, but she's not here.

Miles is lying on the sofa and has gone from moaning to crying. Mr. Evens tells me that he'll be right back and then he just takes off. I don't know where he's going. I look up what to do on YouTube, and they say he should gargle with salt and warm water. I get him to do that, but it only helps for a little while. I'm trying not to panic, but I can't take hearing my little brother in pain.

Should we go to the emergency room? Where's Mr. Evens? Why did he just leave?

I sit next to him and tell him that everything is going to be just fine, but I'm not sure. He knows that I'm panicking; he can hear it in my voice. I call Rue, but I think she's still in class because she's not picking up.

"ARGH! Where is he?!" I shout.

"Sunny, it hurts."

"I know, Miles. I'm gonna make you some tea. Nanna always makes tea, and then you're okay again. Remember?"

"Okay," he says softly.

I have made tea in the microwave before, but all of a sudden, I don't even know where to start. Before I can put water in a mug, I hear someone at the door—Mr. Evens is back!

He enters the apartment with an older lady who has red hair, glasses, and who is wearing PJs.

"Sunny, this is Ms. Burns. She's a dentist; she lives on the tenth floor. She's gonna help Miles, okay?"

"Yes! Please!" I reply. We walk over to where Miles is on the sofa, and Dr. Burns asks him to open his mouth. She takes a look and says, "He has a cavity and needs a filling. I'll get dressed and you all meet me in my office." Mr. Evens thanks her and gets ready. And although Miles is in pain, he's well enough to ask if he's gonna go to the office in an ambulance.

"You're not gonna need one, Miles. We'll drive you. Her office isn't far," Mr. Evens says. We hear Miles reply, "Aw, man! Can we please go in an ambulance?"

Mr. Evens and I look at each other; we're relived that he's okay enough to act like himself.

When we get to her office, Dr. Burns takes him into the room to work on his cavity. Miles is afraid at first, but Mr. Evens says he'll come in the room with him. In the meantime, my job is to call Rue to let her know what happened and that Miles will be okay.

When Dr. Burns is done, Miles is not in pain anymore. He's acting really goofy and has a silly look on his face. Dr. Burns says it's because of the medicine she gave him but that he should be back to normal soon. She also told him that he was not to have any more sweets—or, at least, not as often as he did before. Mr. Evens assures her that he will put the whole house on a no-sweets regimen. I'm not sure what that means, but I'm sure I won't like it.

When we get home, we put Miles to bed and Mr. Evens says good night. But before he goes to his room, I run and hug him tighter than I have ever hugged anyone in my life. I don't say thank you, but the way he hugs me back, I don't think I needed to say the words.

Chapter Eighteen
The Return

THE DAYS ARE MOVING way too quickly. Mr. Evens does keep his promise and lets us know how Nanna is doing. He tells us that she's starting to settle in and she seems happy. Rehearsals are going well, and I can hold notes much longer now since Mr. Evens showed me how. But that's the only good news right now. It's been days, and still no manticore hair! Miles and Mr. Evens are being polite to each other, but not really friends like before. I don't know how to help them yet.

All I know is that both of them miss each other. I know because I watched Mr. Evens pick out a tie and then walk toward Miles to see what he thought. But then at the last minute, Mr. Evens turned back. I know Miles misses Mr. Evens because he keeps telling me how much he *doesn't* miss him.

But something good does happen during lunch today. I walk inside the cafeteria and find my best friend waiting for me, with a brand-new Science VR & Chemistry Kit!

"Where'd you get that?" I ask.

"I traded it in for the makeup kit."

"But you said—"

"I know, I know. But yesterday, the Ha-Ha Girls asked me to come over and hang out. And when I got there, all they wanted from me was the makeup kit. I forgot it at home, and when I told them that, they started to ignore me. Then I thought about it, and Strawberry Shortcake should not be a color! I'm sorry, but it shouldn't. And the kit had six different kinds of mirrors. How many different ways can you see yourself? So I went to Mrs. Free, and she let me exchange the makeup kit for this chem set!"

"That's great! Did she get mad at you for changing your mind?"

Folake replies, "No. It's funny because when she saw me standing in front of her classroom, she wasn't surprised to see me. It's like she was waiting for me. Also, the chem kit wasn't in the closet anymore. It was in her desk."

"Guess she knew you'd change your mind."

"Yeah, I don't know what I was thinking. Look at this, Sunny, real glass beakers, full-size test tubes, and a microscope!" She looks at the box with a dreamy expression and sighs. She's in love.

"I'm glad you're back. Does that mean no more studying the Ha-Ha Girls or anyone else?"

"No more Ha-Ha Girls. Or studying anyone else. From now on, I will just be myself and not go overboard. I promise."

I smile. "Good."

"Did you know that the new security guard is also a mime on the weekends? He does parties for little kids."

Oh no . . .

"I wonder what it's like to hold a pretend box in your hand . . ." she says.

"Folake!"

"Do you think he'd give me a few lessons? Look, I'm already pretty good at it," she says, holding out both hands, pretending to be stuck inside a box. "So what do you think?"

She's terrible at it. The size of the imaginary box keeps changing. It's uneven and it looks nothing like a box at all. She's my best friend, and I really believe with enough work, she can be anything, even a mime.

"Sunny, do I have the talent to be a mime?"

I smile. "Maybe. Let's see that box one more time . . ."

It's late, and Miles and I have just finished brushing our teeth to go to bed. Miles looks to see if Mr. Evens's bedroom door is open. Yes, it is. He starts talking to me but speaks loudly to make sure that Mr. Evens can hear him.

"I made a new friend today. He's really nice. He loves dinosaurs, spiders, and he likes regular milk!"

"Miles, just go make up with him," I whisper.

"And my new friend doesn't get upset with curious people. He's nice!" he adds, loud enough for everyone in the building to hear.

"And where did you meet this new friend?" I ask.

"Our class is talking to another school on video. This school is in Canada. I might go visit my new friend. All the way in Canada and never come back!" Miles informs me—or actually, he informs Mr. Evens.

"All right, Miles. I get it. You don't need me as a friend anymore," Mr. Evens says, coming out of his room. "But you know what? I still need you as a friend."

Miles looks at him to see if he's telling the truth. "You do?"

"Yes, Miles. I need you as my friend. I like when we hang out and do things together. Don't you?"

He shrugs. "Yeah, kind of."

I try not to smile too wide. Miles adores spending time with Mr. Evens.

"I owe you an apology. I should not have yelled at you. There was a better way to handle things, and I didn't do that. I should have sat you down and told you why you could not look into the trunk. I hope you can forgive me and we can still be friends."

"Well . . . you did yell pretty loudly," Miles says.

I poke him in the ribs with my elbow and whisper, "Miles! Be nice."

"Okay, okay. I guess I kind of missed being your friend, too," Miles says.

"You did?" Mr. Evens says, acting surprised.

"Yeah. I did. I tried to match what I was wearing with what Sunny was wearing and, well, she doesn't have our sense of style," my brother says. Mr. Evens laughs and says they can go back to choosing ties and socks together.

"Yes!" Miles shouts.

"But before that, is there anything you want to tell me?" Mr. Evens asks.

"Um . . . no."

He narrows his eyes. "Miles . . ."

Miles sighs and looks up at the ceiling while he talks. "Well, I guess I kind of want to say sorry for touching your stuff. You told me not to, and I guess I should have listened— even though it was very hard not to look."

"Yes, I'm sure it was hard. But from now on, I expect you to be strong enough to do the right thing and not give in to temptation. You need people's permission to touch their things. No matter what, okay?"

"Yeah, okay. Sorry," Miles says.

"You're forgiven, we can move on now," Mr. Evens says.

He goes back into his room and comes out with the tie he plans to wear in the morning. It's dark blue with polka dots. Miles runs to get a handful of his socks to see which pair would work best with Mr. Evens's tie. When they are done coordinating, Miles says, "Just tell me one thing. What's in the trunk—is it a good thing like toys? Or a bad thing like one of Folake's sandwiches?"

Mr. Evens thinks it over for a little while and then says, "It's mostly a good thing. A very good thing."

"Oh. Then why would you hide a good thing?" I ask.

"Does it have to do with Maya, your wife?"

"Miles!" I scold.

"Oh, sorry. I've been holding that question in forever!"

Miles admits. "But it's okay if you don't want to tell us."

Mr. Evens sits down on the sofa next to us and says, "It's all right. We should talk about Maya. She was amazing and, yeah, if you two have any questions, you can ask."

Miles and I know better, so we stay quiet. He tells us again that he is okay with us asking questions. Miles looks at me, unsure. I nod, and he takes a chance and asks the first question.

"What was she like?"

"Maya . . . She loved ice cream, more than any kid I ever met. Once she left our nice and warm apartment in the middle of a blizzard to get a triple-decker ice cream sundae. She tried to act tough when it came to scary movies, but she'd spend most of the time with her face buried in my chest. She loved roller coasters, the faster the better. She could never wait until Christmas morning. One year I caught her red-handed under the tree, trying to steam the tape off the gift wrapping so she could see what was inside. She pretended she was sleepwalking.

"If you told her you liked something, even if years went by, she'd remember, and when the chance came, she'd get it for you. Rue told her how much I wanted this firefighter action figure when I was a kid. But we could not afford it. She hunted it down and paid twice what it was worth just so I could finally have it. She had a thing about little dreams. She'd say, 'I can't make your big dreams come true, but you send me all the little dreams, and I'm on it!'

"She was in foster care growing up, and it was really

rough on her. So she wanted to make sure that when we had the money, we would adopt two kids from foster care and give them the home she never had when she was growing up. She promised that we would only get two kids, but knowing her, she probably had a plan to make sure we'd end up with ten of them!

"Whenever she'd hang out with Rue, she'd end up on the news, protesting one thing or another. The two of them went out for dinner and came back home with their heads shaved. Another time they went down the street to get Chinese take-out and came home with tattoos! Those two couldn't be trusted to stay out of trouble.

"She was insanely good at math but had no sense of direction. She'd get in the car, drive two miles, and get lost. She loved to travel for work and meet new people. But her favorite thing to do was come home . . ."

Mr. Evens's voice starts to drift off. I think he's really far away in his head. I think he's picturing everything he's telling us. "What's Oz and why don't you want to go?" I ask.

His voice cracks when he speaks at first. He inhales and tries again. "Oz is a park that she loved. There's a bench there where we sat on, on our first date. It's also the bench that we were sitting on when I asked her to marry me. After Maya passed away, Rue paid to have the bench named after her. They just finished it, and now it's ready to be seen. Rue wanted me to go and see it, but I think it's too hard. I don't think I could sit on our bench alone."

Miles wrinkles his forehead. "That's silly, Mr. Evens. You

wouldn't be alone. You'd have us. Duh."

He nods to himself and says, "You know, I didn't think of that. Yeah, maybe we'll all go together and see the bench."

"What did she look like?" Miles asks.

"You know what, why don't I just show you?" He turns to Miles. "Go ahead, get the trunk." Miles runs into Mr. Evens's room and slides the trunk out from under the bed. Mr. Evens unlocks it and signals to Miles that it's okay to open it.

There are a ton of photos of Maya. I pick one up and take a look at the woman Mr. Evens married. Her skin was the same color as almonds; her big, bright eyes were light hazel. She was short, slim, and had perfect teeth, the kind that belong in a toothpaste commercial.

"This is one of my favorites," he says, holding up a picture of the two of them dressed as clowns.

"Was this for Halloween?" Miles asks.

He laughs. "No. Rue talked Maya into taking a clown class. She didn't want to do it alone, so I came along."

"You look so silly!" I add.

"Excuse you, I got an A for juggling!"

"You did?" Miles says.

Mr. Evens goes into the kitchen and comes back with three apples he took from the fruit bowl. He starts to juggle. He can actually do it! We clap when he's done. He laughs and takes a bow. He shows us more photos of them on vacation, at work, going to fancy parties, and goofing off at home. It's hard to think that Mr. Evens was ever goofy, but we have the pictures to prove it.

"You said we could ask you stuff, right?" Miles says.

"Yes, ask away," Mr. Evens replies.

Miles looks at me, and I already know what he wants to ask. I think Mr. Evens does too. It's the question everyone always wants to know.

"What happened to Maya?"

The big grin Mr. Evens had fades away quickly. He wraps his hand around the back of his neck and drops his head, like it weighs a million pounds. He's not goofy anymore. We're not laughing anymore. That's why I never like that question.

"She was away on assignment, studying a new breed of insects in Uganda. This was going to be her last trip out of the country. We were going to start fostering our first kid. We did all the classes and all the paperwork. She was so excited. She wanted the kid to be about your age, Miles. She picked out the furniture, the school she wanted him to attend. She had all these plans . . .

"She came home early from the trip because she felt so tired. We thought it was just the flu or maybe some kind of temporary bug. But then the headaches started. We went to the doctor. Glioblastoma. It's an aggressive brain tumor that ravaged her so quickly, we didn't even have time to process what was happening. One day she was racing me to the ice cream place, and the next, she was telling us what she wanted for her funeral.

"She was always brave. She never let anyone see her being upset. But one day, she didn't know I saw her, and there she was looking at that stupid catalog of kids' bedroom furniture.

And she burst out crying. She cried for all the mom moments she would never get to have.

"I just wanted to do something for her, anything to make it better. She knew that. She said what she wanted was ice cream, and that was my job. So every day she'd send me out to get her ice cream. She'd take one bite and that was it. That's all she could manage. But she made me go out and get it because she knew I needed to feel like I was helpful. I came back to the apartment after one of my ice cream runs, and Rue had this look on her face. She told me my Maya was gone.

"I couldn't face it. I took all her pictures down. I put away anything that reminded me of her. Sometimes I'd pretend like she was alive and that she had just gone on a trip; she'd be right back. I'd tell myself that so I could fall asleep: She's alive. She's okay. She's just out of town."

I don't think Mr. Evens realizes he's crying. Miles goes over to him and embraces him. That makes Mr. Evens cry harder. But it also makes him hug Miles back.

"Mr. Evens, if you want us not to ask about her anymore, we won't. We promise."

Mr. Evens pulls away from Miles and wipes his eyes. "No, you can ask. She was a wonderful person, and you should know all about her. Just like I hope you tell me all about your parents someday, when you're ready. Okay?"

"Okay," I reply.

"Do you think Maya would have liked us? If we were in foster care, do you think she'd pick us?" Miles asks.

Mr. Evens takes a deep breath and thinks about it

carefully. "You know what, I don't think Maya would have liked you two. I think she would have LOVED you two. And I think she did choose you two. She picked the two best kids, and she sent you both to keep me company."

"And also to help you make better milk choices," I add.

He laughs. "You never gave goat milk a real chance. But don't worry, I found a new kind of milk at the market last week—I'm gonna buy a whole gallon of it. You'll love it."

Miles and I look at him suspiciously. "What kind of milk?" Miles asks.

"Skunk milk!"

Miles gasps. "NOOOOOOOOOOOO!"

Chapter Nineteen
He Said What?

IT ALL STARTED WHEN I asked Rue to do my hair. She took me to the hair supply store, and we got a lot of stuff. When we got home, she put all the supplies on the table, and she grumbled about how much the small bottle of argan oil cost. It's the oil my nanna puts in my hair so that it's soft and shiny. Miles said the reason it costs so much is because of the tree-climbing goats.

Rue and I had never heard of that and thought he was joking. But then he showed us a video and we were amazed! There they were, goats climbing trees! The goats live in Morocco. They go up there so that they can eat something called argan fruit. And when they spit it out, the farmers pick them up, clean them, and then crush them to make the oil that's in the bottle. It turns out to make just one liter of argan oil takes the workers two whole days! So that's why it costs so much.

"You're so smart!" Rue said to Miles as she starts to prep my hair for washday.

"Smart but not so brave. I wish I could climb like the

mountain goats, but I'm scared—they are so good at it, they never fall," Miles says.

"Well, you have to work on it," Rue replies as she sprays my hair with the water bottle.

"I could try and climb a bunch of trees, but I don't think Mr. Evens would like that."

"No, I would not," Mr. Evens says as he enters the kitchen. "You could fall. If you want to work on being a better climber, I'll take you to an indoor rock-climbing place—where it's safe and you have a harness."

"Really? Can it be just us guys?" Miles asks.

Mr. Evens looks at me. I nod slightly. "Yeah, that sounds good. Why don't you get dressed and we'll head out now?" Miles runs to get ready so fast, he almost knocks me down. Rue says she's glad the boys are going out so that we can have a girls' night in. But she also says we could switch the next weekend, and we would go rock-climbing and the boys would stay home.

Rue and I have the best time! After she's done doing my hair, she lets me do hers! I have to make a part, and I work hard to make sure it's straight. I don't know how Nanna gets my part straight the first time; it takes me six tries with Rue. She says she doesn't mind that I took a long time because she was the same way when she was a kid. She promises that I will get better at it, the more I do it.

By the time Mr. Evens and Miles get back, both of us are finished getting our hair done and we look really cute! We model our freshly braided hair for them and pretend to be walking down a runway.

Miles can't stop talking about the activity center he went to with Mr. Evens. They played laser tag, got on bumper cars, and even played arcade games. But the part he loved the most was climbing the wall. He told us he was afraid at first, but it got easier. He says, "And now, I'm basically a mountain goat!"

Later, when we are drifting off to sleep, Miles says, "Do you know what the best part about climbing was, Shine?"

"Yes, you told me—you were a goat."

"No, the best part was that Mr. Evens was waiting at the bottom. I knew if I fell, if the belt holding me broke or something bad happened, I knew I'd be okay. Mr. Evens would catch me."

Suddenly, Miles gets up and starts pulling the comforter off the sofa. He grabs the pillows and the sheets, too.

"What are you doing?" I ask.

"I'm going to sleep in our room," he says confidently. "Are you coming, Shine?"

The next morning, I hear Mr. Evens enter the living room. He calls out our names when he doesn't see us sleeping on the sofa. I hear him walk down the hall to the bathroom. When he finds the bathroom empty, he stands still for a few moments, and then I hear his footsteps coming toward our bedroom. I don't know why I'm nervous, but I am. My heart is racing, and my mouth is dry. What's he going to say when he sees us taking over the bedroom, like it's our own? I know he said we could stay in here, but what if he changed his mind?

Mr. Evens opens the door slowly. He finds me sitting up with a worried look on my face. Behind me, Miles is tangled up in the covers, one leg sticking out. His eyes are shut, and his mouth is wide open, in deep sleep.

I swallow hard and squeak out, "Good morning."

Mr. Evens takes in the scene for a few moments. Then he smiles—just a little—and says, "Eggs for breakfast?" I feel relief from the roots of my hair to the tips of my toes. I nod. "Yeah, eggs, please." He leaves and closes the door behind him.

Later that morning, over breakfast, Mr. Evens tells us he heard from social services and that they might have a place for us to go. It's an emergency foster home and they have space now; they can take both Miles and me. We stop eating and look at him. I try to act cool.

"What did you tell them?" I ask.

Mr. Evens looks up from his bowl of whole-wheat cereal and says, "I told them they could give the spot to someone else. We're good." Miles and I look at each other, not sure what to say. Mr. Evens laughs nervously and adds, "We are good here, right?"

My brother and I nod. "Yup! We're all good," I reply.

He looks at the both of us and then says, "What are we thinking for ties tomorrow, Miles? A bold solid color or a checkered look? Hey, maybe a floral print to shake things up?"

Miles says. "Tomorrow feels like . . . ducks. Yup. Feels like a duck tie day tomorrow."

"Oh. I don't have any duck ties. We have a little time before school starts, should we look for some online?"

Miles puts his spoon down, brings the bowl of cereal to his mouth, and drinks what's left. Then he and his BFF head to the laptop and go on a serious duck hunt.

I'm gonna miss this place when we go back home to Nanna. I was really starting to like it here . . .

It feels like weeks since Folake came to school and said she had news for me. The truth is it was just this morning. But that's still a really long time. I asked her to tell me her news before class started, and she refused. I even pleaded and gave her my very best "Give me what I want because I'm cute" look. It didn't work.

She insisted we needed ambience. I had no idea what that word meant and had to ask her. It basically means she wants to make sure that we're in the right setting before she talks to me. So we rush through lunch and run outside. We stay inside the yard, but go as far away from the crowd as we can.

"Okay, now tell me! Tell me!" I demand.

She clears her throat. "I have to set it up just right."

"Folake!"

"Okay, okay!" she says. "This morning, before school started, my mom ran out of eggs. She made Abeo get them and told me to go with him because last time he bought the wrong kind. We go to the supermarket, get the eggs, and on our way back, who do you think we run into?"

"Who?"

"Tessa!" she replies.

"Whoa . . ."

"She's coming toward me, and I'm not sure what to expect. She was really nice that time in the locker room, but maybe it was just that one time. Maybe she's back to being a bully. Or maybe she's changed. I had no way to know for sure. As she comes closer, I freeze up and stop walking."

"Oh no! Did she look angry or upset at all?"

"Before I have time to really study her face, my brother asks me why I stopped walking. I figure if he's about to get beaten up, he should at least know why. And if I decide it's better to flee, he should know why I dropped the eggs and suddenly started running."

"So you told him about Tessa wanting to fight us?"

She nods. "Yup. I stood there and told him everything. I told him that I tried really hard but was still a little afraid of her."

"Did he tease you about it?" I ask, getting upset with Abeo in my head.

"Sunny, he said words that I never thought I would hear him say: 'Folake, I wouldn't let anyone bully or hurt you. I'm your brother, I got you!'"

My mouth rolls down to the floor. "He said what?" I ask, making sure I heard right.

"I know! I was so surprised, I didn't even pay attention to the fact that while we were talking, Tessa got closer. And before I knew it, she was punching distance from us. My whole body got cold. Like I was in a winter storm with only my PJs on. There was no time to think of a way to get out of it. Tessa was now in my face!"

I look her over. "You don't look like you're hurt. What happened?"

"Tessa walked by me and said, 'Hi, Folake.'"

When the words come out of my best friend's mouth, I feel like I'm in a dream. There's no way that can be real. So Tessa is just . . . nice now? Is that a thing that really happens?

"Wait, she said hi?!" I ask.

"Yup! She just smiled and said hi."

We look at each other and speak at the same time, "Whoa . . ."

Folake takes my hand and looks into my eyes. She has the same expression as the people on TV when they find out they won the lottery. "Sunny, that's not even the best part!"

"Wait, there's more?!" I ask.

"Yes! So I snap out of my shock and say hey to Tessa. And we keep walking. Abeo says he's glad that she didn't bother me, but that he would never let anyone bully me ever! And that's when I thought about my Backyard Buddies collection and all the stuff Abeo had done to me and, well . . . I told him the truth!"

My stomach flips with worry. If Abeo was mean to her, he's gonna have to face me. I'm not sure what I would do really, but I would have to do something. "What did you say to him?" I ask.

"I said, 'Someone has been mean and bullying me—you!'"

I gasp. "You said what?!"

"Yeah, I know! And then do you know what he said, Sunny? He said, 'Folake, I'm just teasing when I do that. Brothers do that.' And I said, 'Some do that, but some are nice and don't make their little sister scared of them.'

"He said, 'My bad. I was just playing with you. I didn't think you were taking it so seriously.' I told him I did and that it was never fun to be around him because he was always being mean. And then, something happened—something even bigger than Tessa saying hello—my brother apologized!"

"Abeo Musa said he's sorry?!"

"Yup!"

"What did you say?"

"After I made sure that I heard right, I accepted it, and I admitted that I was the one who messed up his sneakers."

"Were you able to make it back in the house before he chased you?"

"He didn't chase me."

"Really? But was he mad, right?"

"Yes, he was upset. But then I said I was sorry and that I would not go in his room again. I also gave him an idea on how he could waterproof his sneaker boxes so that they would never get wet again. He was happy with my idea and actually said that he owed me one—especially after what he did to my dolls!"

"He remembered that!"

"Yeah. He admitted it got out of hand. He said he always felt bad about it."

"That's fantastic, Folake! And you were right, this story

was way too good to waste in the lunchroom. I can't believe it. So Abeo is nice now?"

"Well, *nicer* . . . He still yanked on my hair before he ran up to his room to get ready for school. But it was different because this time he ran slow enough to let me catch him. We tumbled around and even laughed when we hit the floor. My mom thought she was seeing things! We never played together like that."

"This is your lucky day, Folake, I'm so happy for you!" I say, giving her a big hug.

"Actually, this is your lucky day, Sunny."

"What do you mean?"

"Remember Abeo said he owed me one?" she says.

"Yeah . . ."

"Well, I told him how he could pay me back for destroying my dolls. He thought it was a really strange thing to ask for, but he gave it to me anyway."

She takes a small white envelope out of her coat pocket and hands it over to me. I open the envelope, and inside is a small lock of hair from the manticore himself! I scream with joy, and both Folake and I jump up and down. We officially have the second item!

Chapter Twenty
Feeding Time

FOLAKE AND I HAD to work really hard to figure out where to find the first two items for our quest. It looks like it'll be just as hard or maybe even harder to find the third item. Tomorrow is Halloween, the last day in October. We are going to see Nanna on Sunday. And if I haven't finished my quest by this weekend, she won't get better and Mr. Evens will send us off to foster care. I have to find the Gorgon. I just have to!

"Sunny, are you okay?" Mr. Evens asks.

"Huh?"

He looks down at my bowl of oatmeal. It's thick and gross now because I let it sit too long. But I have things that are far more important than soggy cereal. I hear Miles in the background talking to Noodle. I was so lost in my head I didn't even realize Miles had left the table.

"You've been in outer space all morning. What is it? Are you worried about the concert?" Mr. Evens asks.

If I can cure Nanna, singing the solo won't be a problem because she will be there. But if I can't find the last item . . .

"Mr. Evens, if you were looking for a Gorgon, where would you start?" I ask. He furrows his eyebrows and puts down his knife and fork. "You mean like in Greek mythology? The three sisters with snakes in their hair?"

"Yes! Where would they be if they lived here in Chicago?"

"Is this for some kind of assignment?" he asks.

"It's . . . something like that. Where should I start looking?"

He tilts his head up and bites his lip. "Well, I'm not sure why you would need to find a set of sisters with snakes on top of their heads, but if you did, I guess I would start by asking around or maybe posting flyers for them. That sounds like a fun creative writing homework assignment. Is this for English class?"

"It's complicated. Let's say you were me and you already asked around and no one has seen Gorgons and you have no leads at all. What next? What would you do?" I plead.

He leans back in his chair and crosses his arms over his chest. "Well, this a really hard one. Wait, I know. I would call up Indiana Jones and ask him to check out the Temple of Doom and see if there's a Gorgon there," he says, laughing.

I look back at him, confused. "Who's Indiana Jones? And where's this temple?"

"Indiana Jones! One of the greatest movies—okay, that's it. This weekend, we are having movie night. I can't believe you don't know who Indiana Jones is!"

"I'm not looking for Indie whatever-his-name-is. I'm looking for a Gorgon!" I remind him.

"That's the problem, Shine. You're looking for a Gorgon,"

Miles says as he walks past me and goes over to the sink to wash off Noodle's food dish.

"What do you mean?" I ask.

"Do you remember when we first got Noodle and his cage didn't lock right? He kept getting out."

"Yeah, he escaped twice," I reply.

"And I found him both times because I didn't go looking for a hamster—duh! I went looking for the places around Nanna's place that had fruit and nuts because that's what they like to eat. Gorgons own snakes and, well, they gotta feed them, right? So try a pet store that sells snake food."

Mr. Evens and I look at each other, shocked. It's such a clever idea; how did we not think of it? "That's brilliant, Miles!" I reply. I leap out of my seat and run toward him. I hold his face in between my hands and kiss him on the cheek over and over again.

"Argh, gross, Shine!" he says, using the back of his hand to wipe my kiss off his face. He hates it when I do that, but I don't care. My little brother just helped me figure out how to get the last item!

Don't worry, Nanna, we're almost there! Soon, you'll be back to your old self and back with us where you belong!

There's a lot of things I love about Halloween: Waiting until the end of the night, taking the big bag of candy and pouring it onto my bed, and watching it "rain" candy! Going to the store to choose which spectacular costume to wear. Oh, and best of all, I love that Miles and I have a system. We map out all the apartments in the area that give out full-size candy. We don't mess with that mini fun-size stuff. Nope! We are serious about getting the biggest and best candy.

We would let the other kids use our map (for a small fee— one piece of candy for every handful they receive). Every year, Nana swore that she was going to hand out fruit because it was the right and responsible thing to do. But when it came time to shop for the big night, she always gave in and bought bags and bags of chocolates. And yup, I made sure they were the full-size ones. But as much as I love Halloween, I have to stay focused on the quest.

Mr. Evens had some work to do after our one-on-one rehearsal. So when we asked him to take us to the pet shop, he had Rue come over and take us instead. But that was only after she swore over and over again not to let Miles come home with any more pets. He said Noodle was more than enough.

Rue picks us up, and we pile into the car. She thinks the reason why we're going to the pet shop is so that Miles can see the new animals that have come in. She has no idea we are on the hunt for a Gorgon.

On our way there, she asks what my costume will be for later tonight. I mumble something about being a wolf and that Folake is going as Little Red Riding Hood. Rue loves the idea. And just as she pulls the car into the pet shop parking lot, she asks Miles what he's going to be.

"Wait, let me guess! You're gonna be some kind of animal, right?"

Miles shakes his head. "I don't think I should make fun of them by pretending to be them. Animals have feelings. I wouldn't want anyone going around pretending to be me." Rue looks at Miles with admiration. "You are so deep and so right! My bad. So what are you going to dress up as?"

"Well, I want to be something really scary this year, so Mr. Evens took me to the costume shop and I picked out the scariest thing I could think of," Miles says.

"A zombie? A vampire? A ghost?" Rue says, getting more and more curious with each guess. Miles shakes his head every time.

"Okay, I give up. What are you going to be for Halloween?" Rue says.

"The scariest, most horrible thing I can think of—broccoli," Miles replies.

Rue bursts out laughing. "You're going as a vegetable?"

"Can you think of anything scarier?" he says.

She smiles. "Nah, you right!" We get out of the car and enter the first pet shop. There are five shops that sell snake food in this area. All five of them are on our list. Is it too much to hope that the first one is the right one?

If each of the Gorgons owns a bunch of snakes, that means they buy a lot of snake food. So when we enter the first pet shop, the first thing we ask is if anyone has bought a large amount of snake food. The owner says no. The next three pet shops give us the same answer.

"Okay, Miles, this is the last shop. I have to get you two

235

back home after this," Rue says as we enter the fifth shop.

"Okay, last one," Miles replies. "Sunny, there's the owner. Her name is Zoe. Let's go ask her." He guides me down an aisle full of parakeets to the back of the pet store.

"Hi, Zoe!" Miles says to the short, plump woman with the pretty smile.

"Miles! It's so good to see you," Zoe says.

"How do you know my brother?" I ask.

"We had a very grumpy lizard named Samuel, and nothing we did cheered him up. And then Miles came in, and within twenty minutes, he had solved the problem," Zoe gushes.

Miles shrugs and says, "I knew Sammy since he was a baby. He's always been extra sensitive to heat. So I figured there was something wrong with the temperature in his tank."

"Well, you were a lot of help. Thank you," the owner replies. She asks how she can help us, and we ask if any of her customers buy snake food—a lot of snake food. Zoe thinks about it for a moment and shakes her head. Miles and I both sigh and thank her for her help.

We are headed back to the front of the store when Zoe says, "Hey, wait! How could I forget?! The Powell sisters! They don't come here often, but when they do, they really stock up on snake food. It's like they are running some kind of snake town or something." Zoe laughs.

"Really? Do you know where they live?" I ask.

"Oh, sure, they live about half a mile from here, in a gray-and-black old house that looks a little abandoned. It's at the very top of the hill. You can't miss it."

"All right, times up, y'all. Better c'mon!" Rue says, heading toward the front door.

"And you're sure they own a lot of snakes?" I ask.

"I have a protest march to get ready for, and signs don't write themselves. Miles, say goodbye to your pet friends. We gotta go!" Rue says.

I take Miles by the hand, and we dash out of the store. On our way out, Miles yells, "Thanks, Zoe!"

She yells back, "Anytime, Miles! Oh, and we just got a shipment of tarantulas. They could use a good home."

Miles lets go of my hand and turns back to face Zoe. "Really? What kind? Mexican redleg, Chilean rose, or Costa Rican zebra?"

Zoe beams at him and says proudly, "Pinktoe!"

"*Avicularia avicularia*! Really? When did you get him?!"

"Miles!" I shout, trying to pull him along.

"It's not a him. It's a her!" Zoe says.

I gently begin to drag him through the front door; he fights to stay in the shop. "But, Shine, it's a pinktoe female. They're adorable! Just five more minutes."

"Rue is already in the car! Let's go, Miles!"

He shouts as he's going through the exit door, "Sorry, Zoe, I'll be baaaack!"

Later that night, as we're getting dressed, we ask Mr. Evens what he's going as. He says, "A guy in a suit."

"But that's you every day," Miles replies.

"Wait! I have an idea," I announce. I grab a black marker from my backpack and ask Mr. Evens to give me one of his button-down shirts. He hands it over. I draw a picture of a pumpkin and write the word "MISSING" at the top.

"I'm a missing pumpkin poster?" he asks.

"Yup!"

He thinks for a minute and then nods. "I like it."

We get ready to go. Miles wants to come with Folake and me, but his friend from class is having a party, and Mr. Evens is making him go to that instead. He wants Miles to get more human friends to add to all his animal ones. Also, Mr. Evens is staying with Miles the whole night because he doesn't trust him not to eat all the candy in one night. Mr. Evens lets me go trick-or-treating with Folake and her family as long as I promise that I will not wander off alone.

If tonight were like all the other Halloween nights, Folake and I would be super excited and happy to go trick-or-treating. But since we are about to come face-to-face with three sisters with evil snakes on their heads, we're more anxious than excited. We do a little trick-or-treating, and when we get the first chance, we go back to Folake's house and change into our regular clothes. We can't face Gorgons looking like Little Red Riding Hood and a wolf.

It feels like we are walking for a long time, but really it's more like fifteen minutes. I think it feels like forever because we have no idea what to expect when we get to where we're going. But we don't come unprepared. The third item we need is a tear from a Gorgon, so we each brought along a sandwich bag with a plump, super smelly onion. That way, once we get inside the house, we can hide it somewhere and the Gorgons will start to smell it and their eyes will tear up. We'll capture a tear in the small clear vial we brought with us.

On the way there, we don't talk much. I think we are saving our energy for when we really need it. Also, I think if I talk, Folake will hear the fear in my voice, and if she talks, I might hear it in hers. So we walk silently, headed for the Gorgons' home, hoping that we're not making a terrible mistake.

Chapter Twenty-One
Run!

WE CAN SEE THE house a whole block before we actually get there. It's hard to miss.

It sits on top of a hill and looms before us. It's painted in two dark and dreary shades of gray and black. There's a wooden porch in the front that's old and has parts that are rotting. One thing I know for sure, just looking at it even from a distance: the house is angry. I didn't know a house could have feelings, but I think this one does.

The closer we get to it, the smaller Folake and I become. It's like the house is growing; as if at any moment, the rotted-out wooden pieces that make up the porch will split into a row of sharp wooden fangs, swoop down, and swallow us in one giant bite.

There's a pathway we have to walk through to get to the actual door of the house, but we can't get any closer because of the towering black iron gate. The tips of the gate are sharp like the teeth of a great white shark.

On the other side of the gate is a winding trail that leads

up to the house. The trail is made of big concrete squares, with huge cracks in the centers. It looks like the weeds are fighting to break through the concrete and take over the whole walkway.

I wonder what else besides weeds are trying to break through from underneath . . .

There's only one tree behind the gate, but it's the biggest one I've ever seen. The trunk of the tree is so wide, it could swallow an entire Chicago city bus. The leaves are all gone; it has only a few branches left. Its bony fingers are made of twigs and seem to be reaching out to us. It's as if the tree is trying to tell us that it's time to feed it. And guess what the tree likes to eat?

"Um, Sunny, does that tree look like it's screaming to you?"

The moment Folake says that, I see it. The tree is now even more terrifying than it was before.

"Do you remember my list of things I'm afraid of?" Folake asks.

"Yeah, number one, dogs. Two, small spaces. And three, airplanes."

"I would like to change my list and add this house to the top. Like the very, very top," Folake says.

"It made my list, too."

"Are we really going in there?" she says.

I nod. Slowly.

"Okay, just making sure," she replies, trying to hide the fear in her voice.

I take her hand. "I'm scared, too. If we make it past the gate of black ice, the sidewalk of doom, and the mean-looking tree with the big mouth, we'll be just fine."

"No, then we will face the real danger: the Gorgons," she reminds me. "How are we going to make it past them? Maybe we should have planned this out better."

"I don't think there's a perfect plan for getting a tear from a Gorgon. I think we just have to go in and deal with whatever is on the other side."

I see a small orange glow coming from one of the windows on the first floor, but it's faint and I can't be one hundred percent sure. I tell Folake, and together we wrap our hands around the bars and push against the metal to try to get a better look at the house beyond the gate.

"Is that a light? I think it's flickering," Folake says. We stretch as far as we can, but we can't see very well past the gate.

"The metal bars are making my fingers numb," I confess.

"Mine too." We pull our hands away from the gate and shove them in our coat pockets.

Folake does her best to sound calm. "So . . . are we sure it's this house and not that nice yellow-and-white, friendly-looking house across the street?"

"Yes, I'm sure."

She groans. "Aw, man, I knew you were gonna say that."

"This house looks like every scary house in every scary movie ever!"

Folake takes a deep breath and says, "Maybe it only looks

scary. Think about it. So far this has been peaceful. If this place were really creepy, we'd hear noises out of nowhere."

The moment the words come out of her mouth, we hear something or someone howling from the other side of the gate. We scream and take off running. We're halfway down the block when we finally stop.

"What do you think that was?" I ask.

"I . . . don't . . . know," Folake admits, still trying to catch her breath.

"I never want to go back there. What if there are more than one of whatever that thing is?" I ask.

Folake agrees. "Yeah, we should never go back!"

I feel something in the lining of my coat pocket. I suddenly remember what I'm feeling; this coat was torn, and Nanna went out to get thread to fix it. I had forgotten all about that. That night was windy and snowing, but she went to the store because she wanted me to have my best coat for Sunday service the next day.

My heart twists inside my chest. Even though she had to go out in the awful snow and stay up late to fix my coat, she didn't complain. She was always fixing things for us. And now, it's my turn to fix something for her.

"Folake, I can't run away. I have to go back and find the Gorgons. Nanna would do the same for me and for Miles. You can stay behind if you want, but I have to go."

She twists her face, anguished. "Okay, fine. I'm coming, too. But if I don't make it out of that creepy house, my ghost will never forgive you!"

We get back to the gate, this time more determined than ever to get past it. We can't climb it; it's too high. And even if it wasn't, the bars on top are too pointy. We walk along the gate and try to find some way in. I've almost given up when Folake says, "Sunny, this bar is loose." She's standing near the gate where it curves and wraps around. I go over to her. She's right; the bar is loose. It's not loose enough for us to pull it out totally, but maybe we can try and squeeze through it.

"I'll go first and you look out for whatever might be on the other side."

"On it!" Folake says. I get low to the ground and try my hardest to wiggle in between the loose bar. It takes a while, but I manage to slide through. I'm glad we didn't wear our costumes; there's no way a wolf outfit would have fit through there.

"Okay, Folake, it's your turn." Folake makes the same wiggling movement I made and gets past the bars. But her hair gets caught on a loose scrap of the black metal on the bar. I try to free her, but it's not working.

"Ouch!" Folake yells.

"I'm sorry. It's just really caught."

We're facing each other, but Folake can see over my shoulders and out to the rest of the big yard. Her eyes grow to three times the size they should be. She stops squirming. She whispers in a voice so small, I'm not really sure she actually spoke.

"Sunny, run!"

There's a giant man in a thick, long, dark coat and hat. He's running toward us, shouting something. He's gotta be the one we heard howling—a big wolf man created by the Gorgons to guard the house.

"Sunny, go!"

"Not without you!" I work harder to free her from the bar, but it's just too tangled up.

The man shouts, "Hey, you! Stop!"

He's only a few yards away now. I try one last time to yank my best friend free.

"C'mon, c'mon!" I yell at Folake's hair and the piece of the bar that's holding on to it. I almost have it . . . "I got it!" I shout.

Folake is free! We take off running toward the house. The man keeps coming after us. We reach the front porch with the man right on our heels. We're going too fast to stop in time, and we crash into the front door. It bursts wide open. There, on the other side, are three old women with venomous looks in their eyes and snakes coming out of their heads!

I block Folake so that whatever powers they have can't be used on her. "Hey, stay away from us! I'm warning you!" I shout.

"What in the world is going on?!" the tallest woman says. All three of them are wearing long dark dresses. Next to the tall one is a redhead with beady eyes. "Who are these children?" she asks.

"They must have come to see us for Halloween! Well, you two are going to be so very sorry!" the last old woman says. "Isn't that right, sisters?" They all agree and come toward us.

Folake and I hug. I say a silent goodbye to all the lovely

things this world has—ice cream, video games, laughing. Nanna and Miles. I'm going to miss them the most. The Gorgons come close enough to touch us, the snakes on their heads hissing and snapping wildly at us. This is it.

"Folake, I'm sorry I got you into this."

"It's okay. I love you, Sunny."

"I love you, too."

The man who was running after us closes the door loudly behind us. We're tired. There's nowhere to go. Now they have us all surrounded. It's over . . .

"Sunny, Sunny, wake up!" I hear someone calling my name. I open my eyes; the face in front of me is blurry. I have to blink a few times to see clearly. It's Folake. I'm lying down on a pretty pink sofa; she's sitting beside me.

"What—how—I don't understand. What happened?" I ask. She helps me sit up.

"You passed out for a few minutes, dear," the shortest older woman says, standing behind the sofa. "My name is Eugenia Powell. I'm a nurse. I checked you out, and I promise you're fine."

"You're a nurse?" I ask.

Do Gorgons have full-time jobs? Don't they just go around scaring people with the snakes? The snakes! They aren't on her head anymore. Where are they? Folake reads the confused look on my face.

"I saw snakes," I tell her.

"Yeah, me too! They looked real," Folake adds. "But I will let them explain."

"Did you girls really think they moved like actual snakes? That's so nice of you to say," the tallest woman says. "Sisters, I think I might actually have a good chance this year."

"What is she talking about?" I ask my friend.

"Oh no, I should explain," the tallest lady begins. "My name is Jenny. My daughter goes to MIT. It's a really good school for super-smart kids. She's really into animatronics and building robots. I started to get into it, too. Anyway, there's a competition every year at the community college to see who can create the best robot that mimics the fluid movement of some organic life-form. This year, it's snakes. These here are my prototypes. We were goofing around, and we attached them to some old hats we found in the back of the closet." She shows me a mechanical snake.

Now that I'm sitting here in much better light, I guess they don't look like real snakes after all . . .

"But wait, one of you said that we would be sorry we came," I say, still suspicious.

"Oh, that was me," the shortest one says. "I'm Nora. I meant you'd be sorry because we just gave out our last big batch of the good candy. I'm afraid all we have are raisins and yellow marshmallow Peeps."

"Oh . . ." I reply, trying to get things straight in my head.

"And the man who was chasing us, that's Joe. He's the caretaker, and he was worried that we'd hurt ourselves going through the gate the way we did," Folake says, pointing to the man across the room. Now that I see him up close and with good lighting, he doesn't look like a wolf man.

Joe comes close and shakes my hand. "I was trying to tell you to use the other entrance. It's where all the other trick-or-treaters go. But you all took off running. I have to go see to that loose bar. I meant to fix it last week," he says, heading out the door.

"Well, what about the snakes—the real snakes? The lady at the pet store said you get food for them there," I add.

"Oh, yeah, we have lots of real snakes. You see Nora works for a reptile conservation center. And sometimes she likes to take her work home with her," Eugenia says as she walks toward the wall and pulls back the curtain to reveal a huge tank full of lazy, sleepy, happy-looking snakes.

"Say hi, fellas!" Nora says.

"I'm sorry, I thought . . . Doesn't matter. We should go," I say, standing up.

Eugenia says, "Not until you two have had something to eat and drink. I put out some juice for you and Folake on the table. It will help get your energy back." Folake goes over to the table and hands me the glass of orange juice that the nurse placed there.

"We're gonna fix you two a nice snack. And when we get back, we need to call your folks and make sure they know where you two are and that you're safe," Jenny says. The three sisters go off to the kitchen.

"This is great, Sunny! We got it all wrong!" Folake says as

she gulps down her juice. I turn away, not wanting her to see the tears in my eyes. "What's wrong?" she asks.

"They aren't Gorgons. They are just nice old ladies who care for snakes. That means their tears won't work. I failed..."

"I've read *The Girl of Fire and Light* a million times, just like you. And I don't think they said anything about all Gorgons being mean. You were looking for three sisters that have snakes and are magic. Well, the three sisters in there own snakes, and when you passed out, Nora rubbed some peppermint oil on your forehead and that's what helped you open your eyes. Why can't that be magic?"

"I never thought about it that way..." I admit.

Folake puts her arm around my shoulders and says, "Now all we need to do is get one single tear."

I look around and see my coat on the edge of the sofa. I look in the pockets. "I think I must have dropped my bag of onion when we were running."

"Yeah, mine too," she says.

Suddenly we hear loud, booming laughter coming from the kitchen. Folake and I go to see what's happening. The women explain that Eugenia has been trying to get a TikTok dance for days now and still can't get it right. She is offended by what her sisters say and insists on defending herself by showing us the dance.

She begins to dance around the kitchen table with the fake snake on her head, and it's the funniest thing I've seen in forever! I don't know what dance she's trying to do, but I'm pretty sure she's doing it wrong. The more she dances, the more we all laugh. She's laughing along with us, too. And soon, the sisters are doubling over with laughter.

"Stop, stop! You're gonna make me laugh so hard, I'll cry. I promise!" Eugenia warns. And sure enough, she laughs so hard, tears come out her eyes—happy tears, but still tears!

Where did I put the vial I brought to collect the tear? It's in my coat. There won't be enough time to get it before the tears dry up. Someone taps me on the shoulder—Folake. She opens her hand, and in it is the vial I was looking for.

"Thank you," I whisper as the sisters continue to laugh. A single tear falls from Eugenia's face and lands on the kitchen counter. I quietly collect it and place it into the vial. Relief washes over me. It's done! The quest is done! Nanna is saved!

Chapter Twenty-Two
Nanna Jo

ON SATURDAY, MILES DECIDES to unveil his art masterpiece. Now that the quest is over and I have everything I need, all I want to do is put everything together.

But I know how hard Miles has worked on his project, and I figure, as his big sister, the least I can do is be there when he shows it off.

He said he wants a grand "unveiling," so he makes all of us, including Rue, take him to a fancy lunch. He keeps us in suspense until after we eat. Then, when it's time for him to show us his work, he starts off by saying he's already scored ninety-four percent on it from his art teacher. We clap for him, but he assures us that he does not make art for the grades but for the world. We try hard not to laugh at his very serious expression.

"This project is called 'Home,'" he says. Rue helps him take off the cloth and reveal a medium-size white canvas. We're really shocked by what Miles has painted: ties! He painted a bunch of ties with different designs and made it into the shape of a house. He tells us Rue helped him a lot, but Rue says, "I helped a little. But the concept was all Miles." We clap really hard for him, and Mr. Evens clears his throat and looks away. He wipes his face before he looks at us again. Rue squeezes his hand.

"Miles, you did an excellent job!" he says.

"He's right, I love it!" I reply.

"Sunny, your little brother has talent. I can see him being really big in the art world," Rue adds.

"Really?" Miles says.

"Yes!" Rue says, squeezing his cheeks. I shake my head. When I do that, he gets upset, but for some reason he doesn't mind it when Rue does it.

"Does that mean we can have dessert?" Miles says.

"Yes, but not here. I want to show you guys something," Mr. Evens says as he pays the bill. He leads us out of the restaurant and back into the car.

Mr. Evens takes us to get sundaes at Maya's favorite ice cream shop. Then we walk across the street to Oz, the park with the bench that has her name on it. The park is just as pretty as I imagined it. There's an archway with flowers draped on top, a playground with swings, and a pond. We walk up a small hill and find a bench under a huge oak tree. On the bench, a plaque reads *"Beloved wife, sister-in-law, and ice cream lover."*

We sit down on the bench and look out at the same things that Maya must have seen when she was here: kids playing on the playground, tree leaves swaying in the wind. We don't talk, not even Miles. It sounds strange, but I think we keep silent because we don't want to interrupt Mr. Evens and Maya's conversation.

Later that night, I wait until everyone has fallen asleep and then head to the kitchen. It's time to make the potion. The book doesn't tell me exactly how Luna created the oil that saved her family. It doesn't say whether she added the items into a drink or if she put them in a frozen treat and let them eat it like a Popsicle. But now that I have all three items in my hand, I think I know exactly how I am going to apply it.

I go over to my backpack and take out my small shiny tin of shea butter. I love the smell of shea butter—it reminds me of washdays with Nanna and summers playing in the park with Miles. Rue came over the other day, and I smelled it on her. I told her how much I love it, and she bought me one just like the one she has. She said, "I can't have my li'l sis out here with no shea butter! No, no, no!"

Rue makes me laugh. She's really good at that. She comes into a room and lights everything up. I'm going to miss her. Once I make this mixture and rub it into Nanna's hands, she'll be her old self and we'll move back home. But I try to remember that just because we are not living with Mr. Evens anymore doesn't mean that Rue and I can't hang out. Also, Mr. Evens will come visit us. He likes me, even though sometimes he pretends he doesn't. And he'll definitely come to see Miles. The two of them are inseparable.

I mix the shea butter around with my index finger. The

trick to shea butter I learned is that to make it soft, you have to warm it up before you apply it to the skin. I rub the butter back and forth in the tin until it turns soft and gooey. Once it's soft, it has a new smell: melting chocolate. I inhale the scent; it's so good.

Once the shea butter is nice and gooey, I add the tear from the Gorgon, the single hair from the manticore, and embed the mermaid-kissed seashell into the center. The butter hardens up again, and now it looks like a bright yellow bar of soap with a seashell in the center.

When I see Nanna tomorrow, I'll warm the butter up and rub it into her hands. She'll come back to life. I can't wait. I've missed her so much. I know Miles has, too. Sometimes I hear him crying at night 'cause he misses her. I don't want to embarrass him, so I pretend that I don't hear. But the next day, I try to be extra nice to him.

I know that I have everything I need to make Nanna well again, but still, it can't hurt to say a quick prayer over the tin. I close my eyes and think of happy thoughts that have to do with Nanna. And I say out loud, "Please let this work. Please let this work."

When I get under the covers, I feel everything all at once. I'm excited that we'll finally be able to save Nanna. I'm nervous about applying it to her hand; I want to make sure I don't miss a spot. I'm thrilled to be going back home, but I'm also a little sad because this place has started to feel a little like . . . home?

I look up at the ceiling and tell myself that I need to get

some sleep. I don't want to be unfocused tomorrow and risk messing anything up. That means I need a good night's sleep. I'm finally about to drift off when Miles says, "Shine, no matter what happens tomorrow, I love you. And Nanna does, too."

I am the first one up the next morning. I shower, brush my teeth, and pack our stuff as neatly as I can. We have a lot more things now since we moved in here. But I figure we can come back and get the rest. Right now, I pack as much as we can carry to go back to our old home.

The book didn't say how long it would take Nanna to get well again. It could be a few seconds, or it might be really long, like thirty minutes. But since it's fantasy magic, I'm pretty sure it will only take like two or three minutes at the most.

So after we see Nanna and cure her, Mr. Evens will drive us back to Nanna's place. Things will be just like they were before. I put our overstuffed backpacks by the door, ready for when the time comes.

I look at the clock in the living room. It's six in the morning. The nursing home doesn't open until nine! I try to keep my mind occupied. I watch cartoons, eat cereal, and finally find the TikTok dance the snake sisters were trying to do. I was right; they were doing it all wrong. But still, I had fun with them, and I think I'd love to see them again. I wonder if I can get Nanna to take us to see the robot competition that they are in.

Well, since she'll be one hundred percent better, there are lots of things she'll be up to doing with us.

It's seven thirty, and I can't take it anymore. I go to our bedroom and shake Miles. I tell him to wake up so we can be ready to go. Mr. Evens comes into the room.

"Good morning!" he says.

"Oh, good morning! I'm ready to go see Nanna," I announce loudly.

"Yes, I can see that. How early did you get up, Sunny?" he asks.

"Early. Let's go!"

"I think Miles may want to shower first," Mr. Evens replies.

Miles groans and rolls over in bed. I shake him awake again. "Today is the day!" Miles gives up trying to go back to sleep and gets in the shower. It feels like forever, but eventually both Miles and Mr. Evens are at the breakfast table, almost done eating. Now that he's awake, Miles is much more excited about where we're going. He tells us all the stuff he plans to catch Nanna up on.

"She has no idea how much Noodle has grown. And not just Noodle," he says with a smirk. He points to himself. "Yup, I am much taller now. I think I'm tall enough to go on all the rides at the water park. Okay, maybe not all of them, but a lot of them."

"All right, everyone has eaten. Can we go?" I ask, standing up. Miles gets up, too. We make our way to the door. Mr. Evens asks about the bags that are packed and waiting.

"Oh, that's most of the stuff we came here with. I didn't have space to pack all the new stuff you got us, so we'll have to come back and get it. But that should be enough for us to go back home with Nanna today."

He nods slowly. "Why don't you two come here for a second. We should talk before we go." I groan but go back to the table, along with Miles.

"You two know that Nanna isn't well, right? I'm not sure she can just go back home. I don't think you can either," he says gently.

I wasn't planning on telling Mr. Evens about the quest because he might try to stop me, but now that the quest is over, I think I can tell him. That way he'll understand why I am already packed and ready to go.

"Mr. Evens, Nanna is going to be all better, and it's going to happen today!"

Miles looks over at Mr. Evens, and the two of them exchange worried looks. I don't get why Miles is worried; he knows about the quest, and he knows that I completed it. Well, maybe he's worried that Mr. Evens will be sad once we're gone.

"Sunny, how do you know that Nanna will be okay by today?" he asks.

That's when I tell him everything—well, almost everything. I leave out the part about Tessa almost putting an end to us. And I also leave out the part about being chased by the caretaker. He listens carefully and waits until I'm finished.

"So . . . this cure for your nanna, you made it last night?" he asks.

"Yup! Here, see?" I take it out and show him. "She's gonna

be better today. And she'll want to take us back home. But we'll come back to visit you and Rue. We promise."

"Sunny . . ." Mr. Evens is about to tell me something, but then Miles catches his eye and he doesn't. "Yes, Mr. Evens? You were saying something," I reply.

"Oh, yes. I wanted to make sure that you two remember to layer up. It's cold out."

I'm not sure that's what he was going to say, but it doesn't matter. All that matters is that today is the day we get her back. Just before we get into the elevator, Miles hugs me. I hug him back. I think he's just so happy to have Nanna back he can't help himself.

We get in the car. We usually argue over what music should be played. I like pop music, Miles likes the Disney channel stuff, and Mr. Evens like soul and jazz. But today when Mr. Evens drives off and classical music fills the air, no one complains.

Mr. Evens looks in the rearview mirror and sees Miles looking out the window with a gloomy expression. "Miles, everything okay?" he asks.

Miles keeps his gaze out the window and replies, "I think I'm a bad pet owner. I should have told Noodle the truth earlier. I should have told him there's no friend in the cage with him. It's just a mirror. He's all alone."

The sign reads "Shady Glen Nursing Center." We enter the building; it smells like wet bread and apple juice. I don't like it. It's painted the same dull blue and gray color. There are old people sitting in wheelchairs near the window, and some are playing cards with their friends or a staff member. It's not an awful place. I see a few smiles, and the nurses seem really nice as they help the old people get around. But it's not a place for our nanna. Mr. Evens checks us in at the front desk, and a nurse—Nurse Wilson—takes us to Nanna's room.

"NANNA!" Miles and I call out at the same time. We rush to hug her, maybe a little too fast. Mr. Evens and Nurse Wilson warn us to go easy and not crush her with our hugs. We can't help it. We hold her tightly and squeeze. She laughs. Her laughter makes me feel the same way her lemon-honey tea does—warm and safe.

I look her over to make sure she's okay. Nanna's deep, dark brown eyes are just as warm as I remember them. Her skin color reminds me of the hot chocolate we get at the corner store, near school. She's tall like my mom was and has long graceful fingers. We have the same full lips and nose. She's a little thinner than the last time I saw her, but she's not too skinny or frail.

She's wearing one of her favorite floral dresses. It's cream with small red and yellow roses. Her hair is pinned back in a bun, but there's a stray hair that escaped and is falling off to the side. Nanna would never let that happen before. She never left the house unless everything was perfect.

She looks the same, but somehow she's different. She reminds me of a bar of fresh-scented lavender soap. We used to have a lot of them around the house. When I first take the soap out of the box, the edges are sharp, crisp, and new, but after using it for a while, the hard edges soften. That's Nanna; all her hard edges look so soft now.

"Well, look at you two! Come up in here looking like the finest li'l babies in the whole world!" she says in her usual southern accent.

"No, Nanna, I'm not a baby anymore. See, I'm almost too tall now," Miles says proudly.

"Why, yes. I see that you are. Don't go getting taller than a tree now, hear? If you do, how am I gonna get to hug you?" she asks him. He laughs and promises not to grow to tree size.

I fix her stray hair and look into her face. "Nanna, you look so pretty! I love when you wear that dress."

"Well, thank you," she says, blushing.

Mr. Evens comes closer to Nanna and extends his hand to her. She shakes it. "I'm Darrious Evens, Ms. Williams. I'm looking after these two."

"You are? Well, that's real sweet of you!" she says. Mr. Evens smiles and tells her that she did a good job raising us. She laughs. "What you mean, raising them? Who do these little gumdrops belong to?"

We all look at her and then at each other, confused. The nurse leans in and gently says, "Ms. Williams, do you know who these kids are?"

Nanna thinks for a moment and says, "Oh, yes, silly me. You all are my neighbor's kids from back in North Carolina. June and Richie. It's been so long. How you all doing?"

My heart sinks. I don't know why. I knew that she would not remember. I knew that I would have to apply the mixture first before her memory was fixed. But when we first came here, she was so happy to see us, I thought . . .

Miles wraps his arms around Nanna's neck and gives her a big kiss on the cheek. "It's okay. You can call us anything you want. We missed you."

"That's so sweet. I wish I had a grandchild like you, Richie."

The nurse makes us step a few feet away from Nanna and explains, "Sometimes this happens. She'll forget who people are or get them mixed up with other people she's known throughout her life. Think of it like a photo album but with no labels. Sometimes she might attach a different name to a face she recalls. Don't take it personally. This is the happiest I've seen her. She's really glad you are all here, even if she doesn't know your names at the moment."

"How has she been doing? I call for weekly updates, but I would love to see her doctor and get some questions answered," Mr. Evens says.

"Yes, I think we can arrange that. Let me go and check the doctor's schedule. I'll be right back."

When the nurse leaves, I take out my tin of shea butter and walk toward Nanna. Mr. Evens says something, but I am too focused on Nanna to hear him. I kneel in front of her. I take her hands in mine and study them.

"Nanna, we can't have you with ashy hands!" I tell her.

"Oh, you're right. I know I have some lotion somewhere—"

"It's okay. I brought you your favorite kind—shea butter," I reply.

"Oh, I do like that. How did you kids know?" she says. Miles frowns and looks at the floor. I make eye contact and reassure him with the tin in my hand.

"We're gonna fix her," I promise. He doesn't reply. I warm up the shea butter by rubbing it in between my palms. It gets warm and melty very quickly. Nanna says she loves the smell.

"I do, too. Are you ready?" I ask.

She presents her hands like she's about to get her nails done. I take them between mine and rub the mixture into her beautiful skin. I use all of it, and her hands look radiant and smooth.

"How does that feel?" I ask.

"Lovely. Thank you, young lady," she says.

Okay, she still doesn't recognize me yet, but it's only been a few seconds. Mr. Evens is about to say something, but I stop him. "Wait, let's just all be very still and very quiet while the magic does its . . . magic. Okay?"

They both nod and don't say another word. But the more time passes, the more Mr. Evens and Miles look at each other. It's as if they don't think this will work, but they're wrong. This will work; it just needs a little more time. I look at the clock on the wall. I take deep breaths and look back at it again. It's been three minutes. Is that enough time?

Let's see . . .

"Nanna, who am I?" I ask.

"June, don't play no games now. You need to tend to them chores. You know how your daddy gets."

Miles says, "Sunny—"

"No! She's gonna remember. This is gonna work. It just needs a few more minutes."

We wait. We wait another five minutes. There's lead in the pit of my stomach and melting lava going down my chest. I can't think. It's now been ten minutes. Maybe I'm not asking the right questions. I ask her easy things that I know she'll remember. I ask her what color her favorite Sunday hat is. She doesn't know. I ask about all the cooking shows we used to watch together, and she can't remember any of them. Miles puts his hand on top of mine, but I pull away because I'm not ready to give up on Nanna. I ask her three more questions. The easiest questions I can think of: What color are the curtains in our home? What's Miles's favorite subject in the whole world? She can't answer either of them. And lastly, I ask if she remembers my mom, and she looks back at me, more confused than ever.

"It should have worked by now. What's going on?" I ask Mr. Evens.

He comes close to me. "Sunny, sweetheart, I don't think—"

I get up from kneeling and begin to rub the lotion past her wrist. Maybe that's the problem: I need to spread it out more. I rub it all the way up to her elbow.

"Sunny, stop," Mr. Evens says.

"No! This has to work! It has to work! Just a little more time." I rub and rub my nanna's arm. The more frantic I get, the harder I rub. Mr. Evens tells me to stop. I don't; I can't.

"Nanna, who am I?" I beg as tears fall down my face.

"You?" she asks.

"Yes, who am I?" I plead with her.

"You? Well, I . . ." She starts looking around the room and then back at me, even more confused. "Where am I? I can't be here, I'm late for work."

"NO! YOU DON'T WORK! THIS ISN'T RIGHT! NANNA, WHO AM I?"

The nurses quickly enter the room and try to figure out what's going on. They tell me to stop rubbing Nanna and let them tend to her. But I can't. She's my nanna, and I will fix her.

"No! Let me keep trying. I can make more. I'll make more and we'll rub it all over her. It's magic. It'll work. Please let me try!" I sob.

Mr. Evens shouts, "Sunny, enough!" He carefully pulls me away from Nanna. Miles is calling my name and saying that everything will be okay. The nurses speak softly to Nanna and convince her to take a nap. They tell us to wait out in the hall and give Nanna a chance to rest.

I grab my backpack from the chair, take it outside, and frantically search for the book. I find it at the bottom of the bag. I open up the story, *The Girl of Fire and Light*. Miles and Mr. Evens enter the hallway with me.

"Sunny . . ." Miles says.

"It's gonna be okay. I must have done something wrong. But I'm checking the story right now. I'll see where I went wrong and try again."

"Sunny," Mr. Evens calls out sadly.

"LET ME THINK! PLEASE LET ME THINK!" I shout as I flip through the pages.

I flip through the storybook over and over to find what it is I am missing. I look inside every page, but I just can't find it. I know it's here somewhere, the thing that I forgot to do or forgot to add. Where is it?

Mr. Evens puts his hand on my shoulder. "Sunny, let's take a walk."

"No, I have to stay here and reread the book to figure out what I did wrong. What did I do wrong?" I ask.

"You didn't do anything wrong. Your nanna's memory isn't fading because of you. It's no one's fault," he says.

I shake my head repeatedly. "No, it's something I did. It has to be. Nanna told me the story, and she read it to us over and over again. She wanted me to do exactly like Luna did: go on a quest and fix her family. I messed it all up!" I hurl the book at the wall and run down the hallway.

I don't know where I'm going, but I need to get out of the nursing home. Mr. Evens calls my name and tells me to stop running. He says he needs to talk to me, but I don't want to talk. I want him to leave me alone. I want everyone to just leave me alone!

I get to the back of the nursing home. There's a small garden with flowers and a bench. I sit with my head in my hands. The more I cry, the harder it is to stop. I don't hear Mr. Evens walking up to me. I just suddenly hear his voice.

"Can I sit with you?" he asks.

"Please go away," I beg. But Mr. Evens sits next to me

anyway. It's cold, but I can't feel anything other than my heart breaking. I can't feel anything but the cracks splitting my heart in two.

"Sunny, we need to talk about your nanna."

"I couldn't fix her. Why couldn't I fix her?" My whole body is shaking, and I am sure I will never feel anything but pain again. Mr. Evens hugs me, but I try to fight him off. I don't want to feel better.

I was the one who was supposed to fix Nanna and I didn't. I don't deserve to feel better. But when I try to pull away, he holds me even tighter. Maybe I will hold on too—just for a little while. He rocks me back and forth and tells me that everything is going to be okay. But I know he's wrong; nothing will ever be okay again.

When we pull apart, I don't expect to see tears in his eyes, but there are. He takes a pack of tissues from his coat pocket and wipes my face. There's no point in doing that because I will cry again. That's all I will ever do.

"What did I do wrong, Mr. Evens? How did I mess up the quest? I thought I had it. I thought I could save her."

"I know you did."

"I can't lose Nanna. When my mom and dad died, I was sad because I thought they were gone forever. But Nanna told me that she would tell me everything about them so that their memories could stay with me forever. She said if you can remember someone, they never really die. But now . . . Nanna can't remember us. Now she's gone and my mom and dad are gone—again. Please, please, help me fix her." I cling to him and cry so hard, I can't catch my breath.

"Sunny, you have to calm down. You're hyperventilating."

The more I try to do as he says, the worse it gets. I feel like I'm in quicksand, and the more I struggle, the more it pulls me under. Mr. Evens picks me up and carries me back inside. He takes me to the nurses' station and asks them to help me. One of the nurses gets me a brown paper bag and tells me to breathe into it. I can't. I'm sinking.

"Sundae Williams, you listen to me right now!" Mr. Evens's voice is firm but not mean. He kneels in front of me so we are eye to eye.

"You aren't just some little girl. You're the bravest little girl I know. Now take deep, slow breaths . . . please."

I do what Mr. Evens says. I let the air come back in my lungs. I can breathe now, but everything still hurts. Mr. Evens walks away for a few minutes and comes back with a cup of water. He thanks the nurses and says he will look after me. He hands me the water and says, "Drink it slowly." I do as he says.

"Will you tell me how to fix her, Mr. Evens?"

"Sweetheart, there's nothing wrong with your nanna. Not in the way that you think. Sometimes when people get to be her age, things begin to change. It can start out small—she may forget where she put her coffee cup or her purse. But then she starts forgetting bigger things until one day she forgets members of her family. And it's really, really hard to watch it happen to the people you love. But, Sunny, I promise you that it's not your fault. There was nothing you could have done. No quest would have changed things."

"No, there has to be something I can do. Nanna always helps me. She's the reason why I can sing in front of people. The first time I got up to sing in church, I was so nervous my voice didn't come out. That night, we made up our own signal so that I would never be nervous again: our signal is she fans herself when I start singing. That means I'm singing so well, she nearly fainted. It's our thing. Now she doesn't remember that. She doesn't remember anything. Nanna is lost forever," I say, fresh tears springing to my eyes.

"Absolutely not!" he says with certainty. "How can she be lost when she has the biggest sunshine in the world there to guide her? Your nanna is very lucky because she has family that will make sure she doesn't get lost.

"Sunny, you don't just show your love to people by remembering events and places you share with them. You can also show you love her by the way you make her feel. Some days, she might not remember the name of the gorgeous little Black girl with the puffy pigtails and big ideas. She might not know that her name is Sundae or that she taught that little girl how to do her hair and how to tie her shoes.

"But if that little girl talks to her, sings with her, she'll remember that she feels good when that girl is around. The same goes for your parents, Sunny. You don't have to remember every single thing about them in order to love them. Just close your eyes and remember how they made you feel. That is the way to keep them alive, keep them close in your heart forever."

I think about what he said and ask, "Is there a way I can

make it like it was before?"

"No, sweetheart. You can't. No one can."

A new wave of tears streams down my face. "I'm sorry," I say, unable to control my sobbing.

"Don't be sorry, Sunny. You cry as long as you want. It's okay to cry because this is a very hard thing to deal with. You know, grown-ups aren't that good at it either."

I sniff and wipe more tears away. "Really?"

"Yeah, we're not always good with change. But if you have people around to help you get through it, it gets easier. And, Sunny, you have so many people around you who love you and are here to help you: Miles. Folake. Rue. And me. We will all be here to help so that you can turn around and help Nanna."

"But how, Mr. Evens? What can I do?"

"You can help her by remembering where things are when she forgets. You can help her get to bed when it's late and time for her to rest. Or just by asking her how she's feeling."

"Do you think I can tell her a story? Just like she used to do for us?"

"Yes, I think that's a great idea. This isn't the end of your relationship with your nanna. It's just a different version. But it's still strong, and it's still special. That part won't change. Ever."

Miles comes up to us and sits on the other side of me. He wraps his scrawny arms around me and puts his head against me.

"Miles, did you know the quest wouldn't work?"

He looks up and smiles sadly at me. I kiss his forehead.

"Don't worry, Shine. Nanna will be okay. She has us, Mr. Evens, Rue, and Noodle too! That's a lot!"

"Your grandma doesn't have Mr. Evens to help her out," he says with a stern voice. We both look up at him, worried.

"Mr. Evens is gone. You all need to start calling me Darrious. That's what Rue calls me. It's what family members call me."

I'm surprised, but Miles isn't. It's like he was just waiting for Mr. Evens—Darrious—to realize what he knew all along. We're a family . . .

When I finally stop crying and start to feel a little better, I go to the bathroom to wash my face. I'm still sad that the quest didn't work, but I think Mr. Evens is right. I think Nanna remembers me, but in her own way. And even though it's a different way than what it was before, I will make it work. That's what Nanna would do for me. She'd find a way to make everything work out.

When I come back from the bathroom, Miles rushes up to me, speaking way too fast for me to understand.

"Miles, slow down," I tell him.

He takes a big breath of air and says, "Mr. Ev—I mean, Darrious—said that I was only looking out for Noodle by not telling him that the reflection in the mirror wasn't another hamster. I was protecting Noodle's feelings. That means I'm a good pet owner. Then he said that since Noodle thinks he has a friend, let's get him one—for real! We're getting another hamster!"

I congratulate Miles, but he's so lost doing his dance of joy, I don't think he even hears me. He starts talking about finding the perfect hamster and how much responsibility it'll be to give him the perfect hamster name.

Nurse Wilson comes out of Nanna's room and says, "We're trying to get her to take a nap, but she's not settling down. Do you want to come back later?"

"Is it okay if I try to get her to rest?" I ask.

Nurse Wilson thinks it over. "Well, she did light up when she saw you all this morning . . . Okay. Let's give it a try."

We go back inside the room with the nurse. Nanna is looking around the top of her dresser for something. Darrious asks her what she's looking for, and she tells us she misplaced her keys; she's going to be late for work.

I go over to where she is and gently take her hand. I tell her that she doesn't have to worry about anything, and that all she has to do is go to bed. I tell her it's very important that she gets plenty of rest. That's what she used to tell me when I didn't want to sleep. I'm not sure when I decide to sing to her; it just happens. I start singing her very favorite Stevie Wonder song—"As"—the song about loving someone forever.

I think she likes the melody because she stops looking for her keys and slowly lets me guide her to the bed. I pull back the covers and help her get under them. It feels like it's just the two of us; I'm singing to her the same way she's sung to me a million times before.

Once she's under the covers and her head is on the pillow,

I kiss her forehead, tell her to get some rest and that we love her. I turn around to face Miles and Darrious. I give them the thumbs-up sign.

"Hey, Sunny, look," Darrious says. I follow his gaze, and it leads me back to Nanna lying on the bed. She's waving her fan!

"NANNA!" I gasp. She gives me a huge grin and waves her fan again! I wave my fan back at her. There are tears in my eyes, but this time they are the happy kind. Nanna isn't gone. She's in there, and she is still looking out for us.

In the book *The Girl of Fire and Light*, Luna had the magical tree and the red dragon to look out for her. I have people looking out for me, too. And just like Luna, I found a way to bring my nanna back. The only difference is, Luna used magic; I used music. I don't mean to brag, but Luna and I, well . . . we're kind of heroes!

Epilogue

IT'S BEEN A WHOLE year since we moved in with Darrious. He's gotten better at all the important things: picking out junk food, buying normal milk, and laughing. He didn't laugh a lot when we first met him, but now he does it all the time. He doesn't remind me of a pencil anymore. Well, actually he has perfect posture and can be kind of stiff, so . . . still a pencil. But now, he's more like the fun pencil that curves around into a loop. Darrious even dresses more casual. One weekend, Miles and I actually got him to wear jeans!

Darrious isn't the only one who is doing better. Folake and her brother get along now—mostly. The two of them even hang out once in a while and play in the park. And as for Miles and me, we're super happy now. We love our new home. Darrious helped us put pictures up throughout the house. My favorite is the one that has Nanna, Miles, and me all dressed up in our Sunday best. We also created a special area just for the people we love who can't be with us anymore. We call it "the Angel Wall." We have three angels: our parents and Darrious's wife, Maya. Darrious choose the wall near the front door so that we could lay eyes on our angels every day before we leave. Miles thinks that Maya and our parents are now friends. Darrious agrees and says all three of them are watching over us now.

We also do stuff we never did at Nanna's house—we have family meetings. That's when we all sit at the dinner table, and we get to say whatever is on our minds. And if there's an issue, we take a vote on how to solve the problem. Some of the meetings are really fun—like the meeting to figure out where we would go on a family vacation. But some of the meetings are less fun, like the meeting about how much TV we can watch on a school day.

The best part about our new lives is that we still get to have our nanna. Darrious had her moved to a nursing home that's only two blocks away, so we get to see her anytime we want! I read to her, and Miles shows her videos of animals doing goofy things.

Sometimes we get to sign Nanna out, and she stays with us for the weekend.

She still forgets who we are sometimes, but I know that in her heart, she knows who we are. And just how much we love her.

It's been a few days since I saw Nanna because we're practicing for this year's fall music concert. The one last year went even better than I thought it would. I remember that day, and even though a whole year has gone by, I still get butterflies in my stomach when I think about the concert.

I remember walking onto the stage, feeling like all eyes were on me. My fingers went ice-cold and started to tingle. I opened my mouth and nothing came out.

Darrious knew I would be nervous about singing in front of so many people, so he made sure that Nanna was there, sitting right in the front row. She wasn't the only one; Miles, Rue, and Folake were also there.

I was about to panic, but then I saw Darrious fanning himself like Nanna does when she hears me sing. And then, Rue, Folake, and Miles did the same thing. That's when I knew I had no reason to be scared. I took a deep breath like Darrious taught me to do before I sing. And then I closed my eyes and remembered all the times I sang with Nanna. In my head, all the people disappeared; it was just me and Nanna.

I started singing.

My voice was a little shaky at first, but eventually I was able to steady myself by remembering that I was not onstage alone. I have a family in the audience and three angels watching over me. I sang out just like Nanna and Darrious taught me. And the more I sang, the easier it became. Soon, I was hitting all my notes, and my voice filled the auditorium. When the song was over, our chorus got a standing ovation!

I thought that since we did so well last year, we could just relax for this year. I thought there would be fewer rehearsals. But Darrious said, "Sunny, always endeavor to do better than you did yesterday." So, instead of practicing less, the chorus practiced even more. I don't mind. Music is fun, and Darrious always helps me find pretty harmonies to make the song even better.

Rehearsal ran late today, and by the time we get home, it's already dark. Darrious orders pizza. When the food comes, he lets us eat right from the box. He never does that. He also doesn't make a face this time when I put ketchup on my pizza. A few minutes later, Miles puts Noodle and his new hamster friend, Soup, in their cage. We told Miles that "Soup" was an odd name for a hamster, but he said it worked well with "Noodle" and he wanted them to know that they belong together. So, now we have "Noodle Soup" in a cage, on top of the dinner table. And Darrious doesn't say anything. He didn't even notice! Also, he hasn't taken a bite of his pizza.

"Darrious, are you okay?" I ask.

He nods slowly and says, "Yes, I'm fine. But there is something I would like to show you two after dinner."

"If it's the new species of eel called *Pyrolycus jaco*, I already saw it," Miles says proudly.

Darrious smiles. "Close, but no."

I'm not sure if I should be happy or nervous about what he has to say. What could it be? Well, there is only one way to find out—get through dinner. I eat the pizza fast, taking big bites. Miles does the same.

"Okay, done!" Miles says, a string of cheese dangling from his chin. I take a napkin and wipe his face. He grumbles. He hates when I do that, but it's my job as his big sister. And also I like the way he scrunches his face when he's upset with me.

"Darrious, what did you want us to see?" Miles asks.

Darrious swallows hard and looks up at the Angel Wall. He walks over to his briefcase in the corner. He opens it and takes out a big manila envelope.

"I . . . um . . . well . . . the two of you are . . . we . . . ahh . . ." Darrious can't seem to find the words he wants. So I try to help him.

I pretend to talk like him. "Take a deep breath, let your lungs fill with air."

He starts laughing really hard. "Thank you, Sunny. Great advice. I think I'm good now."

He sits down at the dinner table with us and hands me the envelope. I open it. Miles leans in close so he can read over my shoulder. I don't know I'm crying until I feel tears slide down my face.

"That says adoption order," Miles says. "You want to adopt us?"

"Yes, I want that very much. I wasn't expecting you kids in my life, but . . . I'm very glad it worked out this way. And, well, I would like to make this current arrangement permanent. What do you two thin—"

We never let him finish what he's saying. We leap out of our chairs and embrace him tightly. He exhales and hugs us back.

"So . . . that's a yes to adoption?" Darrious chuckles.

"YES!" Miles and I shout at the same time.

I was worried that I would never see Nanna again and that Miles and I would get split up. I thought I'd lose my family. But instead, my family got even bigger. I think I really am like Luna. She went on a quest to find something special, something that would make everything better. I, too, went on a quest, and I found something special that makes things better, too: Darrious and Rue.

Darrious tears into his pizza. He watches a crumb fall to the floor and doesn't go get the vacuum! He just lets it stay there and continues to eat. Miles challenges him to a competition to see who can finish two slices of pizza first. While the two of them race, I look over at the Angel Wall. I want to tell my parents and Maya that we found each other and that we're going to be okay. Not just us; Nanna will be okay, too. But I don't think I need to tell them that. After all, they're angels. I'm sure they already know.

Acknowledgments

The author would like to thank cover artist Lamaro Smith, book designer Jenna Stempel-Lobell, book editor Monica Perez, production editor Erika West, and production manager Trish McGinley.

Don't miss more Marie Arnold!

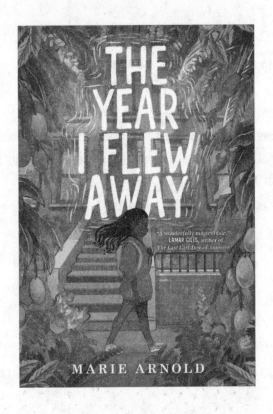